MW01139323

This book has been edited and revised by Newadi-Waya (SkyWolf) Uwetsi Aniyvwiya GreyEagle with Daniel Greyeagle and Ruth Peaceful Dove Govindasamy.

Cover Art
Great Smoky Mountains National Park Scenic Sunrise Landscape
ID 28574749 © Daveallenphoto | Dreamstime.com

A sincere thank you is due.

To my amazing Brother, Daniel Greyeagle. Namesake and spirit of his ancestors.

Ruth Peaceful Dove Govindasamy who invested countless hours making this manuscript readable.

And to my Sons...who keep the spirit alive.

Unto These Hills

Unto These Hills

UNTO THESE HILLS

Robert Greyeagle

Unto These Hills

CHAPTER ONE

A Trail of Tears A Tale of Courage

"I lift up my eyes to the hills.
From where does my help come?
My help comes from the Lord,
the Maker of heaven and earth."
~ Psalm 12:1-2

In 1838, two years after the Alamo fell and spurred the formation of the Republic of Texas, the U.S. government ordered the army to round up all Cherokee Peoples. They were to be gathered from the Carolinas, Alabama, Georgia, Tennessee, Kentucky, Arkansas, and a few other states and the army was to force march them in the dead of winter to the Oklahoma Territory. Fifteen thousand Cherokees made the trip. Four thousand or more died of exposure along the way. Some were shot by the soldiers. It became known as the "Nunna Daul Tsuny", the "Trail Where They Cried". Today it's known as "The Trail of Tears."

As the Cherokees' land and homes were being taken from them by the Government, there were some, a thousand or so they say, who escaped and fled far back into the

Cherokee Mountains - today's Blue Ridge and Smoky Mountains - where they hid in caves and caverns existing off the hunting skills of young warriors and the farming skills of what they planted with seeds they had brought with them.

This is the story of one young Cherokee warrior and his family who refused to become pawns to a government. His name was Denali Unegiyusdi Uwohali (Daniel Greyeagle).

Denali had learned English at one of the mission schools where he was an attentive student and soon caught the attention of the head minister. It was this minister who first called him Daniel. Denali liked the sound of Daniel and learned the biblical history behind the name. One evening at home, after gathering wood for the evening fire, he told his mother and father he had taken a new name, the name of a great word warrior - a Spirit warrior. Daniel's mother, Invigati Agiya (Tall Woman), liked the name and the story behind it, so from that time on he was called Daniel.

Then the soldiers came.

As the fire began to barely take hold, - it was not quite dark, the sun was just going down - eight soldiers busted into the family's compound roughing up Daniel's family, knocking Tall Woman to the ground and running a bayonet through Running Elk's stomach. Running Elk was Daniel's father. Daniel's father died then, blood gushing from his mouth, while Daniel's younger brother and sister screamed and tried to reach their father, but were held back by two soldiers.

Tall Woman was up in a flash, eyes cold as steel. As she

came up she grabbed a large stick of firewood and hit the soldier - he was pulling his bayonet out of Running Elk's mid-section - so hard under his nose that it drove the nose bone into his brain. The soldier screamed, dropped his rifle, and was dead when he hit the ground. It happened so fast the soldiers had no time to react. They hesitated. But Daniel Greyeagle did not.

His long knife in one hand and a tomahawk in the other, he fell upon the two soldiers holding his brother and sister killing the soldiers quickly and without mercy. At the same time, Tall Woman picked up the dead soldier's rifle, shot another soldier and run another through with the rifle's bayonet. The other three young soldiers were so scared they dropped their rifles and ran from the compound.

Daniel, right on their heels, caught up with and killed two of the three with his tomahawk and knife. One almost got away, but Tall Woman had picked up another rifle. She shot the last soldier through the back of his head while he was running away from her. Tall Woman was a Beloved Woman, known for being a crack shot with a long rifle. A Beloved Woman was a female warrior and Clan leader.

Daniel was eighteen years old at the time. Until this incident, he had never taken a human life. Whenever he had to kill a deer for food, he always asked the deer's forgiveness. "I hope you understand that I have to feed my family," he had said humbly.

Now, he knelt beside his dead father crying tears that no one saw because they were deep inside. Until now, Daniel had always had good feelings toward white people. Now he felt only hate.

Kneeling there beside Running Elk, he made his father a

vow: "I will never pass another white eye and let him live."

He felt his mother's touch on his shoulder. "We must gather a few things and leave this place, my son. Soon more soldiers will come. We will bury Running Elk like the white man does, but we will leave no marker. Running Elk is no longer here - he is now with the Great Spirit."

Daniel knew there was not time for Tall Woman to mourn the death of Running Elk now, and he dreaded the day on the trail when she would sing her mourning song. It would be a another time of great sorrow for all four of the family remaining.

All over the several states, Cherokees were being rounded up and placed in stockades until such time as there were no more Cherokee to gather. They were being held until they could be marched to Oklahoma Territory. They were given little food. Soldiers ransacked Cherokee homes, trampled their gardens, beat them, stole their livestock. Many Cherokee were killed in the process.

President Andrew Jackson, supposedly a friend of the Cherokee, caused this "American Holocaust" when he signed the Indian Removal Act. This act was the result of white men's greed for Cherokee land and gold in the ground. By 1838, the Cherokee had lived as a peaceful people among the whites, and some even intermarried and took Anglo names. They had farms and raised cattle and everything from corn to cotton. John Ross, the Cherokee Chief at that time, had even been to Washington and addressed Congress. Still he walked the Trail of Tears as a superintendent of his people. His wife dying along the way.

The Cherokee were a literate people. Having Sequoya's

9

Cherokee alphabet they could read and write when many whites could not. They even had a newspaper, the Phoenix. They were industrious, hardworking - one of the "Five Civilized Tribes". Many wore white man clothes, had horses and wagons. The cause of the removal boils down to greed for land and gold. A whole peaceful people displaced by greed called manifest destiny.

Tall Woman, Daniel, and the two children, had dressed in buckskins for the long trek through the mountains with the few goods and food items they could carry from their cabin. They had brought four rifles, powder, and lead shot taken from the soldiers. Tall Woman and Daniel each carried a knife and a tomahawk. Daniel had also brought his bow and quiver of arrows. The two buffalo rolls were heavy on their backs, but would keep them from freezing when winter covered the mountains. It was beginning to get cold.

The children, Usd Tawodi (Little Hawk) about thirteen, and his sister, Sunali Noquisi (Morning Star), about ten, carried what they could. Little Hawk carried a rifle, his tomahawk, and his knife, while Daniel carried two rifles, plus one of the buffalo rolls high on his shoulders. He also carried two water skins. Tall Woman carried a rifle and a buffalo roll, plus a sack with smoke-cured venison. She also had some corn, squash, and pumpkin seed. They would need the seed to grow a garden in the spring whenever they found a safe place to live.

Morning Star carried Daniel's bow and quiver. She wanted to carry more, but her mother denied the request. Morning Star was a feisty little girl. Daniel thought that she would probably grow into another Nancy Ward. Nancy Ward had been a Beloved Woman, like Tall Woman. She

10

had been a warrior and leader in the Wolf Clan during the 1700's.

They were not overly concerned about water because of the many cool, clear streams that could be found throughout the mountains. Their major concern was skirting the areas where soldiers might be found. This meant off-trail traveling - rough going in a mountainous region, and it was now dark. After several hours of walking, Daniel looked for a good place to camp until early morning. He found a level place near a small stream that had large boulders in a semi-circle about ten yards from the stream. The boulders would block whatever wind that might blow during the night, and would shield a small fire from spying eyes.

After a meal of smoke-cured venison, Daniel spread one buffalo roll on the ground and covered his mother, brother, and sister with the other roll. He was not yet ready for sleep. He sat by the fire starring into the darkness, listening to the gurgling stream, and thinking of what might be ahead. Off in the distance he heard a coyote cry, while another answered. The dark was filled with sounds of animals, birds, and insects who only came out at night. A mountain lion, wolves, or an occasional bear could be a threat so he kept two rifles primed and ready.

His thoughts drifted back to the incident at their cabin home: "O Great Spirit, my mother and I did not want to take the lives of those men. But they attacked our family and killed my father. I ask that you forgive us and watch over us as we travel. I ask that you lead us to a safe place where my mother, my brother, and my sister will be safe from those who would kill or capture us. Because we had to kill those soldiers, the white eyes will place a death warrant on us. They will not hesitate to shoot us on sight, so we must travel far and fast."

Another coyote cried his mournful song, but this time there was no reply. Daniel put two more sticks on the fire. The fire would keep the wolves away, but not a cat or bear. He knew his mother, Tall Woman, was in charge of the family, but he also knew he had been cast into his father's roll as provider of food and protection. There was no garden, as yet, for his mother to grow vegetables or corn, but in season there were plenty of wild berries, nuts, and edible roots his mother could harvest in the mountains. It would be up to him to hunt for meat. Finally, when his eyelids became heavy, he put several more good sized sticks on the fire, and made sure the two rifles were loaded with shot and had powder in their flash-pans. Only then did he crawl beneath the buffalo roll next to Morning Star.

Daniel slept fitfully. Subconsciously, he was aware of the night sounds. He had dozed off thinking about the events of the day. When he awoke, a foggy mist still covered the area and would not dissipate until the sun appeared. He knew it was early morning, but he could not, yet, see the stream because of the fog. He stoked the coals and rebuilt the fire so the others would wake to a warm glowing fire. As soon as he could see twenty-five yards in front of him, he would take his bow and arrows and bag several squirrels for breakfast. Daniel had worked with the bow since the age of six and was a very proficient bowman.

Back now from the hunt, he skinned and gutted the squirrels, washed them in the stream, and made a fixture from two forked hickory sticks and stuck the sticks in the ground on either side of the fireplace. Another slender stick was run through three squirrels long ways and placed in the forks of the fixture. He sat turning the squirrels slowly over the fire when the others opened their eyes.

"Breakfast is ready," he said in Cherokee. "Wash your faces and hands. We must eat and leave this place. We have many miles to travel and mostly uphill."

"Well," remarked Tall Woman, "appears we have a true man warrior among us, children." She smiled at Daniel, appreciating the roll he had taken.

"I am a warrior too," offered Little Hawk, pushing out his chest.

"You are not!" Laughed Morning Star. "You're just a few years older than me! When I get Daniel's age, I will be the best warrior these mountains have ever seen!"

"I don't doubt that, little sister," Daniel came back. "You both are very capable." They both shined to Daniel's comment. They accepted his leadership without question.

The family traveled from daylight until dusk each day, going further and higher into the Cherokee Mountains. On the fourth day, they came across another Cherokee family of three, a man, his wife and a young girl around nine. The little girl had beautiful long hair. Tall Woman's family knew the group. They had lived in a village near where Tall Woman's family had a cabin. It was a good reunion. Both families socialized and ate venison around a good sized fire.

"They found the eight dead soldiers," the head of the other family told them. "You will need to be very careful. They are seeking to shoot you ." He said the army did not know that Running Elk was dead, and did not believe that a small family such as Tall Woman's could kill eight soldiers. "They believe you had help. They are searching all over for you."

The man said he did not believe the army would search this far into the mountains because they were busy rounding up all Cherokees to march them to Oklahoma Territory. There were 7000 soldiers involved in the roundup.

"Just the same," remarked Tall Woman, "we are going further and deeper into the mountains. I want to find a safe place my family can live without jumping every time a twig is snapped."

The other family was traveling in the same direction, but figured it would be more safe to travel separately, so they parted company after a long farewell. They were hiding from the soldiers also, not because of killing anyone, but because they did not want to go to Oklahoma Territory.

After a week and two days of walking in the cold mountains, Little Hawk was stalking a doe one morning when he came upon a cave that looked good to him. He ran back to where his family was camped, excited with his news. The cave was about half a mile from where they were camping. When Tall Woman saw the cave, she knew Little Hawk had found the right home. But first the cave would have to be checked out. Tall Woman and Daniel made torches from dry moss, kindling, and Pine bark. They searched the cave checking for bats and evidence of a bear den while the children stood watch at the cave's mouth.

The cave was clean, as far as caves go, with no signs of any animal ever having lived there. Even the floor was of stone, and the sides of the cave looked solid, as did the roof. The mouth of the cave was about ten feet across and about the same distance in height. It would be easy to enclose with strong timber and hidden with brush. Once that was done, it would be difficult to make out from the forest.

Daniel sensed air movement toward the back of the cave because the flames of the torches bent that way. When he checked it out, he found that air was coming in through the cave's mouth and escaping through several large crevices at the rear of the cave near the ceiling.

He said. "This is perfect mother. We can have a fire and cook in here and the smoke will go out and up through those cracks. We can build a fireplace of stone near the cave's back. It will give light and warm the cave."

Daniel and Little Hawk found dry wood in the forest. Meanwhile Tall Woman and Morning Star started a good fire. The smoke acted just as Daniel had said - very little remained in the cave. The boys kept bringing in wood until one side of the cave was lined with wood three feet high. That took three days. Another two days the boys had found and carried in enough good sized stones to build a workable fireplace. They also carried in four large stones to use as stools.

"This place is shaping up," giggled Morning Star, her hands on her hips. "Now you warriors must find some good timber to close up the mouth, yet let enough air in to carry the smoke out the back! You must not get lazy, now."

The others laughed, but in the next several days, the boys enclosed the cave's mouth with upright timber, just like Morning Star had pictured. On one side of the cave's mouth, they left an eight inch opening from top to bottom so air could enter. On the right side, they made somewhat of a door about, four feet high, that swung open on hinges of rawhide. They had to stoop going in and out, but they didn't mind. It worked. In the days to come they piled brush on the outside that hid the cave's enclosure and also acted as a windbreak. Enough air came through to force smoke out through the crevices at the cave's rear.

As Daniel surveyed the cave, he thought that at sometime in the far distant past another family, probably, had lived in this cave. There were ancient hieroglyphics on the wall he did not understand. The Cherokee were of the Iroquoian race, and had been in North America since 2000 BC. This particular cave seemed suited for family living. The old folks had told stories around the sacred fires about wars between the Cherokee and other tribes, about the bravery of Cherokee warriors who were peaceful, but feared no one. They had spoke of the ancient Cherokee of by-gone years, about their traditions, the four directions, the myths and stories that thrilled him as a young boy.

Many learned scholars have traced modern peoples and races - going back to the sons of Noah - and have written that the Cherokee, are descended from Canaan, the fourth born son of Ham of the Bible. Because of the actions of Ham, a curse was placed - not on Ham who did the deed, but on his son Canaan. Scholars believe that the North American Indians migrated to these shores from ancient Israel - specifically from ancient Canaan.

If a curse was placed on Canaan, son of Ham, son of Noah, is it possible that the curse, through millennia, also was upon the North American Indians which included the Cherokee? If so, this could account for the ill-treatment of all American Indians throughout modern history.

Daniel recalled his father, Running Elk, and became sad at the loss of such a brave warrior. He remembered how Running Elk had began teaching and training him to be a warrior since the age of six. He smiled when he recalled the first time he pulled back a bowstring. The bow came back on him bruising his forehead. Gone now, his father, but not the memories.

On the inside, the cave was about thirty-five feet long and fifteen feet wide - plenty of room for a family of four. There was a clear running stream some fifty yards from the cave, so water would be no problem. During the really cold months, surface ice would have to be broken to reach the water, but that, too, was no real problem. Their task now was to find game, build a cabinet to smoke-cure the meat, and store enough to last awhile. Their clothes would be made of deer skin. Like Morning Star had said. Things were shaping up.

Snow came to the mountains without warning. The family went to sleep in the warm cave, and when they awoke a one foot blanket of snow covered the ground.

It was sleeting and snowing on the Trail of Tears also. A great distance from the cave, thousands of Cherokees were struggling along a snow covered trail trying to keep warm with what little they had as cover. The line stretched for miles. On each side of the trail rode soldiers on horses yelling orders for stragglers to keep up the pace and stay in line.

Old and young alike tromped through the slush and mud made slippery by so many feet trudging on the ice covered trail. Slipping and sliding, some fell, and one old woman could not get up. A soldier on a grey mare rode up and whipped her across her shoulders with his rope. The old woman wailed and cried, but the soldier kept hitting her. An outraged young warrior ran up to the woman, grabbed the rope and pulled the soldier off of his horse. He began beating him with his own rope. Another soldier shot the warrior. They left him dead on the side of the trail. Others helped the old woman up and helped her along, but that evening when the column stopped for the night, she died from exposure.

Chief John Ross, who was on the trail with his sickly wife, tried to reason with General Winfield Scott, the officer in charge, to have mercy on his people. But a junior mustached officer spat a wad of tobacco juice at Chief Ross and said "We give no mercy to wild dogs, why should we show mercy to you scoundrels?" The officer rode off in a huff. The General said nothing. During the freezing night, the wife of Chief John Ross died of pneumonia. Another chief and his family refused to move unless the abuse stopped.

Private John G. Burnett later wrote "Future generations will read and condemn the act and I do hope posterity will remember that private soldiers like myself who were forced by General Scott to shoot an Indian Chief and his children, had to execute the orders of our superiors. We had no choice in the matter."

This barbaric removal of the Cherokee in the dead of winter along a trail of death and dying was called in Cherokee Nunna Daul Isunyi - the Trail Where They Cried or The Trail of Tears.

18

No better symbol exists of the pain and suffering of the Trail Where They Cried than the Cherokee Rose. The mothers of the Cherokee grieved so much that the chiefs prayed for a sign to lift the mother's spirits and give them strength to care for their children. From that day forward, a beautiful new flower, a rose, grew wherever a mother's tear fell to the ground. The rose is white, for the mother's tears. It has a gold center, for the gold taken from the Cherokee lands, and seven leaves on each stem that represent the seven Cherokee clans that made the journey. To this day, the Cherokee Rose prospers along the route of the Trail of Tears. This is the legend of the Cherokee Rose.

When Daniel, Little Hawk, and Morning Star opened their eyes, they peered outside the cave and saw the snow, but they did not see their mother anywhere. They became concerned, but Daniel quieted them. In the distance he heard the chant and wail of a Cherokee wife mourning the loss of her husband - Tall Woman was singing her mourning song. Remembering the death of their father, tears filled the children's eyes, and great sadness filled the cave like thick smoke that could not be vented. Daniel told the children to stay in the cave. He picked up two rifles and followed his mother's trail to where she was kneeling in the snow, her arms raised toward the heavens.

He stood behind a large evergreen tree, not to intrude, but to protect in case some wild animal was attracted to Tall Woman's mournful dirge. For two hours she sang her song of loss and death. She entreated the Great Holy Spirit to accept Running Elk into the great unknown because he had been a loving mate, a good provider, a strong warrior,

19

and a great father to her children. Daniel cried on the inside where some of his father's spirit now lived. His face was stoic, but his heart was breaking like the thin ice on the slightly frozen stream. Unadulterated hate filled his thoughts as he remembered the vow he had made to Running Elk. He wished he could cry real tears that would wash away his hurt, but he could not show what his soul felt. It would not be becoming to a Cherokee warrior. Daniel just stood there - waiting, hurting.

Daniel was behind the tree as Tall Woman walked toward the cave. She looked not to the right or left, but she knew he was there. She had seen his tracks in the snow and felt his presence. She thought, he has grown several years in the past few weeks. He had become a true warrior, the son of a great warrior - the son of Running Elk. His heart was broken, but he walked back to the cave with pride. He was Cherokee.

Throughout the weeks and months that passed, Daniel and Little Hawk kept the family in meat. Whenever they stalked a single buck or doe through the snow they used the bow, but when they come upon a deer's lair Little Hawk went back to the cave and brought Tall Woman. She was the best shot with a long rifle, and their ammunition was limited. With three rifles, she could bring down three deer in a matter of seconds. They butchered their game in the field. It took several trips to haul the meat to the cave.

The family now had smoked venison to spare, and many skins for shirts, trousers, and moccasins. Daniel and Little Hawk worked steadily throughout the winter plating rawhide ropes that would be useful for many things. Daniel also made Little Hawk a bow from hickory and arrows from strong reeds found along the banks of the stream. They flint-napped stones for arrow heads, and made several spears that they stood along one wall of the cave. These would be used for spearing fish; the spear heads were made from bone and were barbed. They also made ornate necklaces for Tall Woman and Morning Star. Nothing was thrown away.

"Mother," asked Morning Star, as she and Tall Woman prepared the evening meal, "Will we ever go back home?"

"Much too soon to tell, little one. We are safe here for now. There, our family might not survive. Try not to think about yesterday" Tall Woman told her daughter. " We must live in today."

"Will you, then, teach me to shoot the long rifle so one day I can become a Beloved Woman?"

"I will," answered her mother. Like Daniel, Tall Woman recognized that her daughter was strong willed. She would grow into a beautiful, intelligent woman. Her raven colored hair was already past her shoulders and shined like sunlight on still water. One day, she would become a great leader, her mother thought. All three of her children would soon need the companionship of others their age.

Several months had come and gone when Daniel and Little Hawk came in from a hunt. They were empty handed. Although meat was plentiful, Tall Woman thought it odd they came home without game.

"We are not alone here, mother," Daniel informed her slightly apprehensive. "We came upon the tracks of another human - a white man! The man was not wearing moccasins."

Tall Woman did not need to be told if the boys had been

21

seen or not. A Cherokee warrior is seen only when he wants to be seen.

"We will stay inside the cave for a few days," Tall Woman instructed. "We have plenty of food and water. When necessity calls, we will go out only at night. Always Daniel will be nearby. When the snow clears, Daniel, you will track this white man to where he lives. Without snow on the ground, the man cannot backtrack you. You will watch his habits and determine what he is about, and if he is a danger to us."

Winter fought hard to stay, but spring would not allow it. The snow melted and the ground was soon dry with flowers and springtime things blossoming all over the mountains. Colorful birds began singing their cheerful songs. Squirrels were again chasing their tails. Deer grazed in the meadows ever alert, ears searching for sounds of danger. The grass was a verdant green and the sky was trimmed with various colors of blue and long streaks of white. The air carried an aroma of new life as bees went from flower to flower sampling the nectar. The woods, the valleys, the meadows came alive and pushed winter far into the background.

But in the back of Daniels mind, he knew he had a job to do, a job that could prove dangerous if he were not careful. He donned his large knife, his tomahawk, his rifle, and his bow and quiver of new arrows. He bade farewell and hugged each of his family members.

"I will to go with you," Little Hawk said plaintively.

"Not this time, Little Man," replied Daniel. "A warrior is needed here to protect the women." Daniel handed Little Hawk one of the rifles. "you will carry this, your knife and tomahawk, and your bow and arrows everywhere you go. I will be gone a few days. I want to rest easy knowing that mother and Morning Star will be well protected."

"You can count on me, Daniel!"

"I know that I can, brother," said Daniel. "From this day forward, you will not be known as Little Hawk. Your name is now Ta-wo-di (Hawk). You have gained a year since we left our home. In many ways, you have become a man. You can shoot the long rifle as well as I can, and you have become almost as good as me with the bow and arrow. You are a good tracker. From this day forward, be as wise as the hawk and strike only when you have figured out your prey's habits. When you do strike, strike quickly and with vengeance."

With those parting words, Daniel left the cave. Darkness covered the mountains. He had planned his departure to be at night because he wanted to get to the place where he first saw the white man's footsteps, find a good hiding place, and wait for this man that could possibly be a danger to his family. He figured the man would come some early morning to place traps in the places he had found during winter. There were several beaver dens along the stream, so he hid himself on this side of the stream opposite the first beaver den. It was now a waiting game.

Daniel took a piece of smoke-cured venison from his food pouch and ate. He loved the Springtime. It was cool, but not cold, and the moon gave ample light to see his surroundings. He lay back on the soft, green grass, folded his arms beneath his head and gazed at the stars while listening to the night sounds he loved so well. Soon he was asleep.

Early morning awakened him to day sounds. These sounds, different than those at night, but to his ears they both were music - just different musical sounds. He rolled over on his stomach and watched through foot-tall grass at the stream twenty yards away. His eyes were focused on the beaver den, but his peripheral vision took in a larger area. He watched all day, but his prey did not show. Three days passed.

Early on the forth morning the birds stopped singing - a clear sign that something or someone was moving about. Soon the white man appeared on the opposite side of the stream carrying eight traps over his shoulder. As the man moved up the stream on the other side setting traps, Daniel moved parallel to the man on this side, but about twenty yards from the stream. Cover was good, so Daniel had no worry about being discovered. Besides, the man was so noisy in everything he did, it would be difficult for him to hear even a wolf creeping upon him.

Daniel never understood why a white man was so noisy. They talk loud and they walk loud, he thought. A Cherokee became a part of nature and his surroundings - they blended in with what is. The white man tried to dominate nature, which was unnatural and caused discordance - like an out of tune piano; they hurt the ears.

After the out of tune piano man set all of his traps, he sat on the bank of the stream smoking a pipe, looking but not seeing anything except what was in his head. The man unloaded his pipe and struck out walking away from the stream and over a slight rise. Daniel waited an hour before crossing the stream and following - just to the left of the man's trail. He would not be hard to follow.

After three or four miles, the trapper came to his lean-to style abode. The man had an hour's start on Daniel and had started an outside fire with a black, metal pot hanging from an iron rod over a fire. Two iron rods stuck in the ground with a Y at their tops held the cross bar. A thin line of smoke angled into the air. Daniel moved off to the left of the trail a few yards and about twenty-five yards from the lean-to. All day, Daniel watched the habits of the white man and noticed that he never got more than six feet from his long rifle.

The bearded man wore a large Bowie style knife on his left side, and had a long percussion-cap pistol stuck inside his wide belt on the right side. He was just as noisy in the camp as he was on the trail. Shortly, the man started sipping from a jug that Daniel figured was white man whiskey. The rest of the day he drank from the jug until he fell asleep. Daniel had seen enough for today, and it was now getting dark, so he, too, went to sleep.

The next morning, Daniel heard the clanging sounds of the man at the lean-to cooking breakfast. Soon he threw eight more traps over his shoulder and headed up the same trail to the stream. Daniel waited an hour then went down to the lean-to to have a look. Inside, Daniel saw something that caused his mind to scream silently with fury - rage, pure complete rage! On a pole inside the lean-to, he saw three scalps. One had belonged to a child. His mind raced back to the family he had met on the trail. Had to be! The hair was Cherokee!

His mind was made up - he knew what he had to do. Still fuming, he softly backed out of that place, but this time he hid only ten yards to the right of the lean-to. Daniel lay on his stomach in tall grass and waited. When the sun reached the three o'clock position, the big man returned and went through the same ritual as yesterday. Daniel watched, his blood boiling to a fervor's pitch.

Finally, Daniel stood up and yelled "Osiyo, (Hello) you son of a pig!" The man, startled, stood straight up, turned to face Daniel and grabbed for his pistol. As the pistol cleared the man's belt, Daniel squeezed his rifle's trigger. He felt the rifle jolt against his shoulder and saw smoke come from the barrel. He shot the man through the heart. The power of the shot knocked the big man backward four feet and on top of the fire.

Daniel started to leave him there, but thought better about it and dragged him away a few feet. He took the scalps up the rise to an evergreen tree and ceremoniously buried them beneath the tree. He spoke prayers for the family - telling them that they had been avenged. He said no prayer for the dead man. After burying the white man, Daniel took the man's rifle, Bowie knife, pistol, a powder horn, and all the powder and shot he found in the lean-to and started back to the cave. His mood was somber. His face looked cloudy enough to rain.

Back at the cave, Daniel explained what had happened from the time he had left the cave until his return. The cave was filled with anguish and great sorrow when he spoke of the scalps. His family cried painful sobs. There was not a dry eye anywhere in their world. Morning Star went to the far end of the cave and bawled. Hawk joined her with his arm around her shoulders. Tall Woman fell to her knees, arms in the air. In Cherokee, she cursed man's inhumanity to man. Daniel went outside where it was dark, where no one could see his face.

After several days, Daniel took his family by a short route to where the lean-to stood. There were items there that would help his family survive - no use leaving the items to rust and corrode. The family paid respects at the spot where Daniel had buried the scalps, then they torn down the lean-to and scattered what was left over a large area. In a few months grass and weeds would claim the spot where the lean-to had been. Hawk wondered if the scalper's remains would contaminate the soil where he was buried.

Daniel and Hawk built a travois from poles that had held up the lean-to, and stretched several rawhide skins onto the travois. On it they placed the large metal pot, three smaller pots, two large metal spoons, the cooking rods, a bag each of beans, corn, coffee, sugar, salt, and a small music box that Morning Star had found and liked. Very important was the double-bladed axe Tall Woman had found. Daniel and Hawk pulled the travois to the cave.

The next day, Daniel and Hawk searched for and found the dead man's traps. They buried them in the forest where no one would again use them to harm more animals needlessly. "We take from nature only what we need to survive," Daniel told Hawk. "It is not good to trap animals to sell their hides. It is not our way."

When the weather was right, Tall Woman and Morning Star made a garden while Daniel and Hawk stood guard at either end of the short rows , rifles cradled in their arms. Daniel now carried the trapper's long pistol inside his belt. Although the family had lived here almost a year, they weren't sure of what was beyond their valley, or beyond the forest, or the next mountain ridge. Daniel would explore an

27

area fifteen miles in diameter using the cave as the center. They must know if more trappers were in the area, but even more, if other Cherokee families had made it to these mountain ranges safely.

Tall Woman had planted seed corn, squash, and pumpkin, and had soaked the brown beans they had taken from the lean-to in water overnight and planted them also. Soon the family would eat corn on the cob, fried and boiled squash and pumpkin bread. They could also husk corn, boil the corn in the kettle they now had, along with ash from the fire, and make hominy. The ash would remove the hard outer skin of the dried corn. Boiling several times with new water would produce great, tasty hominy.

They could also grind dried corn into meal for Cherokee fry bread. When the brown beans grew about two feet tall, they would produce green beans. Let some of the bean plants grow completely, and more dry beans would be produced. Wild onions grew in many places in the mountains. And in season wild blueberries, blackberries, and sassafras roots could be harvested. Sassafras tea was loved by the family. Today it is called root beer.

"Thoughts of all this good food is making me hungry," smiled Morning Star. "It is so beautiful here, and game is so plentiful, I don't know if I want to go back home!"

Morning Star voiced aloud what each family member had been thinking for awhile. Once Daniel explored the area and found it safe, they could consider building a cabin like the one they had left. There were abundant trees in the forest, and plenty of stones to build a real fireplace and a chimney. And now they had an axe to work with.

Tall Woman stood to stretch the kinks from the small of

her back. Her hands were beginning to blister from using the hoe Daniel had made for her. It was a long piece of hickory with a hook at one end. Daniel had carved the hook so that it had a three inch wide blade of a sorts. She looked out over their valley to the edge of the forest - wondered where they would build a cabin if Daniel found the area to be safe.

Hawk was now somewhat past fourteen. Morning Star eleven, and Daniel a little over nineteen. She watched her children as she stood there, and thanked the Great Holy Spirit for each of them. Daniel was almost six feet tall, and weighed around one hundred eighty pounds. His long coal-black hair reached his shoulders, his black eyes alert and clear. To her he was beautiful - an image of Running Elk. A sadness flushed her body thinking about her husband.

Hawk was tall for his age and looked like a smaller version of Daniel and Running Elk. His actions reminded Tall Woman of Daniel, even his hair and eyes. She remembered her promise to Morning Star. Soon I will teach her to shoot the long rifle, she thought. Daniel and Hawk had already started teaching Morning Star how to track animals and people. She was quick to learn. She was also the apple of her brothers' eyes.

Now arrived in Oklahoma Territory, the last of the long line of Cherokee arriving in a strange barren land felt the sting of the Oklahoma winds blowing cold plains dust into their eyes. This place had not the beauty of the mountains of the Carolinas or the their other mountain state homelands from which they had been driven. This pale land was battered to monstrous thunder storms and powerful tornados that often plowed through the country like so many thundering horse herds.

The Cherokee, herded together in a giant make-shift reservation of thousands, guarded and oppressed by soldiers, were not the only displaced Native Americans. There were Choctaw, Creek, Seminole, and Chickasaw. It was as if the American government, guilty over its treatment of Native Indians, wanted the first Americans far from Washington, placing their guild far from mind, and far from thought. Mainly, the government wanted the rich Indian lands for settlers.

Trail of Tears Timeline -- 1838

February: 15,665 people of the Cherokee Nation petition congress protesting the Treaty of New Echota. In this unauthorized treaty, a few Cherokee headmen made a treaty that sanctioned removal for lands in Oklahoma Territory.

March: Outraged American citizens throughout the country petition congress on behalf of the Cherokee.

April: Congress tables petitions protesting Cherokee removal. Federal troops ordered to prepare for roundup.

May: Cherokee roundup begins May 23, 1838. Southeast suffers worst drought in recorded history. Cherokee Leader Tsali escapes roundup and returns to North Carolina. He is later executed by the Army.

June: First group of Cherokee driven west under Federal guard. Further removal aborted because of drought and sickly season.

July: Over 13,000 Cherokee imprisoned in military

stockades awaiting break in drought. Approximately 1500 die in confinement.

August: In Aquohee stockade Cherokee chiefs meet in council, reaffirming the sovereignty of the Cherokee Nation. Chief John Ross appointed superintendent of the removal from the Cherokee side.

September: Drought breaks -- Cherokee prepare to embark on forced exodus to Indian Territory in Oklahoma.

October: For most Cherokee, the Trail of Tears begins.

November: Thirteen contingents of Cherokee cross Tennessee, Kentucky and Illinois. First groups reach the Mississippi River, where their crossing is held up by river ice flows.

December: Contingent led by Chief Jesse Bushyhead camps near present day Trail of Tears Park located near Cape Girardeau, Missouri. John Ross leaves Cherokee homeland with last group, carrying the records and laws of the Cherokee Nation. 5000 Cherokees trapped east of the Mississippi by harsh winter -- many die.

Trail of Tears -- 1839

January: First overland contingents arrives at Fort Gibson. Ross party of sick and infirm travel from Kentucky by river boat.

February: Chief Ross's wife, Quati, dies near Little Rock, Arkansas on February 1.

March: Last group headed by Ross, reaches Oklahoma. More than 4000 Cherokee die on Trail of Tears, 1600 in stockades and about the same number en route. 800 more die in Oklahoma in 1839.

April: In Oklahoma, Cherokees build houses, clear land, plant and begin to rebuild their nation.

May: Western Cherokee invite new arrivals to meet to establish a united Cherokee government.

June: Old Treaty Party leaders attempt to foil reunification negotiations between Ross and Sequoyah. Treaty Party leaders, Major John Ridge and Elias Boudinot, assassinated. Ridge and Boudinot were responsible for the unauthorized treaty with U.S. Government.

July: Cherokee Act of Union brings together the eastern and western Cherokee Nations on July 12, 1839.

August: Stand Watie, Brother of Boudinot, pledges revenge for deaths of party leaders.

September: Cherokee constitution adopted on September 6, 1839. Tahlequah established as capital of the Western Cherokee Nation. Within a few decades the Cherokee that went to the mountains to escape the Trail of Tears would become a part of the Eastern Band of the Cherokee Nation at Cherokee, North Carolina.

The Cherokee people are a strong independent people - strong in bravery, strong in valor, and strong in the attitude of never giving up. Back in the Cherokee Mountains, Tall Woman and her small family never gave up or even considered that thought. They were isolated from actual events of the Trail of Tears and the facts of what happened along the way to Oklahoma Territory. Her concern was for her family's survival and staying out of the clutches of the government and its soldiers.

Tall Woman had been a Cherokee woman warrior since the age of eighteen. She had distinguished herself in battles with the Cherokees' long time enemies, the Creeks. Following the actions of Nanye-Hi (Nancy Ward), a

Cherokee woman warrior of the 1700's, when a male
warrior fighting beside Tall Woman was killed, she took up
his long rifle, and a tomahawk, and led a charge that ended
in the defeat of the enemy.

For her bravery and leadership, Tall Woman was given
the honor and position of Beloved Woman. A Beloved
Woman was respected as leader. They, like their male
counterparts, made decisions of life and death. Her love for
her people made her a woman sought after for advise and
decisions effecting her clan.

Now, sitting outside the cave on a ledge, looking off into
the distance, she thought, I have only my family to lead.
And since her family was her prime concern, she had to
think about their future. She must find other Cherokee
families that had come to these mountains. She felt deeply
that there were many families that had done as her family
had done, sought the mountains instead of Oklahoma
Territory. She must find these people, bring them together
and build another Cherokee nation, a nation of mountain
Cherokee.

Tall Woman was a beautiful, statuesque woman. Her
long black hair, down to her slender waist, glistened in the
sunlight. Two very thin streaks of grey highlighted the
beauty of her hair, and indicated that here was a wise and
capable woman. Before she chose Running Elk, she was
sought after by many a brave warrior. There was not a
Cherokee in North Carolina that had not heard of this brave
Cherokee woman warrior.

Spring had just turned to summer, but in the mountains
it does not get as hot as it does in the lowlands. There were
still cool breezes blowing into Tall Woman's valley when

she called her family together. They were sitting by the
stream that gave them water.

"I have a mission for you, my son, Daniel." Daniel perked
up because he
knew his mother was speaking as a Beloved Woman.

"With morning light, I want you to explore beyond our
valley, to find other Cherokee families and tell them you
have a message from Tall Woman. Tell them that I would
speak with them here in Tall Woman's valley. Tell them
there is plentiful game and water here. Tell them I wish for
them to live here because there is much room for many
Cherokee families, that together as a clan, all will be more
safe than we are scattered throughout the mountains. Fall
will come, and following that winter. Tell them to come
before winter so we can build shelters for them. That is the
message."

Daniel left the cave early the next morning. He had
gathered the food, equipment, and arms he would need on
his journey, and Tall Woman had given him a large piece of
dried deer skin rolled into a bundle and several pieces of
charcoal she had saved from their fires. He was to make a
map of his travels, noting streams, valleys, ridges, and
places where he found Cherokee families or white men. He
was told not to engage in combat with any white trappers
he might run across unless absolutely necessary. He would
start with a five mile circle around Tall Woman Valley then
extend the circle in five mile increments until he had
reached fifteen or twenty miles. He was then to come home
whether he found any Cherokee or not. At a later time, it
would be decided if he should explore beyond a twenty
mile radius.

The going was rough in some areas - traveling up and down ridges, in and out of valleys. When night came on the first day, Daniel had no problem going to sleep. He built a small fire next to a stream he had found, heated venison on a stick, and ate fry bread his mother had made. He slept like a baby full of its mother's milk. When morning came, he ate more venison and fry bread and was on his way.

Near the end of the second day, he noticed a wisp of smoke rising from an enclosed valley a mile away. He was about five miles into the circle. He headed toward the smoke. Since it was almost dark; Daniel chose to sleep and watch that place in morning light. When morning came, he lay in tall grass some twenty yards from a well built lean-to. He could tell it was Cherokee made, but he wanted to wait until he could see people.

It wasn't long before a Cherokee woman came out of the lean-to and started a fire to cook breakfast. Daniel walked toward the woman speaking Cherokee as he went. "Osiyo, mother! I am Daniel, son of Tall Woman. I have a message to you from her. I ask permission to enter your camp."

A Cherokee man came from the Lean-to, rifle in hand. Behind him were three children. "Come forward, brother Cherokee, and welcome," he said. "I know of Tall Woman. You are welcome in this place."

Daniel ate breakfast with Brave Bull, his wife, Fawn, and their children, Little Fawn and Stonecalf. He relayed the message from Tall Woman as broad smiles crossed their faces.

"I was beginning to think we were the only Cherokee in these mountains," remarked Brave Bull. We have little to pack. We will do that and follow you to your valley."

Daniel explained that he had more traveling to do in search of other families, but gave them directions. He helped the family pack, and again was on his way. After a month of searching, Daniel had located twenty-one Cherokee families, all eager to be associated with Tall Woman and other Cherokee. Even with an average of three children per family, thought Daniel, that would be over a hundred Cherokee. That thought brought a smile to his face.

Daniel had finished his circuit. He had been gone a few days over a month. Several times he had to replenish his food supply from the field with rabbit, squirrel, and a deer he shot with his long rifle. The day before, he had seen a large ridge to the north, and had to see what was beyond it. Most of the day he traveled to, and up the ridge. When he finally got to the top, he was awe stricken. Below was the most beautiful valley he had ever seen. It was like someone had painted a picture of Eden.

Daniel sat for several hours just gazing at the beauty of that valley. It was protected by surrounding hills, and had forests with trees of pine, oak, hickory, cedar and species he could not name. There was a waterfall there feeding a plush, green carpet that stretched for several miles. Other streams fed off of that waterway throughout the valley. He saw more deer and elk there than he had ever seen in one place. It was so pleasing to his eyes, he decided to stay on that ridge a day or two.

One day, he thought, if and when I ever marry, I will come here and build my family a great cabin. I will raise my children here, and they will raise their children here. I will care for Tall Woman when she gets old, here in this valley.

He named his place Ulanigida Adanvdo - Strong Heart Valley.

On the way home, Daniel stopped one evening to rest and eat. He was sitting beside a clump of small bushes when he heard voices. He stopped chewing so he could hear better. Off to the right, about fifty yards, he saw six Creek warriors cooking something on a small fire. He could not make out what they were saying, but he knew that the Creek were bad medicine. They were age-old enemies of the Cherokee. Tall Woman and the wolf clan had fought the Creek many times when she was a young woman. There were several hours of daylight left, so when the warriors left, he decided to follow them. After an hour or so, they led him to their village. He lay on a rise and watched as the warriors entered the camp of some seventy-five people, half of them warriors. This was not good. He backed out of his hiding place, brushed his tracks off of the trail, and set off for Tall Woman's Valley in a long sustained trot.

Morning Star was the first to see Daniel as he walked out of the forest toward the cave.

"Mother, look! It is Daniel! He is back!" She ran to meet him, grabbing him in a bear hug as if he had been gone a year.

"Look at all the people, Daniel! They have been coming in, a few each day. Is that not wonderful?"

She gave him no time to speak, instead, she took his hand and pulled him along to where Tall Woman and Hawk were talking to new arrivals. He was hugged by his mother and Hawk with pats on his back and smiles a mile wide.

"Look at what you have done," said Hawk! "Mother is beside herself. All the time you were gone, mother

37

wondered if you would find one family. So far, we have nineteen!"

Tall Woman's eyes glistened with love and pride in her son. She put both of her hands on his face and kissed his forehead. Then the four of them walked to the cave hand in hand. They had to know everything that had happened from the time he had left on his mission until now. Tall Woman fixed Daniel some food, and while he ate he was bombarded with questions. No sooner had he answered one, they asked three more. When he told Tall Woman about the Creek village, his mother became silent. She shrugged her shoulders as if to say: Just when everything was beginning to come together - now this!

"The Creek are thieves, murderers, and kidnappers," she finally said. "They kidnap girls to make slave wives, young men to make slave workers. Those they don't like, they burn at the stake. I have fought these people. They have no morals and no scruples. This is bad news, my son, bad medicine."

She said she would alert the newcomers to be vigilant and on guard at all times. Finally, when he had satisfied their questions, he curled up on a Buffalo roll and closed his eyes. Soon he was dreaming about Strong Heart Valley.

The next week saw Tall Woman and Morning Star busy with organizing the Cherokee. New arrivals that came in daily. Daniel and Hawk made furniture for the cave. They made an eating table, four chairs with deer hide bottoms, remade the cabinet where they smoke-cured meat and placed it outside, and made two beds - one for Tall Woman and Morning Star and one for Daniel and Hawk. As mattresses, they stretched cured deer hides across hickory-

38

pole sides and laced the hides tightly with the plated ropes they had made during the winter. The beds stood on hickory legs two feet off of the cave's floor. They were held together by strong rawhide ropes. They also made two brooms from hickory sticks and wrapped wheat grass at one end, using rawhide as twine.

Daniel was not in a hurry to build their cabin. He and Hawk would probably start that after the coming winter. The cave was comfortable and cozy and it had become home. Besides, there were families that would need their help in building living quarters that would see them through the coming winter. He and Hawk would also have to help the families lay up and smoke meat before cold weather set in.

With the Cherokees' approval, Tall Woman laid out plans for the village. It would be a semi-circle starting on the left of the cave and coming around to the right of it. The valley was large, plenty of room available for the families to have large gardens. In the center of the village they constructed a place where people could gather for special festivals, ceremonial dances, and pow-wows. Benches were made and placed in a circle where families could sit. Later, when each family had a permanent home, a stockade-like fence would enclose the area for protection.

By the end of fall, all the families had suitable structures that would see them through the winter, and had at least a cord of firewood stacked beside their dwellings. There were several axes in the group now, and one man had a two-handed, cross-cut, long saw. These implements made gathering wood and building much easier. During a hard winter, the men would only need to find game if they ran short of meat, haul water from the stream when needed, and cut wood for the fires if they ran low. Other times they could sit by the fire, smoke their pipes, and tell the children stories and tales of by-gone years. These were the times Daniel loved and remembered when Running Elk was alive.

Winter came with a fury of sleet and snow. Bristling winds whipped through the valley whistling like a banshee, while ice-cycles hung down a foot from tree limbs - some occasionally falling, disappearing in a foot and a half of snow. White covered the valley. But inside the cave it was warm and cozy. These were the times when Tall Woman's family ate her good cooking, slept when they felt like it, told stories, and mended and made useful items of deer skins, wood, and other materials. Tall Woman and Morning Star made four warm coats from heavy rawhide lined with deer skin. They also made mittens with rawhide strings that attached to the coats so the gloves would not be misplaced.

Daniel and Hawk made snow shoes from willow-wood and rawhide strips. Each of the family now had warm deer skin boots that reached halfway to the knee, and Hawk made Morning Star a flute he soon wished he had not made. More or less, the family hibernated much like the bear. The cave was a good winter home. The days passed smoothly, but then came calamity:

"Mother!" Yelled, Hawk, coming into the cave from the cold. "I can not find Morning Star anywhere!" He was beside himself. "I have searched the village! She went with her little friend, Raven, to fetch water, but they are nowhere to be seen. I found their tracks by the stream among some adult tracks; it is as if someone lifted them up and carried

40

her and Raven away!"

"Creeks!" Tall Woman said loudly and apprehensively. Daniel was already putting on his cold weather clothes.

"Daniel, you and Hawk arm yourselves heavily. Follow the tracks and leave me some clear sign. I will rouse every able bodied man in the village. We will catch up to you," his mother cried.

Filled with dread, Daniel followed Hawk to where he had found the tracks. Besides those of Morning Star and Raven, there were enough footprints in the snow to indicate eight warriors. There had been a struggle, Morning Star had fought the abductors fiercely. A wooden water bucket lay strewn nearby. From the evidence, Daniel concluded that the Creeks had tied the girls hands and feet, and lifted them onto their shoulders before crossing the frozen stream. Two sets of prints were deeper in the snow than the others.

Without any words spoken, the boys crossed the stream. They each carried two rifles - one in each hand in addition to their knives and tomahawks. Daniel and Hawk wore snowshoes and walked on either side of the Creek's deep tracks in the snow. The snowshoes imprints would be sign for Tall Woman and the Cherokee warriors who were, even now, following the boys. Hopefully, the two young warriors could catch up to the Creeks because of the snowshoes, but it was doubtful. The Creeks had too much of a head start. It was obvious the Creeks were laboring through the snow with no snowshoes, and one had fallen down, but had gotten back up. Daniel

estimated the Creek village to be twenty miles from Tall Woman's Valley, and figured he and Hawk had, by now, covered half or more of that. Farther, on down the trail, one

Creek had veered off to the right of their path - his prints very deep in the snow. Daniel remembered something his father had told him long ago:

"We were tracking some Creeks in the snow after they had raided our village," Running Elk had told him. "They are a shifty people. One warrior had picked up a smaller one onto his shoulder and veered off the trail. The smaller warrior, after a time, jumped from the strong warrior's shoulder and lay in the snow to ambush us. The strong warrior came back to the trail and continued on..."

Daniel motioned for Hawk to lean near. He told Hawk of what he suspected, and since the tracks led off from Hawk's side of the trail, it was up to him to find the Creek. Hawk nodded and followed the tracks. Up a ways was a single snow bank. It was here Hawk figured the man was hiding in the snow, waiting to ambush them. He did not want to fire a rifle because that would alert the Creeks that they were being followed. Hawk rested his rifles on his left shoulder and took his tomahawk from his belt. When he got close enough to the snow bank, he gobbled like a wild turkey.

The Creek stood up, ready to fire an arrow, but was too slow. Hawk had already thrown his tomahawk. The sharp blade embedded itself into the warrior's forehead. He fell backward as Hawk rushed up with his knife, and with a wide swing of the arm, Hawk's knife blade caught the Creek's throat. The man died in red snow.

When Hawk came back to the trail, Daniel saw the bloody tomahawk. No words were exchanged. They traveled on. It did not bother Hawk that he had killed the Creek warrior. The Creek would have killed him if Daniel had not taught him how to use a tomahawk, and how to throw it with precision at close range. Daniel had caused Hawk to practice hours upon hours until his arm had felt like a lead weight. Tonight, a chapter had turned in Hawk's life. He would never be a youth again.

Dusk had come, and the boys had finally reached the Creek village. A foreboding quietness seemed to envelope the land - like something had happened that disturbed nature to the point that time seemed to stand still for Daniel and Hawk. Leaves on trees were not rustling. There was no breeze, no wind. The only sounds were in the Creek village below. Daniel and Hawk hid behind some scrub bushes watching as the villagers war danced around the two young Cherokee girls tied to posts in the center of the camp. Hawk, seeing his sister and Raven, started to rise, to run head long into the camp killing as many Creek warriors as he could, but Daniel quieted him.

"We will wait here for Tall Woman and the Cherokee warriors," he explained to Hawk. "They will not kill Morning Star, because some brave will want her as a wife. The little one, Raven, they might, but they will wait for day. Tonight they will dance and talk and convince themselves of how brave they were to kidnap two Cherokee girls from under our noses. They may leave the girls at the poles, or they may move them later to a hut. If they do, we need to know which hut."

They waited, watching, for what to Hawk seemed like an eternity. He had not yet learned Daniel's patience. He felt the rush that war brings to a man - he wanted to kill every Creek in sight because they had abducted his little sister, and now she was tied to a pole. Looking down at her, even from this distance, she reminded him of Tall Woman. Her hands were tied behind her back, but her shoulders were erect, her face held high. It wasn't long before Tall Woman eased up beside them. The Cherokee warriors, twenty strong, waited ten feet back, low in the snow.

"Who killed the Creek back on the trail?" asked Tall Woman.

"Hawk did," answered Daniel. Tall Woman placed her hand on Hawk's shoulder as if to say, well done, but said nothing.

"Do you have a plan?" Tall Woman whispered to Daniel.

"Now yet, but here is what I think: They won't harm the girls tonight, and maybe they will move them to a hut after a bit in order to better guard them. If they do, we need to know which hut. Maybe some of our warriors can create a diversion by setting fire to a couple of those huts on the far side of the village."

"Two of our warriors can handle that," offered Tall Woman. "The rest of our people will move down quietly, staying out of the fire's light, while you and Hawk sneak into the hut where the girls are guarded and bring them to safety. If they leave the girls tied to the posts, you will rescue them there as we storm the village. When the girls are safe and guarded by Raven's father and brother, we will sweep through that village killing every warrior there! No warrior is to be left alive to kidnap another Cherokee!"

"What about the women" asked Hawk.

"Harm no woman, child, or old man unless necessary." she replied. " I speak some of their tongue. When the battle is over, the women, children, and old men will be gathered into a group, and I will speak with them. They will leave

this place and never return. We will burn the village.
Nothing will be left standing. The Creeks brought this upon
themselves, and I feel no qualms about doing this."

The Cherokee warriors waited until, finally, the Creeks,
tired of dancing, wandered off to their huts. Daniel and the
Cherokee watched as the girls were moved to a hut on the
side of the village where they lay. Mentally marking the
hut, they watched as only one guard was posted outside the
hut. How stupid thought Hawk. Morning Star could handle
that one guard if her hands and feet were not tied! Tall
Woman had informed her warriors of the plan, and when
she raised her hand, Brave Bull and another Cherokee
moved out and circled the village. Soon, two huts began to
blaze lighting up the camp with an orange glow. Loud
shouts were heard as Creeks came out of their huts in a
rush toward the fires, concerned that the whole village
might go up in flames.

Tall Woman raised her hand a second time. Daniel and
Hawk ran to the hut where Morning Star and Raven were
being held. The guard was looking toward the fire when
Daniel ran upon him, knife and tomahawk in hand. He hit
the man at his neck with his tomahawk severing the Creek's
jugular vein, and them plunged the knife into the man's
belly and ripped upward as far as it would go. The Creek
slumped to the ground, gurgling. Hawk was already inside
the hut. Only one warrior was there, and a woman -
probably his wife. The girls lay on the floor tied and
gagged. The man, half awake, stood up as Hawk swung his
tomahawk so hard it almost took his head from his
shoulders.

The other Cherokee warriors, led by Tall Woman, were

45

now in the village. They had run in so fast and furious, the Creeks were caught off guard and surprised. A massacre was in the making. Tall Woman shot one warrior with her rifle, then downed two others with the rifle's butt as she ran forward. The stock broke. She dropped the rifle's remains, grabbed her Tomahawk and knife and waded into the Creeks like a woman gone berserk.

The Creeks had not taken time to retrieve their weapons because of rushing to help put out the fires. Cherokee warriors were yelling war cries, slashing, cutting, shooting, as women and children ran screaming, and Creek warriors were falling everywhere. It was a bloody night. There was bedlam! In a few minutes the horror show was over. The Cherokee had killed every warrior in the village. Only women, children, and four old men were left.

But in the hut where the girls had been kept, there was sadness. Hawk walked out of the hut with Raven's limp body in his arms.

Tears rolled down his young face as he told Daniel, "Morning Star told me the woman killed her while she was sleeping - plunged a knife into her fragile body while she was gagged!" He walked away from the hut looking to the heavens screaming a Cherokee war cry that ripped through the night air like a mountain lion screaming into the darkness.

Morning Star, right behind Hawk, said sobbing to Daniel, "The woman was jealous because her husband was going to take Raven for his wife!" Morning Star stood there slumped like a rung-out dish rag.

In a rage, Daniel went into the hut and dragged the woman out by the hair of her head. She was trashing and kicking when he threw her hard to the ground. Tall Woman and the Cherokee warriors were now gathered around Hawk and Raven, Daniel and Morning Star. Hawk's shrill war cry had brought them on the run. Hawk handed Raven to her father searching for words to ease his pain, but found none. The father slumped to his knees with his daughter's lifeless body in his arms. He looked from one staring face to another - as if to say, WHY? Her brother fell to his knees sobbing.

"What about this crazy woman?" bellowed Hawk.

"Her fate is up to Raven's father." Tall Woman knelt down and touched Raven's hand, a deep sadness in her eyes.

The father, his face contorted with pain, beckoned several Cherokee warriors to tie the woman to the same pole where Raven had been tied. He handed Raven to her brother, picked up his rifle, and walked to within ten paces of the woman.

"We were going to let all the women live," he told her, tears streaming down his face. "But you...may the Great Holy Spirit have mercy on your soul. I cannot!" He shot the woman in the face taking off most of her head. Her body fell limp against the ropes that tied her. The father turned and walk away.

The Cherokee warriors gathered the remaining Creeks into a group where Tall Woman addressed them in their own tongue.

"You Creeks have brought this disaster upon yourselves," she told them boldly. "You came to our peaceful village and kidnapped two of our daughters, and murdered one of them. Now all of your warriors are dead! Now you have no

47

village because I am about to burn it to the ground! We are
a peaceful people, but throughout the generations you
Creeks have sought war with us rather than peace. What
have you gained by taking our daughters? What have you
gained by murdering a girl in her youth?

"Your warriors were not men! They were dogs that harm
children! And where does the fault lie? It lies with you
stupid women who could have led them to a good path!
You disgraceful women will leave here tonight and never
return to this country. Tell other Creeks what happened
here tonight, and why! If you are found anywhere in this
country, you will be killed on sight. Now gather what you
can carry and get out of my eyes before I have my warriors
slaughter every last one of you! Tall Woman has spoken."

As the Creeks trailed off in a long line into the snow, the
Cherokee warriors burned the village to the ground. The
Cherokee people, by nature, are a peaceful people, but if
necessary they will fight to the death. It takes a lot to get
them started, but once started, it takes a lot to stop them. If
the few Cherokee living at the time of the Trail of Tears had
the same armament as the U.S. Army, and the supplies the
army had at that time, the outcome would have been very
different.

The trip back to Tall Woman Valley was long and cold.
When they arrived, there was deep mourning for Raven.
The Cherokee buried their dead under a mound of earth. A
section of land was set off from the village as a cemetery,
and the next morning the whole village was present for
Raven's funeral. After the funeral, the people went back to
their homes. The first burial mound stood as a sentinel to
the village. There was a quiet that prevailed throughout the

village during the mourning time which lasted for several weeks. For a year, according to Cherokee custom, Raven's name would not be mentioned. A month later, Tall Woman gathered her family together in the warmth of the cave.

"Morning Star, she said, "from this day forward you will be called Star, because you shine bright in the eyes of your family morning, noon ,and night, and always. You fought the Creeks bravely at the stream like a warrior, and you conducted your self as a Cherokee while you were their captive."

To Hawk she said, "My son, you have become a true warrior at a young age. It was, in some ways, forced upon you, but you lived up to the challenge. I had hoped that war would not come to you until you were older. You will walk as a true warrior from this day forward and you will be treated as such. Daniel did what was expected of him as a warrior. He told me of your bravery on the trail, and I saw your bravery in the Creek village. Daniel also told me that if he ever had to go to war again, he would want you by his side over any other man."

Hawk felt ten feet tall, because his brother did not say things he did not mean, nor did he give compliments without them being merited. From then onward he was treated by his family and the Cherokee as an adult and a warrior. Whenever a council was held, he took his place beside his brother.

Life sometimes throws the young into situations where either they survive or they die. If they survive, their life changes - sometimes for the good of that person, sometimes they react poorly and it does not pan out. In Hawk's case a good change. A good lesson. As time passed he became a confidant to his brother and mother. He became a wise leader, a fearless fighter, a good friend, and to his enemies a devil with a tomahawk.

Two years passed since the kidnapping of Star and the murder of Raven by the Creeks. All the Cherokee families now had log cabins and sizable gardens, food and meat were abundant. Still, Tall Woman's family had not built a cabin for themselves, preferring to live in the cave. Daniel and Hawk had done away with the brush that had hid the cave from spying eyes, and had built a real log door at the cave's entrance. From the outside, the cave looked like a cabin set into the mountain's stone framework.

There was now a stockade-like fence made of upright logs and sunk deep into the earth around the village and a log gate that allowed people entry and exit. Two heavy crossbars made the gate secure. Star was now fifteen, Hawk pushing seventeen, and Daniel was a few weeks past twenty-one.

Occasionally, the men of the village scouted the countryside out to twenty miles and more. They found other Cherokee families and brought them to the security of Tall Woman Valley. There were now close to one hundred families living in the village. Tall Woman had appointed four sub-chiefs, Daniel, Hawk, Brave Bull, and an experienced warrior named Big Tree. Like his name, this warrior was big and as hard as a hickory tree. These four took much of the weight that previously had fallen on Tall Woman's shoulders. She was now free to plan for the village without dealing with everyday affairs. She let her sub-chiefs carry out her plans and deal with problems that come up from time to time.

One thing she dealt with personally was the young Cherokee men that had taken an interest in Star. Tall Woman had implicit trust in her daughter, and since coming to the valley, she had been training Star to one day step into her moccasins. Even at fifteen, Star could out shoot, out run, and out maneuver any of the young men that courted her. Tall Woman said nothing, but she did watch her daughter's doings. She would not permit her daughter to marry at fifteen, and even when she did finally marry, the man would have to be a proven warrior with an intelligent mind. He would have to be a strong man to live with a strong minded girl like Star.

Both Daniel and Hawk had been courting several of the village girls, but neither one had seriously entertained marriage. Tall Woman gave her sons their heads. In her mind, her sons were adults and she knew they were proven warriors. In time, when her sons did married, she knew whomever they chose would be special. Daniel, Hawk, and Star excelled in the sports played by the Cherokee, and Daniel was a star lacrosse player.

Lacrosse was a rough game played much like hockey is played today, but without skates and not on ice. Each player carried a stick with a small net at one end about the size of a large coffee cup. Each team tried to get and carry a ball to a goal. Snatching the ball from the ground was one thing. Carrying the ball through young, strong warriors, or passing the ball to another team member, was another.

Very often, the Cherokee held contests with the long rifle, the bow, and tomahawk throwing. Tall Woman's sons and daughter always finished in the top categories. No one could match Hawk with the tomahawk, unless it was Daniel. It was as if Hawk had been born with a tomahawk in his hand. And although Daniel had taught Hawk, he would readily concede that Hawk was the best he had ever seen. And Hawk worshiped his brother.

"Mother," spoke Daniel at an evening meal, "I have been thinking about visiting Strong Heart valley. I would like for Hawk to see it. Brave Bull and Big Tree can handle anything that might come up while we're gone."

"I would like also to go," said Star. "That is, if the boys don't mind. I would like to see Daniel's valley, too."

"Could Star go with you?" asked Tall Woman. "I'd like for her to get away for awhile, away from all these boys that are always hanging around like love sick mules!"

Daniel and Hawk did not mind, so the early the next morning the three left the Village and headed out to Strong Heart Valley. They each carried a rifle, a shot pouch, powder horn, knife and tomahawk. The weather was clear and cool and their buckskin clothing was just the ticket for this kind of weather. They traveled all day, found a camp, ate, and the next morning went on their way again.

On the third day they were making their way through a thick forest. Of a sudden, Daniel brought his rifle to a hip firing position and cocked the hammer. Hawk and Star, sensing something wrong, did the same. Three white trappers stepped out from a thicket and stood in front of them, but about fifteen feet away.

"Well, lookie here," belched a red bearded trapper, "Ingins!"

"We want no trouble with you men," spoke Daniel. "Back out of the way

52

and let us pass." .

"Now ain't this sumthin,'" said a trapper with a bent nose, "this un even talks Amerikin. Where'd you learn to talk white man talk?"

"Since we started talking," replied Daniel, "now move aside."

"Tell ya what," said red beard, "we'll take the girl an' let you two leave with your scalps."

"Now, wait a minute," said the trapper who had not spoken until now, "them scalps would bring a purty penny down in the low lands!"

Wrong words! Daniel, Hawk and Star fired at the same time. Smoke belched from all three rifle barrels. Daniel's shot caught red beard in his right eye spraying brain parts backward. Star's shot hit bent nose just above his heart, and Hawk deliberately shot the last trapper in his fat belly.

After the smoke cleared, they re-loaded their rifles. Both boys looked a Star to see her reaction. She appeared calm and unruffled.

"What should we do with their carcasses?" asked Hawk.

"Nothing," answered Daniel. "The animals have to eat, too. Their bones will be a warning to others that this is Cherokee county."

The trapper that Hawk had shot was whimpering like a wounded dog. "Shoot me!" he pleaded with Hawk. "I can't stand this pain!"

"I wouldn't waste a lead ball on you, you piece of nothing. But I'll finish you off with my tomahawk?"

The trapper was about to call Hawk the son of a something when Hawk lifted his tomahawk high, brought it down swiftly, and hard. He severed the man's jugular vein almost to the neck bone. The trapper whised his last breath in a gurgle of saliva and blood. They took the trappers' rifles, shot, powder horns, and knives. They left that place and never looked back. Daniel remembered his vow to Running Elk. Hawk and Star said nothing. That night as they camped both Daniel and Hawk were looking at Star wondering how she felt about what had happened.

"What?" She asked.

"How do you feel," asked Daniel.

"I'm okay," she answered. "I don't like taking a life, any life. It was unavoidable. We did what we had to do."

That was the end of it. They spoke no more of the incident, but Daniel knew he would have to tell Tall Woman when they got back to the Village. Star's life had changed. Like Hawk's life had changed on the Creeks' trail, hers would never be the same again, either.

When Hawk and Star saw Strong Heart Valley they had to catch their breath. The place was so beautiful to their eyes, they were at a loss for words. They reacted much like Daniel had the first time he saw the valley. It took awhile for them to descend down the ridge and reach the waterfall. Hawk and Star had not seen one before. Hawk just stood there with his mouth open in amazement, and Star covered her cheeks with both hands in delight. They built a camp alongside the water, made a fire, and cooked venison on a stick.

The next morning, they explored the water fall and found a cave behind the falling water. There was a walkway behind the falls some eight feet wide - plenty of room for a person to walk about. The sound of the water falling was deafening. Star covered her ears. They came out and left the falls to build torches to explore the cave more fully. Once back inside, the torches revealed dry areas beyond a few yards from the opening, but the sound was still loud. They continued on and around a bend to a place where it was evident ancient people had camped at one time.

Going on farther a good ways the sound of falling water lessened. Soon they saw a beam of lime colored light. They looked at each other questioning, then went on to see where daylight was coming from. They came upon an opening that led out of the cave into sunlight. They were again amazed. In front of them was a large forest that appeared virgin, a place so beautiful no one could speak. Again Star put her hands on her cheeks, astounded. This, thought Daniel, was a valley within a valley. It would take some time to explore this place, so they found a suitable site just before dark and made a camp. Sitting around the fire, they ate and all seemed to talk at the same time. Star laughed.

"I will name this place Unenahida Ugedaliyv (Lost Valley)," said Daniel, taking the floor. "I now have two valleys where I can bring my family if we every need a place to hide from the world. Here in Lost Valley no one can find us if we do not want to be found."

During the night they heard strange animal sounds they did not recognize. Hawk threw more wood on the fire. He and Daniel took turns standing guard while Star slept. At Dawn, they cooked and ate breakfast eager to explore Lost Valley. They checked the soil, it looked dark, rich, and ready to grow things. Some of the trees were very tall with limbs and foliage that stretched a good ways outward from the trunks. Hawk tried, but could not reach around the trunks even with Daniel holding his hands. Grass was tall and green, beautiful flowers grew everywhere, and there were fruit trees - apple, pomegranate, pear, and other fruits they did not recognize. They found pecan and walnut trees, and edible berries galore.

"What is that?" Star jumped back in alarm. It was a large turtle. "That thing would feed several families," she observed.

The turtle payed no attention to them and very slowly inched along its way. They watched in amazement at the turtle for awhile, then slowly moved on, eyes wide open and alert. They saw deer, antelope, elk, jackrabbits, squirrels, raccoons, and opossums. Once, two wild hogs with long tusks jumped from some bushes and ran from them. Only Daniel had ever seen a wild hog before. Hawk and Star were wide-eyed.

"Look at that!" remarked Daniel, "a house in a tree!"

They could not believe their eyes. High up in one of the giant trees was a tree-house. On the ground by the tree they found what had once been a rope ladder made of wood and rawhide. The rawhide had long since been gone, killed by years of weather. The three walked several times around the big tree gazing up at the place where long ago someone had lived, high up and off the ground. As they explored farther, they found other tree houses, all withered and weathered from years of none use.

"There was a reason the people, whoever they were, chose to live high up from the ground," Daniel told his brother and sister. "They were afraid of something that roamed this place. We need to be extra vigilant for whatever that was, or is!"

To Daniel, it was evident that whoever lived in this place

had left long ago, a very long time ago. He wondered what kind of people they were, where they came from, and more importantly, where did they go and why did they leave such a beautiful place so abundant with food and water. He checked his rifle to make sure there was ample powder in the flash-pan. Hawk and Star did the same.

They made their way out of the forest to a plain covered with ankle-high cured grass. Then they saw something theirs eyes did not want to believe. Several hundred yards away they saw horses! Fifty or sixty! There were paint and pinto ponies, grays and blacks and buckskin colored horses. The three Cherokee just stood there, speechless

Daniel finally spoke. "It appears we have stumbled onto a land lost in time, a valley surrounded by high mountains with only one entrance, one exit. Closed to the outside world, this place has grown some of the largest edible fruits, trees, berries, nuts, and some oversized animals like that turtle."

"I wonder what other kind of animals are in this place," questioned Star, "and how dangerous are they?"

"Yes, said Hawk, and I wonder what kind of animals made those sounds we heard last night?"

"You afraid?" laughed Star.

"I am afraid of nothing," braved Hawk. "If it lives and breathes, it can be killed!"

"Just the same," said Daniel, "we should find a safe place to camp tonight until we find out what all is in this place."

They all agreed and began searching for a good campsite. They found a hill not far from the plain. There were no trees on the hill, but it had good three hundred sixty degree vision, and high enough to make them feel safe. They took wood from the forest, enough to burn all night. When they got to the top of the hill, they found a large cage like structure made of flat, metal bars. The cage was twenty foot square. Its top was covered with flat-iron bars also. At the bottom and around the cage was a stone barrier about four feet high.

Outside the cage to the left and to the right, they found the skeletal remains of four human beings. Near the skeletons, were the remains of five animals that looked like very large dogs or large wolves. The heads of the animals were too large for any dog or wolf they had ever seen, and their mouths was extraordinarily big. In each animal was a long, metal spear where once a wooden handle was attached, but had weathered away.

"A vicious fight occurred here between these men and those animals," said Daniel. "Appears some made it into the cage, but those laying here did not! Now we know the reason for the cage and the tree houses."

"But why up here on this hill?" asked Star.

"Don't know," answered Daniel. "Could be their horses were near, or they wanted unobstructed clear vision. In the forest, they couldn't have that."

The cage door was rusted and took all three of them with some effort and a little time to open and close it. Once inside and the door closed, they muscled an iron bar down to lock the door. They felt safe because only a very small animal could get through the cage's square openings. They had a panoramic view in all directions.

Counting those they took from the trappers, they each had two long rifles, and Daniel still had the long percussion pistol. Long before the sun set, they made sure all rifles were loaded and had powder in the flash-pans. The boys still had their bows and arrows. Waiting for night, they gazed at the horses, now farther away, and wondered how they came to be here.

In the center of the cage were remains of what was, at one time, a fireplace. Daniel rearranged the stones and placed wood in the center for a fire for it became dark. In one corner of the cage, Hawk found a metal helmet that had a metal crest on the top that ran from the front down the center to the back. Laying beside that was the remains of a soldier's chest armor, half buried in the cage's dirt floor.

"Look at this!" he told his brother and sister. "I've never seen anything like it!"

"It's an old Conquistador helmet and chest armor," Daniel told him. He had seen a picture of them at the mission school.

Daniel told Hawk and Star the story he had learned about the Spanish Conquistadors exploring the Cherokee Mountains in the 1540's searching for gold. Evidently, they had found this hidden valley and lived here for awhile, and that accounted for the stately horses, but not for the small herd. This was 1841 or 1842. Over three hundred years had passed. Rightly, there should be thousands of horses out there on the plains. Something or someone had been slowly thinning out the herd.

Hoping to find the riches that other Spanish explorers had discovered in Central and South America, Hernando de Soto landed in May 1539 near Tampa Bay, Fla., with about six hundred men, a few hundred horses, packs of dogs, and a large herd of swine. The army set out north and west through Florida. Along the way, the expedition encountered a variety of native societies. Sometimes the encounters were peaceful, sometimes violent. Occasionally, the expedition would stop for a few days of rest; each winter they set up camp for several months. As they moved on, de Soto's army took native men and women along as slaves or willing workers. From Florida, the expedition moved north through what is now Georgia, the Carolinas, and into Tennessee.

Night came with a curtain of deep foreboding, and with the apprehension came the strange night sounds. From the forest came sinister howls like they had never heard. Shivers ran up and down Star's spine. The fire was going and the boys were alert. The horses had long disappeared to some unknown safe place.

"I have never heard a wolf howl like that!" Spoke Hawk. "Sounds like a howl mixed with a bellow!"

"It's spooky," whispered Star, looking all around the cage as if to locate some unknown foe, and appreciating the security of the cage.

Then they saw the eyes, ten or so sets of them, all gathered around the front of the cage. The eyes belonged to huge wolves and the wolves growled fiercely as they stared at the cage's inhabitants.

"Be calm," said Daniel. "They can't get to us. But be ready to fire at their heads when I give the command."

The animals tried to stick their heads through the small openings of the cage, but could not find room. They bit at the bars, growling madly. Some threw their bodies against the cage door with a wham! They were vicious and wanted at Daniel, Hawk, and Star. It was obvious that if they could get into the cage, the three Cherokee would be slaughtered.

"Okay," spoke Daniel quietly, "shoot at their heads."

From the middle of the cage, rifles belched flames, and animals screamed. When it seemed the three Cherokee had killed all the wolves, more ran up from the forest and took their places. They loaded and re-loaded again and again. The rifle barrels turned hot. Daniel gave a command to cease fire for awhile so the barrels could cool. Many sets of eyes now lined all around the cage.

The three Cherokee put their backs together - shooting growling wolves, reloading and shooting more. Some of the lead balls bounced off of the flat metal bars with a ping in the smoke covered cage. They fired their rifles what seemed like an eternity, their arms became numb. Finally, Daniel called a another cease fire so the barrels could again cool and their arms could rest. While the barrels cooled they knelt and re-loaded all rifles. More wolves raced to the cage from the forest below trying desperately to gain entrance.

Continuously, Daniel, Hawk, and Star fought the desperate wolves, killing an untold number. It was a good thing they had the extra powder horns. It was dark and they had only the firelight and the wolves' eyes to target by. Loud gun shots and howling wolves filled the night. Star could no longer hear the wolves' screams - the noise from the rifles had taken its toll on her ears. Finally, she had to kneel, to rest. She slumped, laying her rifle on the ground for awhile. Daniel and Hawk kept firing and reloading, firing and reloading.

Dawn arrived on a cloud of mist and dew. And with the daylight, the few wolves that were left turned and ran back to the forest as if they were afraid of daylight. Daniel restarted the fire. All three of the Cherokee fell into exhausted sleep until noon.

When they awoke they were hungry, but they could not eat because of the stench of dead wolves that piled up like cord wood outside the cage. They could not believe the number of wolves they had killed during the night. It took some mighty hard tugging to open the cage door because several wolves had died up against it. But once out, they counted forty-seven dead wolves, if you could call them wolves. They were three times the size of an ordinary wolf with heads the size of a small watermelon. Their fangs were very large and long, some protruding outside the mouth.

"Well," Daniel finally spoke up, " we can do one of three things. We can stay on this hill using the cage as protection until our food runs out, we can leave this place while it is still daylight, go through the water fall to the valley beyond, or we can track the wolves to their den and finish them off. It appears they come out only at night, so we should be safe during the day. What do you two think?" he asked.

Hawk was the first to speak. "We finish them off! Can't be too many of them left. Best thing I figure is for us to spend one more night in the cage. What's left of them will come for us. Best to battle what's left from the cage."

"I agree," said Star. "I like this place and I want to see more of it, plus I don't like the idea of a bunch of big mangy wolves running us away. Let's finish them off and be done with it!"

"It's agreed then," replied Daniel. " Hawk, grab a few tails and help me pull these critters away from the front of the cage. We'll battle them here again tonight. Tomorrow, we'll find their den, kill any left, and close it up."

When night finally came, as expected, a dozen wolf creatures assaulted the cage with determination. It did not take long for the shooters to finish off the twelve wolves, but, just in case, they stayed in the safety of the cage until morning light. When Daniel thought it safe enough, they backtracked the wolves to a den deep in the forest. It was a cave. Hawk made a torch, lighted it, and threw it into the den. Daniel and Star stood guard. The torch revealed an empty cave.

"Guess that's it," said Star. "That'll teach them to mess with us Cherokee!"

The three took several more days to explore Lost Valley without incident. They had been gone from home almost a month, so they headed back through the waterfall to the valley beyond and toward home. On the way, Daniel shot a deer to replenish their meager food supply. He told his brother and sister that soon they would return to Lost Valley with Brave Bull and Big Tree to break horses for their people. He said Tall Woman would probably want to come along as well.

Tall Woman's face smiled with happiness as she watched her children walk through the stockade gate and into the village. They looked tired and weary, but not too tired to embrace their mother warmly. In the cave, Tall Woman listened intently as her children told of their exploits and adventures. She was thankful they had found the cage in Lost Valley and used it wisely for protection and safety against the strange wolves. Tall Woman was glad they were safely home. She asked many questions about the horses. Although the Cherokee were not a horse people like the Comanche and other Plains Indians, she could definitely see how they could be beneficial to her people.

"Soon, she said, we will gather some men from the village, go to Lost Valley, tame the horses, and bring a few here." She was concerned about the white trappers they had encountered.

"Too many are coming to our mountains in search of beaver and other hides. I fear this is going to be a problem. We ran the Creeks off, but I fear the few trappers we have encountered is only the beginning. In the near future more trappers and white hunters will come, and behind them farmers with oxen to till the earth. White settlements will be scattered throughout these mountains, and the Cherokee will again be pushed to other areas.

"There seems no end to the white man's greed for land and profit. It is as if they wish to push the Cherokee off the face of the earth. We have been here thousands of years before the white man set foot in this land, and in some form, we will be here until the end." Tall Woman's face was grave.

Some scholars believe the Cherokee have been in North America since 2000 BC. They first settled in the southeast between 1000 and 1500 AD. The two hundred and forty year period from then until Hernan de Soto made contact with the tribe in 1540 might be described as a formative one, during which the Cherokee established themselves in their new home an began to shape their society.

The view of current scholars began in 1823, when John Haywood published the first theory of Cherokee origins, and concluded that two nations with different cultures had in the past merged to form the Cherokee tribe. The first of these groups built mounds, erected fortifications, constructed wells with adobe-brick walls, and used seven as their most sacred number. They came from southern Asia, and their culture was linked to that of ancient Hebrews.

When they migrated to North American, they settled in the southeastern area. Later, another tribe, democratic in organization and with a strong military came from northeast Asia, took control of eastern Tennessee and gradually merged with the first group, to form the Cherokee tribe that existed when the first white man arrived in A.D. 1540. Any way one looks at it, the Cherokee people have been in America for thousands of years.

Tall Woman had taken her family from their home farther east in the Blue Ridge Mountains, and had brought them to the Cherokee Mountains in what is now western North Carolina. She and her family had evaded the government's roundup, had escaped from being marched on the Trail of Tears to Oklahoma Territory, and had brought over a hundred families together into a thriving village. And more families were coming in weekly. Tall Woman was a remarkable woman, a fearless warrior, a Beloved Woman, and a leader beyond question. She was Chief now of the mountain Cherokees and was looked upon with respect by village women and men alike. Her being a female had nothing to do with it. It was her person, her personality, her capabilities, that made her larger than life.

In time Tall Woman Village became over crowded when it reached three hundred families. Daniel was now twenty-

five, Hawk twenty, and Star seventeen. And so the
mountain Cherokee grew. They grew gardens, and they
grew children. As the people grew in number, Tall Woman
either had to expand the stockade wall and enlarge the
village, or create another village. She chose to build another
settlement in Daniel's Strong Heart Valley. She let Daniel
speak to a village gathering:

"All of you have heard me speak of the beauty, and the
abundance of food, water, and game in my valley. There is
much beauty here in Tall Woman's Valley, but it cannot
compare to the beauty of Strong Heart. And there is a
waterfall there, the likes some of you have never seen. The
valley is large, surrounded by mountains that give
protection. Forest woods are plentiful, and I have horses in
another valley near there that can be used to pull logs from
the forest to cabin sites.

CHAPTER TWO

Stong Heart and Lost Valley

When the People reached the ridge overlooking Strong Heart Valley, there were Ooos and Ahhs all up and down the line. The families had never seen such a beautiful place, and when they finally walked into the valley below and saw the great waterfall, to a man and woman, they stood wide-eyed and wondered at the sight before them. The weather was warm with a cool breeze, just right for sleeping under the stars when night came. Although there were several hours before dusk enveloped the valley, families were spreading their bedrolls on the soft, emerald green grass, sitting and eating smoked venison and watching the waterfall. They knew they were home, and they liked what they saw.

"You have done well, Daniel," remark Tall Woman. "The people are already happy here. This valley is going to make a wonderful home for our people. And tomorrow, I would like to go behind the falls into Lost Valley. I want to see where you intend to bring me when I am old." She smiled a contented smile. "You are now Chief of these people, my son. Lead them well."

Big Tree had already spread Tall Woman's bed roll near a large cedar tree and spread his not far from that. Daniel spread his roll next to his mother, then walked among the people touching their out-stretched hands as he walked, occasionally picking up a baby and kissing its forehead. It took a long time to go through his people, but he missed not a one. They could see the love he had for them in his eyes, and they loved him for loving them. He was their chief, a man of vision.

Tall Woman watched as Daniel walked among his people, his long raven hair glistening, his pearl-white teeth accentuating his tan face as he smiled.

"A born leader", she thought, then realized she had spoken out loud.

"And also a fearless warrior," answered U'tana' Tsaligu (Big Tree). He did not speak much, but when Big Tree spoke, the warrior's keen mind revealed truth in few words.

As Tall Woman watched her son, for a moment she thought she actually saw Running Elk instead of Daniel. She shook her head and Daniel's image reappeared. She hoped the hate her son felt for the white man would never damage his soul, and as she watched the love emanating from him toward his people, she hoped that hate would stay dormant. She figured Daniel did not hate the white man really, not yet. He hated what the white man was, doing to the Cherokee, and what they had done to his father. Like fear, there were different degrees of hate. Daniel was too strong of a warrior to allow even a small amount of hate to cloud his judgment. She hoped.

Evening sun was setting. Soon the moon would shoot streaks of colors shimmering down the waterfall and send small, white-capped, rippling currents across the water basin that caught the fall's overflow. And as a deep indigo night covered the valley, yellow fires sparkled throughout a hundred campsites. From the ridges above, that encircled the twenty mile long valley, the glowing fires looked like sparkling stars set in a dark blue universe.

The Valley was twenty miles long and fifteen miles wide. Mountains surrounded and protected it from the strong north winter winds. Interspersed throughout the valley were hickory, oak, cedar, pine, cottonwood, ash, pecan and walnut trees. Other hardwoods, some two men with outstretched arms could not reach around, stood tall in the forested valley. Deer, elk, antelope, beaver, wild turkeys, raccoons, opossums, jackrabbits, and squirrels roamed the forest. Ducks and other water fowl frequented the large waterfall basin. In season, geese visited for awhile. Streams and creeks, fed by the waterfall basin, meandered through the valley like undulating snakes bringing cool, clear, mountain water to any who would drink, then passed out the far end through chasms and waterways to places far below the valley.

Daniel was reminded of what the minister at the mission school had said about Moses leading the Israelites from Egypt to a new land. His trek with his people was minor compared to that of Moses, but he knew there was much work ahead. A hundred families depended upon him for shelter and food and guidance.

Serenaded by nightjars (whippoorwills), and other pleasant night sounds, the Cherokee families drifted off to sleep, guarded by a hunter's moon. A coyote howled at the moon from a distant hill. Night had come to Strong Heart

Valley.

At Tall Woman village, Hawk, Star, and Brave Bull had settled arriving Cherokee families into cabins vacated by those who had decided to follow Daniel to Strong Heart. Hawk was now as tall as Daniel and weighed almost as much. With his long Ink-black hair and muscular good looks, he was the eye of every maiden of age. Star was getting her share of looks from the young Cherokee warriors, too, but one newcomer stood out from the rest. His name was Eagle Feather, and he had become a hunting companion of Hawk's. Eagle Feather and his family had arrived only three months before. Tonight Eagle Feather was walking with Star through the village. She was making sure there were no problems with the new arrivals. Eagle Feather was Hawk's age. He was of the Bird Clan, so Star's dating him was staying within the boundaries of Clan taboos.

To understand the Cherokee, their taboos needs to be understood. To the average Cherokee, it is forbidden to kill an eagle, wolf, or rattlesnake. There were few people trained as specialists to deal with killing a wolf, eagle, or rattlesnake. Specialists for taking Eagles come from the Bird Clan and specialists for killing wolves come from the Wolf Clan. It is rarely done, but sometimes they are hired to do this.

The reasons for this division of labor vary, but one of the main reasons is to acquire certain parts of these animals for ritual and ceremonial use. Certain rituals, ceremonies, and dances require this. The Eagle Dance, for example, requires the use of eagle feathers.

As to plants, the killing of evergreens is generally

avoided but sometimes these are harvested and used usually for ceremonial purposes. When this is done, it is done by people who know what they are doing, by people who are aware of the proper forms of ritual associated with the taking of an evergreen. It is more common for a part of an evergreen to be taken and used for medical or ceremonial use rather than the entire plant. In some ceremonies pine boughs are thrown onto the fire. And in some Cherokee families, sprigs of cedar or pine needles are put into a pot of hot coals. This produces a smoldering effect giving off a quantity of smoke which is used for purification.

Evergreen wood is not used for common tools or firewood. Like the evergreens, ginseng, is a sacred plant. When harvesting ginseng, the first three or four plants are picked, when the right plant is found and uprooted with proper prayer, beads are placed in the hole. Traditionally red beads are used.

Warriors preparing for war must avoid sexual intercourse four days before leaving and four days after returning. During these periods they will undergo purification. The same rule is applied when going on a large hunt. After killing a deer, the hunter cuts out the hamstrings and leaves them behind. He would not leave without offering a prayer for pardon to the deer. He would use the tip of the deer's tongue as an offering of thanks by putting it in the fire. It was common for people to throw some of the meat from a meal into the fire as an offering.

For three months after birth the mother did not prepare meals for her husband and avoided sexual intercourse with him. Women in their moon time (going through the

71

menstrual cycle) were separated from the community by staying in a house built by the community for this purpose; they remained there for the duration of their menstruation.

Foods from the opposing realms were not be mixed. For example, foods from the upper world of sky such as birds were not mixed with foods from the lower world of water such as fish.

Members of the same clan were forbidden to have sexual relationships with each other.

When there was a death, the mourning period lasted for one year during which the name of the deceased was not to be spoken.

White men think the stone face (or poker face) they encounter on a Cherokee comes from a dull or insensitive mind. This is not the case. They see only what the Cherokee show them. Around their own kind, the Cherokee are like any other human being. They love, they laugh, they tell jokes, and they do like to play tricks on their friends.

Hawk watched as Star and Eagle Feather dated from time to time, and since Tall Woman was absent from the village, his sister was his responsibility. While his mother was away, he was acting chief of the village. But Hawk approved of Eagle Feather, and had given his consent for Star to date him. Eagle Feather was a bold warrior and a great hunter. Being of the Bird Clan, he was authorized to hunt the eagle and gather their feathers for ceremonial purposes. Hawk had, on several occasions, gone with Eagle Feather to the great mountain heights in search for feathers.

He had witnessed Eagle Feather's great talent and patience in the climb to where eagles could be found.

Eagles were dangerous around their nests, and would attack - sometimes sending a hunter to his death tumbling down a mountain. But Eagle Feather had a professionalism about him. He would soothe the Eagle with coos and easy sounds while reaching into a nest for feathers. He knew how to talk with eagles.

Hawk was impressed with his bravery and talent. He was also impressed by the way Eagle Feather carried himself. He walked with quiet confidence, was not a braggart or blowhard, was kind to women, children, and listened with interest to the old men as they told their stories. Eagle Feather was well liked and respected in the village. Hawk thought he would make a good husband for Star.

When morning came in Strong Heart Valley, Daniel awoke before the others. He went behind the falls to Lost Valley and brought apples, pears, blackberries, and paper shell pecans for Tall Woman and Big Tree to eat for breakfast.

"Where on earth did you find these?" exclaimed his mother. It had been years since she had eaten fresh fruit.

"Fruit and berries and nuts grow in abundance in Lost Valley," he told her. "After breakfast, I will take you there. I intend to take the others in small groups, but today, I take only you and Big Tree. You are going to be amazed!"

Tall Woman and Big Tree followed Daniel behind the Falls, through the cave, and finally into Lost Valley. Their eyes widened when they saw the great trees, the beautiful forest, the fruit trees, the pecan and walnut trees, the many different kinds of berry bushes, the tree houses, the deer, elk, and antelope, then finally, the horses. Big Tree did not

73

believe his eyes. There, just ahead of them on the plain
grazed sixty horses of various strains. He told them the
herd would now increase since the wolves had been
eliminated. In time, he said, there would be plenty of horses
for the Cherokee.

When they saw the cage, and the remains of the large
wolves Daniel, Hawk, and Star had fought and killed, they
stood amazed at the number of dead, giant wolves. The size
of them impressed Tall Woman and Big Tree. Daniel
recounted the battle and told them of De Soto's probable
stay in Lost Valley - how during the day, De Soto and his
soldiers no doubt had built the tree houses for safety at
night. He told them there was no longer a single wolf in
Lost Valley.

"The cage, I will tear down, and those flat metal bars will
be turned into working tools, axes, and plows to be pulled
by horses to break great areas of earth for gardens. We will
have long rows of corn, squash, pumpkins, beans, and
other vegetables." Daniel kicked the ground, reached down
and picked-up a hand full of the earth.

"This earth will grow anything!" he said. "The Cherokee
have always grown food, but now we will farm great areas
of ground. With what is grown, and the food that grows
wild, and the abundance of game, after the first growing
season the Cherokee will never be without food again. And
when needed we will transport all types of food to Tall
Woman Village using the horses and travois.

"Where the cage now stands," he continued, "I will build
a great log cabin with several rooms. The kitchen will be
separated from the living quarters by a covered path. There
will be a family room with a great fireplace and a chimney,

all made of stone. You will have a room of your own. You will not have to cook because someone will do that for you. During winter when snow covers the ground, we will sit by the fireplace, laugh and tell stories. For his services to you as protector, Big Tree, if he chooses to live with us will have a room of his own and a horse to ride. And if and when he should marry, we will build him a cabin next door."

"You do have vision, my son," said Tall Woman. "There will come a day when the Mountain Cherokee are too numerous to count. It will then be up to you, Hawk, Star, Brave Bull, and Big Tree, to lead them. I am still young, but it is good to know that my family is thinking ahead to the time when I will retire. My heart warms thinking about it."

"Lost Valley is four times as large as Strong heart," Daniel told them. "The mountains enclose the valley. There is only one entrance and one exit. It is a natural fort." He said that if the Cherokee were ever threatened there was room to gather them all in Lost Valley for safety.

Tall Woman had seen enough and was glad she came, but she felt needed at her village. She and Big Tree left after a week of exploring both valleys. Daniel turned to the task at hand. His first move was to appoint four sub-chiefs, giving each of them authority over twenty-five families. Then he directed them to stake out plots for the families, making sure each family had ample space and distance from each other with plenty of room for large gardens.

He organized work parties to cut trees, trim them, and saw them into logs. He assigned men to tame and train horses, and now the horses were being used to pull logs to the various building sites. The eight horse trainers continued to work the horses, some for riding, some to be used pulling plows. Men who knew blacksmithing disassembled the cage in Lost valley and made hoes, axes, and plows from the flat bars. When axes were finished, young boys quickly carried them to men in the forest. Women went to work building temporary lean-tos, and carried fruit, berries and nuts from Lost Valley. Daniel selected ten experienced hunters who, each day, hunted deer, elk, and antelope to provide meat for the families while other men built cabins.

One hundred grown men, plus older boys, worked from daylight until just before dusk - taking only one day off each week for rest. Women and young girls fed the men in the fields and forest. Younger boys carried water to the workers. When one cabin was finished, complete with fireplace and chimney, a family moved in - tearing down their lean-to and using it for firewood. The women broke ground and made gardens. They worked all through spring, summer, and fall, and the first days of winter.

Before the first snowfall, one hundred new cabins ringed the valley. A buckskin stallion had been tamed for Daniel that he called Arrow because of its speed, and as he rode through the valley surveying the settlement, pride for his people and their accomplishments swelled up inside of him. He watched as smoke trailed upward from one hundred chimneys into the chilled night air. One hundred and one chimneys - his was the last cabin built. Daniel's cabin stood a hundred yards from the cedar tree where he, Tall Woman, and Big Tree had slept their first night in the valley. After living in the cave at Tall Woman Village for so long, it felt strange sleeping in a cabin.

Due to the rounding up of the Cherokee and force marching them to Oklahoma Territory, different clan members attempting to escape the march wound up in Tall Woman Village or Strong Heart Valley. By far the most numerous were of the Wolf Clan - Tall Woman's clan. About forty percent consisted of other clans. The clans are a traditional organization of Cherokee society, and currently seven clans are recognized by the Cherokee.

Customs of the clans have evolved since ancient times, however, traditionalists still observe clan customs regarding marriage and certain social events.

The Cherokee society is historically a matrilineal society; meaning clan-ship is passed through the mother. Among the Cherokee, women were considered the head of household, with the home and children belonging to her should she separate from a husband. The knowledge of a person's clan is important for many reasons; one of those reasons being that among Cherokee traditionalists today, it is forbidden to marry within your clan as clan members are considered brother and sisters. Knowledge of a person's clan is also important when seeking spiritual guidance and traditional medicine ceremonies, as it is necessary to name the clan. Seating at ceremonial stomp dances is also delineated by clan.

In ancient times, for Cherokees born outside of a clan or outsiders to be taken into the tribe, they had to be adopted into a clan by a clan mother. For a woman who was married to a Cherokee man and given birth to a Cherokee child, she could be taken into a new clan. However, her husband had to leave his clan and live with his wife in her new clan. Men who were not Cherokee but married into a Cherokee household had to be adopted into a different clan by a clan mother because he could not take his wife's clan.

The Blue Clan made medicine from a blue-colored plant to keep the children well. They are also known as the Panther or Wild Cat Clan.

The Long Hair Clan wore elaborate hairdos and walked with a proud, twisting gait. Clan members are regarded as peacemakers, and often peace chiefs would be from this clan.

The Bird Clan were known as messengers. The belief that birds are messengers between earth and heaven, or the People and Creator, gave the members of this clan the responsibility of caring for the birds.

The Paint Clan were prominent healers, medicine people. Medicine is often painted on a patient after harvesting. They were professionals at mixing and performing other aspects of the ceremony. They made red paint and prepared teas for vapor therapy specific to each ailment.

The Deer Clan were fast runners and great hunters. Even though they hunted game for subsistence, they respected and cared for the animals. They were also known as messengers delivering messages from village to village, or person to person.

The Wild Potato Clan were keepers of the land and gatherers of the wild potato in swamps along streams.

The Wolf Clan is the largest and most prominent clan. During the time of the peace chief and war chief governments, the war chief would come from this clan.

Because of the various clans represented in both the Tall Woman Village and Strong Heart Valley, things got done -

for example the Wild Potato people oversaw all planting and garden growing. The Deer people oversaw most of the hunting and ran messages between villages. People of the Paint clan were the doctors, and the Bird clan people raised and cared for fowl life. The Blue clan people were the pharmacists, and the Wolf clan members were the soldiers and protectors. They were known to be fierce warriors.

During the last weeks of winter, a Deer clan runner came to Strong Heart Valley with a message for Daniel from Tall Woman. Daniel asked the young warrior if the message was urgent. When he replied in the negative, Daniel fed the man and let him rest for two hours. Then sitting by the fireplace, the runner told Daniel that his sister, Star, was to be married during the first week of spring. Daniel was full of questions for the young warrior. He wanted to know everything the runner knew about Star's intended husband, and what Tall Woman and Hawk thought about the coming wedding and the bridegroom.

"His name is Eagle Feather," the runner informed Daniel. "He is of the Bird clan. He is the same age as Hawk, and is a hunting friend of your brother. Both your mother and brother approve of Eagle Feather, and consider him to be a worthy husband for your sister. He is a bold warrior, honest, trustworthy, and he, personally, told me he was anxious to meet such a great warrior and leader as you, his future brother-in-law."

"Is he short or tall?" asked Daniel. "Does he shoot the long rifle well? Does he fire the arrow with accuracy? How well does he handle the knife and tomahawk?"

The runner laughed and said: " He is about the same

height and size of Hawk. He handles all weapons like a Cherokee should, plus he is well liked and respected by the other Cherokee. He climbs the high mountains for eagle feathers for the ceremonies without fear."

Daniel questioned the man until late into the night, then let him sleep. His little sister was getting married! Much time had passed since the family had left their home for these mountains. He remembered how feisty Star had been as a young girl, how well she had handled herself when kidnapped by the Creeks, how she had responded when the trappers surprised them on the way to Strong Heart, and how she fought the wolves with him and Hawk in the cage at Lost Valley. Eagle Feather had better be a strong man, he thought, because Star is certainly a strong woman!

The Deer clan runner stayed for two days with Daniel. The morning of the third day, Daniel took him to the corrals he had built in Lost Valley for the tamed horses and picked out a strong, young pinto pony for his sister, and a paint for Eagle Feather.

"Ride this pony and trail the Paint back to Tall Woman Village," he instructed the runner. "Tell Star the horses are my wedding present to her and Eagle Feather. Tell Tall Woman when I come to the wedding, I will be bringing a horse each for her, Hawk, Big Tree and Brave Bull. Tell my mother and Star that I will be hungry for Cherokee fry bread and venison stew when I get there."

After making sure the young man had plenty of shot and powder for his long rifle and food to eat along the trail, he sent him on his way.

Spring came with all its freshness and beauty. Birds sang, a woodpecker tattooed a hardwood tree, the horses were frisky, and things began to grow all over Strong Heart and Lost Valley. The high-pitched squeals of children at play gave mothers a needed rest, and wives were washing clothes in streams of clean, cool water.

Daniel was approaching the stockade gate at Tall Woman Village, trailing four horses for Tall Woman, Hawk, Brave Bull, and Big Tree. As he entered the gate, children and grown-ups alike ran to see the horses. Daniel rode his buckskin, Arrow, up to the cave where his family waited. Standing with them was Brave Bull, Big Tree, and Eagle Feather. Daniel embraced his family and shook hands with his friends. Star held his hand tightly as she introduced him to Eagle Feather. Daniel immediately took a liking to Star's husband to be. He was graceful and thanked Daniel for the gifts, and welcomed him home.

Daniel handed the rawhide reins of a stunning white mare with graceful lines to Tall Woman. His mother was ecstatic. She ran her hands over the animal, appreciatively, then hugged her son again - a great smile on her face. Next Daniel gave Hawk a coal-black stallion that looked as if it could outrun the wind. Hawk immediately swung upon the stallion and was off through the gate, his long hair blowing in the breeze. To Brave Bull, he had brought a strong grey with a long mane, and to his friend, Big Tree, he gave a large, stout dun that would carry the big man with ease. Off went his friends following Hawk, trying to catch him, but Hawk was long gone.

Later, with his family and Eagle Feather, Daniel rode to the stream, staked the horses to graze in spring grass, and took seats on small boulders near the water. Daniel brought Tall Woman up on the happenings at Strong Heart and Lost

Valley, and told her that, in his absence, ground in Lost Valley was being broke for a field of corn. He had brought fruit, berries and nuts to his family, and told them they should come and bring back a load of food items.

"Have you two decided where you will spend your honeymoon?" he asked Star and Eagle Feather. "If you haven't, and would like to, you can use my cabin. I can stay with one of my sub-chiefs."

"We were going to ask if that would be possible," said Eagle Feather. "Star has been wanting to show me your waterfall."

"It's beautiful," stated Daniel. "What better place for a honeymoon than a few yards from the waterfall." Then to Tall Woman, he said "Mother, do you remember that cedar where we slept on the ground when you were there?"

"I do," she answered. "It was beautiful and so peaceful there."

"Well, my cabin is just a few yards from that place. Don't you think it would be great for Star and Eagle Feather for their honeymoon? They can stay as long as they like. Our people would love to see Star again, and they would like to meet Eagle Feather."

"Yes, I do," Tall Woman answered.

"Then it is done," said Daniel. "What a great time this is. My little sister getting married!"

The Cherokee wedding ceremony is a beautiful event, whether it is the traditional or ancient ceremony, or a modern version. The original ceremony differed from clan to clan and community to community, but basically used the same ritual elements. Because the woman holds the family clan, she is represented at the ceremony by both her mother and her oldest brother. The brother stands with her as he gives his vow to take the responsibility of teaching her children. In ancient times, the couple would meet at the center of the townhouse, and the groom gave the bride a ham of venison while she gave an ear of corn to him, then the wedding party danced and feasted for hours on end. In those early days, venison symbolized his intention to keep meat in the household and her corn symbolized her willingness to be a good Cherokee housewife. The groom is accompanied by his mother.

After the sacred setting for the ceremony has been blessed for seven consecutive days, it is time for the ceremony. The bride and groom approach the sacred fire, and are blessed by the priest or priestess. All parties in the wedding, including the guests, are also blessed. Songs are sung in Cherokee, and those conducting the ceremony bless the couple. Both the bride and groom are covered in a blue blanket. At a specified moment in the ceremony, the priest or priestess removes each blue blanket, and covers the couple together with one white blanket, indicating the beginning of their new life together.

The couple drank together from a Cherokee Wedding Vase. The vessel held one drink, but had two openings for the couple to drink from at the same time. Following the ceremony, the town, community or clans provided a wedding feast, and the dancing and celebrating often continued through the night and into the next morning.

When the celebration was over, Daniel, Tall Woman, and the people of the village, waved their goodbyes as Star and Eagle Feather rode through the gate toward Daniel's cabin in Strong Heart Valley. Tall Woman had asked Daniel to stay a few days after the wedding - she wanted to talk with him.

"I will need two more of your horses," she said as they walked toward the cave. "I plan to send a delegation of five to Tahlequah in the Oklahoma Territory. We know that is where the government was taking the Cherokee people, but we don't know what has happened to them. We must know their condition, and they need to know about us.

"Hawk will be in charge," she continued, "and I will send Big Tree, Brave Bull, and two more of our people with them. The last I heard, when they were rounding up our people, was that Chief John Ross was among them. He is a wise man. If he made the trip alive, he will be about organizing the Cherokee."

"Mother, that is a very long way!" Daniel spoke with concern. " There will be many dangers along that trail. And we don't know how the soldiers figure into this, or even where they are?"

"We have never shirked from danger," she said softly. "Especially when a mission was vital to our people. It is most important that we re-connect with the Cherokee Nation. For all we know, we may be the only Cherokee left in the world! I have thought long and hard about this. The government probably has our people on a reservation there. If that is so, they won't be difficult to find."

"The difficult part will be in getting there, Mother. Many

84

miles lie between here and Oklahoma Territory. Seeing five Cherokee warriors riding through the countryside - no telling what the white-eyes will think or do."

"We will dress the five in white man clothes," she answered. "Many of our people came to this village wearing white man clothes. That will be no problem."

When Daniel saw he could not dissuade his mother, he set about thinking of how the mission could be accomplished. Hawk, and Big Tree spoke the white man's language as good as they did. If they ran into white men, communications would not be difficult. But they would need more than two horses. Hawk, Brave Bull, and Big Tree already had mounts, in addition, they would need at least three pack animals, extra ammunition, food, and camping equipment. If they ran short of food, they could supplement it by hunting.

On his return to Strong Heart, Daniel sent five horses back with Star and Eagle Feather - three were strong, good for pack animals. Eagle Feather trailed the three pack horse carrying fruit and nuts to Tall Woman. Star trailed two riding horses packed with smoke-cured deer and antelope. Then Daniel, with the help of many friends, began work on his great cabin in Lost Valley.

It was still spring when Hawk and his traveling companions set out for the Oklahoma Territory. None of them cared for the white man clothes they wore, but they were eager to get started on a new adventure and to see country they had never seen. They took the most direct route from the Cherokee mountains to Oklahoma Territory. Their travels would take them from western North

Carolina, across southern Tennessee, into Arkansas as far as present day Little Rock, then on to Fort Smith. From there they would travel into Oklahoma Territory and up to Tahlequah. It doesn't sound far when you say it right fast, but riding horseback up and down mountains, hills, and through unknown country, was going to tale a long time.

They carried their long rifles, knives, and tomahawks, but their bows and arrows they hid undercover on the pack animals. Seeing five Cherokees with bows and arrows might frighten whatever white men they ran across, but the rifles would not. It was common practice for Indian and white alike to carry long rifles. When needed for silent hunting, they would then bring the bows out from cover.

The men rode from daylight until dusk each day. When they camped the first night, they were still in western North Carolina, and would be, for quite a ways yet. That night they cooked venison on a stick over a small fire, and talked about being chosen for this important mission until sleep came to their eyes. On the forth day, they came across a Cherokee cabin and saw a couple weeding their garden. The couple was glad to see them, and asked them to share a meal and spend the night - which they gladly accepted.

They had much current information to share with Hawk and his group. They told the men that they were on the right trail that would take them into southern Tennessee, and gave them directions to another Cherokee family on down the trail. The man said that family would direct them to others who would help them along the way. The man told Hawk that the Cherokee had, indeed, made it to Oklahoma Territory, but that thousands had died along the way. This news grieved Hawk and his men terribly.

After the evening meal, they all moved out onto the cabin's porch. While smoking the pipe, Hawk learned that Chief John Ross was yet alive and had organized the Cherokee at Tahlequah into the Western Band of the Cherokee Nation. He said the men who had, unauthorized, signed the treaty with the government for Indian removal to Tahlequah had been killed by the Cherokee. He also said that the Cherokee had already built homes, schools, and were growing corn and vegetables. He said they were organized and settled.

Early the next morning the five headed out to find the family who lived some fifty miles away. The trails were getting easier to travel, but the man had told them they would run into rough traveling crossing Tennessee. That night, they rested at a campsite, but hit the trail early the next morning. They found the Cherokee family that evening, ate with them, and gathered more information. This family informed them that the army was not hunting the Cherokee anymore. The news about the army relieved Hawk and his men considerably. This family directed them to a small Cherokee settlement just across the Tennessee line.

After three days, they found the settlement, was welcomed heartily, and they decided to stay there a few days to gather more news and hunt deer to replenish their meat supply. Six cabins made up the village. Corn and vegetables were growing and the settlement looked prosperous and healthy. Big Tree decided to help a family who was building an additional room onto their cabin, while Hawk and Brave Bull went hunting.

Hawk's other two men, Nightbird and Laughs-a-lot,

helped gather corn for the settlers. Nightbird knew the night sky and could find directions by following the stars. That was the reason Tall Woman had chosen him for this trip. Laughs-a-lot was an oddity. He never smiled, never laughed, and seldom talked. He was a prime example of an Indian with a stone face. But when it came to horses, no one knew them better. Laughs-a-lot was Daniel's chief horse tamer and trainer.

Crossing southern Tennessee was rough in places, but the men managed and then passed into Arkansas. At Little Rock they saw other Indians milling around, so felt no threat. After a night in the woods, they continued on to Fort Smith. Getting directions to Tahlequah from a mule skinner, they skirted the town, and set off in that direction. Hawk had expected problems with white people along the way, and was pleasantly surprised when he found none.

Oklahoma Territory was, to Hawk and his men, ugly in many respects. It blew dust into their eyes. There were no high mountains like in western North Carolina, and the wind blew sharp across the land. They found a creek and after watering the horses, took a bath. They camped beside the creek that night, ate a good meal of venison and parched corn, and when morning came, they changed into their buckskins. They were not about to let the reservation Cherokee see mountain people in white man clothes.

Approaching the reservation they saw many white houses, barns, and planted fields. They were not prepared to see so many thousands of Cherokee. The Cherokee were dressed in white man clothes, and stared at them as they rode in. Hawk asked a young man where he might find Chief John Ross. Finding the house they were directed to, they dismounted, tied their horses to a white picket fence, and walked up to the porch. They just stood there. After several minutes, Hawk spoke in Cherokee.

"Osiyo, in the house! We would speak to Chief John Ross!" After a few minutes, a white haired man opened the screened door and stepped onto the porch, holding some papers in his hand. He looked at each man carefully, then said:

"I am John Ross. It appears you men have come a long way."

"We have come from Tall Woman's Village in the Cherokee Mountains. She is my mother. Tall Woman sent us here to learn of the condition of the Cherokee people - to learn if they are still alive - to learn what we can and return to her."

"You have traveled many miles, my sons," said the Chief smiling warmly. "Come. Sit on the porch. We will talk." Offering them water, he asked about Tall Woman's health.

"She is well," responded Hawk.

"I know of Tall Woman. I knew her mother and father, and I also knew Running Elk. You say you are her son? How many children does Tall Woman have?"

"I am her youngest son. I have an older brother, Daniel, and a younger sister, called Star. These are my friends - Big Tree, Brave Bull, Nightbird, and Laughs-a-lot." The men nodded their heads as their names were called.

"When we left the mountains, Tall Woman had somewhat over eight hundred people in two large villages. She wishes to know what will become of the mountain Cherokee."

"That will take some days to talk about," said Chief Ross.

"Tomorrow morning, I will hold a council meeting. You men will attend. You will hear about what is happening here, and the plans we have for the mountain Cherokee. I will want you to speak before the people, to tell them of Tall Woman's people. They will want to know how so many Cherokee escaped the Trail of Tears."

The men ate with Chief Ross that evening. The food was prepared by his cook, a middle aged Cherokee woman. They ate steak, mashed potatoes, corn, green beans, and cornbread. Some of the food was different to them, or at least cooked differently, but they ate and enjoyed the meal. They had never sat at a mahogany dinner table before, and had not eaten with fine china or shining silverware.

That night, Chief Ross invited them to sleep in his house because he had several empty rooms and he knew they were tired from the last leg of their trip. But they declined, preferring to sleep on the porch. They moved the cane bottomed chairs to one side, spread out their bedrolls, and drifted off to sleep thinking about all of the white man furniture they had seen in the house.

The Council Meeting was held in a long, white structure of milled lumber. Outside, whitewashed stones lined a walkway, and there was a flagpole flying the orange flag of the Western Cherokee Nation. In the center was the Nation's Great Seal surrounded by seven stars signifying the seven Cherokee Clans. In future years, official buildings would be made of brick, but here, now, the buildings were made of milled lumber and painted with whitewash.

Hawk, Brave Bull, Big Tree, Nightbird and Laughs-a-Lot followed Chief John Ross into the building filled with fifty leaders of the Western Band of the Cherokee Nation. A

90

hush covered the large room. The leaders were sitting in cane bottomed chairs, all wearing white man clothes, some wore brogans and a few old timers wore moccasins.

From a lectern, Chief Ross opened with a dialog beneficial to Hawk and his men. He spoke of the hardships of the Trail of Tears, the difficulty of organizing the Western Band after arriving at Tahlequah, and finally of the unity achieved after many heated arguments. He spoke of the Council's desire to reunite with the mountain Cherokee to establish an Eastern Band of the Cherokee Nation at some central point in the Blue Ridge Mountains. He told Council members of Tall Woman's efforts in bringing together a great many Cherokee families and settling them in two villages high in the mountains.

Chief Ross brought Hawk to the podium who related in detail the hardships of the mountain people at first, but that now the people were happy and healthy. Hawk told them of Tall Woman's desire to reconnect with the Cherokee of Oklahoma Territory, and waited for instructions of how that could be accomplished. Hawk's humble and pleasant voice, coupled with the fact, "awaiting instructions", won the Council over wholeheartedly. Many voices were raised in the positive, and many questioned were asked and answered by Hawk.

It was evident to them that Tall Woman was a wise chief who wanted nothing more than a people united once again. They voted unanimously on sending to Tall Woman an official charter directing her to establish an Eastern Band of the Cherokee Nation with her as chief of all chiefs. After the meeting Hawk and his men were swamped with attention and more questions. Hawk and his men had carried themselves with quiet humility and dignity and had gained the respect of these tough leaders.

The men stayed at the reservation three weeks. Brave Bull, Big Tree, Nightbird and Laughs-a-Lot moved into an empty bunkhouse, and mingled with the people of Tahlequah, but Hawk stayed with Chief Ross. There was much the Chief had to share with Hawk, much official information for him to relate to Tall Woman. When Hawk and his men finally left Tahlequah, they left with food, ammunition, warm blankets, extra corn for the horses, and the goodwill of the Tahlequah Cherokee. Hawk carried a large leather folder of official documents for Tall Woman.

Hawk and his men had been gone a few days over four months when they finally arrived back at Tall Woman Village. The whole village turned out to greet the adventurers. That evening, Tall Woman held a feast in their honor and publicly praised each man for satisfactorily carrying out the mission she had given them.

"The bravery and endurance of these five men is beyond question," she said proudly to over three hundred families. "They have brought news of our people in Oklahoma Territory. They are alive and well there, and they have established a Western Band of the Cherokee Nation at a place called Tahlequah. The Western Cherokee Nation's flag waves there. Unfortunately, four thousand of our people perished along the way, but many thousands still live."

Tall Woman paused to let the loss of so many sink in. She held up the charter Hawk had given her.

"This," she waved the charter before the people, "is an official charter from principal Chief John Ross, and the leaders under him, giving me the authority to establish an Eastern Band of the Cherokee Nation here in the mountains." Thunderous applause rippled through the village.

"Soon, I will be moving to Lost Valley to live in a cabin Daniel has built for me there. From there, I will be better able to build our new nation. I am promoting my daughter, Star, to chief of this village. Her two sub-chiefs will be Brave Bull and Eagle Feather. Star, as you know is a Beloved Woman, and her sub-chiefs are well known and respected by you.

"I am taking Hawk and Big Tree with me. Hawk will become chief of Strong Heart Valley. Big Tree will continue as my protector. Daniel is already chief of Lost Valley where many families are building cabins and breaking ground for acres of corn, squash, and other vegetables. None of our people in all three villages will ever go hungry again. There are now almost a thousand Cherokee families in our three settlements.

"My efforts will be in building for us a new nation, a nation of Mountain Cherokee, a people of pride and honor. I will be traveling a lot in my new role as Chief-of-all-Chiefs. There are still many families out there. They will be brought to Lost Valley and join those already there. Tomorrow morning, Hawk, Big Tree, and myself will leave for Lost Valley. So, I will take this opportunity to express my love for each one of you. Each of you, I know by name and face. And your names and faces will always be in my heart."

With Hawk now chief of Strong Heart, and Tall Woman living in the cabin Daniel had built in Lost Valley, Daniel felt complete. He could now spend all of his time making the big valley into many homes for those who would soon come, and breaking more ground for growing food. He could now, also, construct more corrals for his growing horse herd. He had made it clear to those living in Strong Heart that access was clear for them to enter Lost Valley any time they wished, to gather fresh fruit, berries, nuts, and corn from the fields.

Hawk had moved into Daniel's old cabin in Strong Heart, and had kept the same four sub-chiefs that had served Daniel so well. Daniel, Tall Woman, and Big Tree had rooms of their own in the big cabin, and Daniel had hired a single, middle-aged Cherokee to cook for them. Her name was Willow. She had no one to care for her, having lost her family during the round-up of the Cherokees. An addition was built onto the Kitchen that gave her easy access to her work. She was a great cook, and she loved the family that had taken her in and cared for her.

The cabin had three bedrooms, a large family room - the kitchen and Willow's room was separated from the main cabin by a covered path - and Daniel had made furniture for the cabin. Each bedroom had a bed, a rawhide bottomed chair, a small table, and deer antlers on the walls for hanging clothing. In Tall Woman's room, there was also a desk and a second chair. The desk had pigeon-holes for storing papers. On the desk was an ink-well and scribes made from turkey feathers.

In the family room was a large, stone fireplace that vented into the chimney outside. The fireplace easily kept the cabin warm during winter. There was a long table with six chairs, a large wood bin, and antler racks for holding coats. Willow's room was kept warm in winter by the kitchen fireplace. In each room there were antler racks holding long rifles. Outside, about fifteen yards away, Daniel had built a toilet with two holes. A corral, with attached barn, stood away from the cabin for their horses - the horses had become accustomed to being led in and out of the falls. Daniel also built a corral on the other side of the falls in Strong Heart Valley, with a barn. Ten or fifteen horses were kept there for easy access. Now, there were horses on either side of the falls. Like Star had said years ago, things were looking up.

Throughout the following months, Tall Woman sent out men on horseback searching for families all over the Cherokee Mountains. They kept coming in, and as soon as they arrived they were taken into Lost Valley. More cabins went up and more ground was broken for planting. The Eastern Band of the Cherokee Nation grew by leaps and bounds.

Beyond the falls, at Strong Heart, Tall Woman had a large structure made of logs with a split rail fence around it. Whitewashed stones separated a stone walkway, and there was a tall flag pole in front of the structure. At the top waved a yellow flag with a circle in its center that read: The Seal of the Eastern Band of the Cherokee Nation. In the center of the circle was a seven pointed star representing

the seven Cherokee Clans. This was the official offices of
the Eastern Band. All the Cherokee from Tall Woman
Village, Lost Valley, and Strong Heart were present at the
flag raising.

There was an enormous celebration with food, dances,
flute and drum music. More than a thousand people were
gathered in Strong Heart. There were speeches made, and
Tall Woman was honored as the Chief of the Mountain
Cherokee. She was the Chief of Chiefs of the Eastern Band
of the Cherokee Nation. She had finally realized her dream
of a united people.

And then Daniel met Blue Eyes. She was the most
beautiful Cherokee he had ever seen. Her waist length hair
was so black, it looked a shade of dark blue, and she was
well proportioned for her height of five foot seven inches -
just a few inches shorter than Daniel. Her eyes were pastel
blue. Odd, Daniel thought. Cherokees had black eyes, yet
here was a Cherokee with beautiful blue eyes. She was
standing beside the new flagpole with her mother and
father. Daniel walked over and introduced himself to the
family and caught her name - Sahani Dikata (Blue Eyes).

"I was wondering," said Daniel to the family, "if you
would honor me by sitting at my family's table?"

"You are Chief Daniel, son of Tall Woman?" questioned
Sahani's father.

"Yes, I am."

"We would be honored," replied the father.

Daniel escorted them to Tall Woman's table and
introduced them to his mother, Hawk, Star, Eagle Feather,
and a few others. Sahani's Family were so impressed by
sitting and eating with such dignitaries they seemed ill at

ease. But Tall Woman, recognizing it, came around the table grasped the father's hands and said "You are welcome here. You are Cherokee, so that makes you family. Please sit, eat, drink, and enjoy the festivities." It wasn't long till the family engaged in friendly conservation with Daniel's family and relaxed.

"You are wondering about my eyes?" Sahani asked Daniel.

"Yes, they are beautiful. I have never seen a Cherokee with such eyes."

"My great grandfather was a white mountain man. He married my great grandmother and lived most of his life as a Cherokee. He was adopted into the Blue Clan and became a great Cherokee warrior. His bravery is still talked about among my clan. His eyes were blue like mine, but his heart was Cherokee. As far as I know, I am the only one in all my family that has blue eyes."

Sahani's father was called, Yona (Bear), and her mother, Woya (Dove).

The second day after the celebration, Daniel showed up a Yona's cabin in Lost Valley with eight fine horses. He asked to speak with Yona, Sahani's father. The family stood outside the cabin.

"I have come to ask permission to wed your daughter, Sahani," he said. "I have brought eight beautiful horses as a sign of respect. If she can be my wife, she will be treated with much love and respect. As my wife she will be the princess of Lost Valley and accorded the respect of a chief's wife. As the parents of a princess, you will gain much stature and will be well cared for."

"I would speak with my family for a short time," said

97

Yona. "Please wait here."

After a time, the family came out of the cabin and Yona spoke. "I have talked with my wife and Sahani and we are all in agreement. This is a good thing."

Daniel broke into a great smile. He handed the horses' reins to Yona, embraced Dove, kissed Sahani's cheek, and told them that he would speak with Tall Woman about the arrangements, and that Tall Woman would soon meet with them to discuss the marriage plans. Daniel walked on air all the way to Arrow, swung upon his back, and rode away a happy man.

The next day, Daniel's chief horse trainer, Laughs-a-Lot, showed up with his men and built a corral and a barn for Yona's horses. They also built a split-rail fence around the cabin and a stone walkway. As the days passed Hawk and Star showed up with baskets of fruit, berries, and nuts. Star had not yet gone back to Tall Woman Village. Finally, Tall Woman and Big Tree came with smoked venison, elk, and turkey. They brought cured and finished doe skins to be made into dresses, pants, shirts, and moccasins. Big Tree gave Sahani a large basket of multi-colored beads, and colored ribbons.

"We have never received so many gifts," Dove told Tall Woman.

"My son is telling you of his love. It is his way. He is very wealthy, and gives generously to those he loves."

Tall Woman spent most of the day talking over wedding arrangements with Sahani and her family. They all had a grand time with much laughter, even Big Tree joined in the laughter. They all agreed the wedding would be held the first moon of fall beside the Waterfall - an outside affair.

There would be many tables laden with all kinds of food. After the wedding, there would be dancing, music, and gaiety. Hundreds would attend the wedding. That afternoon, Daniel brought Sahani one of his best pinto mares, and while the families continued their planning, he and Sahani went for a ride by the stream that flowed beneath tall cottonwood trees. Birds were singing soulfully from the trees that evening.

"What will you name your pony?" Daniel asked, as they walked hand in hand beside the water.

"I will name her Galihelisdi (Thankful), because I am thankful the Great Spirit brought you to me. I have been praying that a beautiful warrior such as you would come and carry me away." They embraced and they kissed for the first time. It was a long, passionate kiss. The first of many to come.

Tall Woman had been planning to build a cabin next to the Eastern Band headquarters at Strong Heart so she would be closer to her work. She had grown tired of walking through the cave behind the waterfall each morning. Usually, when she reached the headquarters there was a line of people with problems, or requests, of one sort or another that did not fall under Hawk's authority as chief of Strong Heart. And now that Daniel was getting married, she thought it best to have a cabin of her own built.

She talked it over with Hawk, and before long a two bedroom cabin, with a family room was built for her. Like Daniel's cabin, the kitchen was separated from the main structure by a covered path, and had a room at one end of the kitchen for a live-in cook. Willow, moved to Strong Heart as Tall Woman's cook. A split rail fence ran around the cabin, and it had a stone walkway. Big Tree's bedroom was separated from Tall Woman's by the family room. Tall Woman was careful not to do anything that would cause rumors, not that there would be any - Big Tree was a loyal protector and nothing more. His whole life was in keeping Tall Woman safe.

Tall Woman had closed the headquarters office late that day - dealing with papers she needed to send to Tahlequah and Chief John Ross. She was tired. Straining over the complicated legal documents had made her that way. Big Tree followed her to the cabin and opened the door for her to enter, then he followed her inside. The cook had fixed their supper, and there was a small fire in the fireplace. It was not cold, but evenings in the mountains brought with it a slight chill. Tall Woman ate, said her "good nights", and went to her room. Big Tree was not sleepy. He felt like talking now that Tall Woman was safe and secure in her room. He felt that he could relax. He laid his percussion pistol on the table where he sat talking to Willow, the cook.

But Big Tree did not know of the danger that lurked on the ridge overlooking Strong Heart Valley, where thirteen Creek warriors hid behind large stones - peeking around the stones at the settlement below. No one would expect a raid on a village with so many Cherokees, but this was not a raid. This was a calculated plot to assassinate the one Cherokee they hated above all people - Tall Woman. This was the woman that had destroyed one of their villages so many years ago. This was the woman responsible for the deaths of almost forty Creek warriors. This was the woman who had sent women and children to brave the winter cold to another land - a land where they had, finally, located a Creek village far away. The women had spread the tale of the slaughter and the burning of their village. They had told and retold the story about a Cherokee warrior that had shot a tied-up Creek woman in the face, blowing half her face off.

Over the years the hatred had built until, finally, a plan was made to send a small war party deep into Cherokee territory to take revenge, to wipe Tall Woman off of the face of the earth, the woman who was now the Chief of all Eastern Cherokee. The Creeks had been on the ridge two weeks - watching, plotting the routine of Tall Woman, and seeing only one man who guarded her. Their plan was for eight Creeks to create a diversion by stealing the horses from the corral near the cabin where she lived, while five specially selected warriors would gain entrance to her cabin and kill all three of its occupants.

They would wait until around midnight, then creep down into the valley under the cover of darkness. One group would go to the corral, while the assassins veered off to the cabin. When the thieves drove the horses off with loud war cries, the killers, using the noise and confusion, would break through the cabin door killing everyone in sight - particularly the hated Tall Woman. The people in the settlement would think the Creeks came on a horse stealing raid, and would chase after them into the night, leaving the killers to do their dirty work and slip off into the darkness amid the confusion. Only later would the villagers know the real reason for the raid.

When the horse thieves reached the corral, the five killers crept around the cabin to the front door and waited in the darkness. At the sound of whooping and hollering the horses thundering from the corral. The five Creek assassins burst through the cabin door expecting no one in the family room. What they saw was the biggest Cherokee they had ever seen holding a long pistol in his hand.

They saw the flame shoot from its barrel, knocking one Creek dead against the cabin wall. The big man hit another Creek so hard with the barrel of his pistol, it killed him instantly. Then pulling his long knife, the giant Cherokee slashed one warrior across his mid-section with such force, his insides fell onto the floor. He spun around ramming his long knife clean through an advancing warrior, while the last Creek ran at Big Tree, tomahawk raised for a fatal strike. As the big man tried to retrieve his knife from the belly of the man he had just stabbed, the human body held the knife firmly and would not let go. A rifle shot echoed the cabin. The warrior with the tomahawk fell dying against Big Tree from a shot to the head. Tall Woman stood in the hallway, smoke coming from her rifle. Willow, the cook, huddled in a corner with her hands covering her mouth, could say nothing.

Hawk came running into the cabin, a knife in one hand and a tomahawk in the other. "Mother, are you alright!" He cried.

"Yes," she replied evenly. "Big Tree has earned his pay this night."

"Can you handle things here?" Hawk asked Big Tree.

"I can," he said.

"I have stationed men outside in case this thing is not over," informed Hawk. "I have sent a man for Daniel and horses. He will be here soon. We will track the Creeks, get back our horses, and leave the Creeks face down in the dirt."

Just then Daniel ran through the door. "Mother..!" he cried.

"I am okay," she said. "Thank the Great Spirit for Big Tree. If not for him I might not be standing here. Go get your horses back and find the other Creeks. If you would, send a couple of the guards Hawk posted outside to help with this mess."

Daniel, Hawk, Laughs-a-Lot, Nightbird, and Yona, Sahani's father, and ten other Cherokees mounted the horses Daniel and his men had brought from Lost Valley and followed Laughs-a-Lot as he walked ahead tracking the Creeks in the dark. There was no hurry. The steep trail leading out of the valley would hinder the Creek's escape. Only one man at a time leading a horse could ascend to the ridge. At daybreak they found most all of the stolen horses grazing in the valley. These would be rounded up later. The Creeks had taken only eight horses, only those they could ride. Leading the other horses out of the valley would have taken too much time.

"Eight men leading horses went up this trail," Laughs-a-Lot told Daniel. "They are about two hours ahead of us."

"No need to hurry," informed Daniel. "There's no way they can escape. There's not a Creek village within fifty miles of here, so they will wear the horses out trying to put some distance between themselves and us. They will have to rest their mounts, or walk. We will follow at a trot and not wind our horses."

Several hours later Laughs-a-Lot motioned for Daniel to ride up to where he stood. "They stopped here," he reported. "They are now walking the horses. They are just ahead. Be careful of an ambush"

Daniel gave orders to stake their horses, and to follow him quietly. After about fifty yards, he raised his hand. The men stopped. Suddenly, a Creek warrior quickly stood and shot an arrow that pierced Daniel's thigh. He fell to the ground trying not to moan. Hawk was by his side immediately.

"Finish them," he told Hawk, grimacing with pain.

The arrow had penetrated Daniel's upper thigh without striking the bone, and was embedded halfway through his thigh. Yona stayed with him while the others laid down a volley of rifle fire, then ran in before the Creeks could recover. A furious knife and tomahawk close combat fight ensued. When it was finished all eight of the Creek warriors lay dead on the ground.

As the men gathered around Daniel, he told Hawk to pull the arrow from his thigh. Hawk placed a piece of folded rawhide cut from his own shirt between Daniel's teeth. He then sat on the ground and put both of his feet against Daniel's thigh - on either side of the arrow. He looked at his brother, and when Daniel nodded, he yanked the arrow shaft out with one fast pull, leaning back as he did so. He then poured a small amount of gun powder into the wound, and lit the powder. The powder's short blaze cauterized the wound. Using pressure, and tightly wrapping the leg with rawhide stopped most of the bleeding, but he would need to get Daniel home, and to a medicine man before infection set in.

Daniel was bedridden for two weeks, and was confined to his house for two months. Sahani never left his side. At night, when Daniel was feverish, she slept on a bedroll beside his bed, checking him frequently. When the fever finally broke, she fed him turkey soup and babied him like a doe babies a new born calf. Tall Woman and Hawk came often, as did his men, but Sahani would only let his men stay a short while - saying Daniel needed his rest. The wedding was postponed until he got well, and once Daniel talked about getting married while he was confined to the house, but Sahani vetoed that. She said the people of Lost Valley would want their Chief up and well and ready to dance the day away when they got married.

Because of what had happened, Tall Woman created the first ever Cherokee Police Force, selecting fifty men to provide security and give warning in case of another attack. They would also be available in an emergency such as a cabin fire, or in case of an accident requiring immediate attention. They wore red ribbons on their left arms. Twenty five men were given the day shift, headed by Yona, and twenty five men headed by Nightbird were given the night shift. They rode in pairs throughout the valley day and night.

Summer ended. Fall came with colors falling from trees in multi-painted leaves, and covered the ground with crunchy sounds as people walked on them beneath spreading limbs. It was coat weather. During the last week of fall, Daniel, who had recovered enough, stood beside Sahani, both wrapped in blue blankets, as a holy man performed the wedding ceremony. Since Sahani was an only child and had no brother, Hawk, according to custom, took the vow and the responsibility to teach the couples future children about spiritual matters. He, Tall Woman, and Sahani's mother stood with the couple as hundreds of Cherokee looked on with happy eyes and wide smiles. Then the holy man removed the blue blankets and wrapped Daniel and Sahani in a single white blanket, signifying that they were now husband and wife.

Loud cheers reverberated throughout the valley as flute and drum music filled the fall air. The sounds of laughter and gaiety, dancing and fun, happiness and mirth, enveloped the people as they celebrated this long anticipated event. Lost Valley now had a princess. Daniel now had a bride.

Tall Woman stood watching her oldest son kiss his new bride. She was happy and sad at the same time - happy that Daniel had, at last, found true love and a person to grow old with - a wife that would bear many grandchildren. But she was sad that Running Elk wasn't here to share her happiness. She looked up Big Tree who was standing beside her. She knew, as women always do, that he had loved her for a very long time, but he, out of respect for her position, had not stepped out of his place to express the feelings he had long repressed. She took his big hand into hers.

"How long have you loved me?" she said warmly. Big Tree took a few

seconds to make sure he had heard her words correctly.

"I have been your protector for a very long time," he said quietly, " I have loved you from the beginning."

"Come with me," she said, taking his hand and leading him toward her   cabin. "We have much to talk about."

The next day, Tall Woman sent a runner to bring Daniel

and Hawk to the headquarters building. She and Big Tree were sitting together by her desk when they arrived. They took seats and peered questioningly at their mother. Tall Woman was never one to mince words.

"I have news," she said. "Big Tree and I will marry." The boys looked at each other and broke out in laughter.

"What?" she questioned.

"This is not news, mother," blurted Hawk. "We have known this would happen for a long time. We just did not know when!" Tall Woman looked puzzled at Big Tree.

"We were waiting to see which one of you would be the first to break," laughed Daniel.

"You mean you knew all along?"

"We knew Big Tree would not step out of his position to ask you to marry him, so we bet on who would break the ice!"

"Who won?" asked Big Tree.

"Neither," replied Hawk. "We both thought it would be mother."

"Then you approve?" asked Big Tree.

"Yes!" they both responded at the same time.

Tall Woman and Big Tree were married a week later in a small ceremony in the headquarters building. Only a few people were invited: Daniel, Hawk, Star, Eagle Feather, Sahani and her parents, Brave Bull, and a few of Daniel's and Hawk's top men. The news spread fast. Tall Woman and Big Tree had, finally, married. All three villages were happy at Tall Woman's choice. While Star was there, she broke the news that she was with child.

She sent Brave Bull back to Tall Woman Village to administer things there, then she and Eagle Feather moved in with Hawk until the baby came. Star wanted to be near her mother and brothers at this special time in her life.

Fifteen miles west of the Cherokee settlement, four white trappers had built a lean-to camp and was preparing for winter trapping in a place the Cherokees called Where the Willows Grow. Cherokee women often came here to obtain wood for baskets. The trappers were butchering a buck killed earlier that day, and one, a young, smoothed faced trapper with a scar on his face, had started a good sized fire.

"I wouldn't build that fire so tall," a grey whiskered trapper with a severely bent nose told him. "This here is Cherokee territory, an' we ain't suppose' ta be here, no how!"

"I ain't skeered of no Cherokee!" the young trapper with the long scar boasted.

"You will be when one of them arrows splits your gizzard," remarked another trapper with a short black beard and beady eyes." The forth trapper said nothing. He just shook his head at the stupidity of young 'uns.

"Anyways," said the young man, "I intend to find me one of them purty squaws to winter with."

"I told y'all we shouldn't have brought that young idiot," the forth trapper with large ears finally spoke. He wore an earring on his right ear. "He's likely ta git us all kilt."

Brave Bull was riding back to Tall Woman Village when he saw smoke, and thought he would investigate. He tied his horse a distance from where the smoke was coming, and moved silently up to a camp where he saw the four trappers cooking something on a large fire. He also saw the remains of a deer hanging from a tree. He could hear the men's voices from where he hid in a clump of bushes, but he could not make out what they were talking about. He figured that he could kill two of the men with two fast arrows, another with his long rifle, then run in and finish the last trapper with his war club. But this, he thought, was news he should take to Star, his chief, who was now staying with Hawk at Strong Heart. Daniel had previously forbidden trappers to camp in Cherokee territory.

When Brave Bull arrived back at Strong Heart and told Star about the trappers camping at Where the Willows Grow, she became alarmed.

"Sahani and her mother, Dove, left earlier for that place!" she exclaimed. "They went to gather wood for baskets. We must catch up to them! They could be in trouble!"

Daniel and Hawk were not available right then, so Star, Eagle Feather, and Brave Bull galloped toward Where the Willows Grow as fast as their horses could carry them. When they got near the place where Brave Bull had seen the camp, they slowed their horses to a trot, then stopped, and hitched the horses to some willow trees and crept up to the camp. The camp had been moved. There were lots of tracks and debris lying around where the camp had been, but no trappers. They began to search the area.

Eagle Feather found the bodies of Sahani and her mother in a ravine not far away. They lay nude, face down, half covered with leaves. When Star saw the bodies she let out a scream and began to cry, her body racked with emotions. Eagle Feather put his arm around her and held her tight, he already knew Sahani and Dove were dead. They had been raped and choked to death. Brave Bull found what was left of their clothes and wrapped the women as best as he could. There was hate in his black eyes. He dreaded seeing Daniel and Yona when they learned of this tragedy.

Sahani and her mother were in a festive mood when they arrived at the Willows, and immediately began gathering wood for the baskets they planned to make. The young trapper with the scar on his face saw the women first. The other trappers were close by. Upon seeing the men, the women dropped the wood they had gathered and tried to run for their horses, but were blocked by the three other trappers. Losing whatever abandon they had, they rushed the women and threw them to the ground. After they had all assaulted Sahani and Dove, they realized they could not leave the women alive to warn the Cherokee or their lives would not be worth a plugged nickel - they choked them to death with no more feeling than a man would have stepping on a scorpion. They left them in the ravine, covered them with leaves, tore down their camp, and left the area immediately.

Brave Bull and Eagle Feather carried the women's limp bodies in their arms as they rode back to Strong Heart. Star and the men were so downcast as they rode slowly through the afternoon - it was as if there was no sunshine anywhere in the world. The Cherokee had experienced so much sadness over the passed years, they wondered if the Great Holy Spirit even cared for them anymore. As they entered the settlement, people began to gather as they slowly rode by with heavy eyes. When the people realized what had happened, wails arose so loud they brought Hawk and Daniel out to see what was going on.

Daniel took the body of Sahani from Brave Bull into his

arms and fell to his knees. He sobbed great sobs of grief and despair. His whole body shook. Tall Woman, Star, and Hawk knelt beside him. After a good while, Daniel recovered his composure and stood. He gave Sahani to Hawk's waiting arms.

"Sahani is no longer here," he said, "and I have died with her." He turned and walked away. When he returned, he was riding Arrow, and he trailed a pack horse loaded with what he would need on the trail.

"We will go with you," said Hawk, looking at Brave Bull and Eagle Feather. Brave Bull had given Daniel descriptions of the trappers.

"No. I will go alone. This is something I must do alone. Take care of Sahani's and Dove's funeral," he told his brother.

And to his mother, he said: "Place someone in charge of Lost Valley. I don't know when I will return. Maybe a month, maybe a year."

Tall Woman tossed him a rawhide pouch containing white man coins. He caught it. Without another word, he rode off toward Where the Willows Grow.

Looking after him, Tall Woman said "He will track the four trappers, but I am not sure that it will end there." His mother had again seen the hate for the white man in her son's eyes. She dreaded what her son might do.

Daniel had no problem picking up the trappers' tracks. They rode mounts that had been horseshoed, and one horse had a loose shoe. Two men trailed pack horses. He followed their trail for two days before the four separated - three horses went left, but one had headed on straight. Daniel decided to follow the one. The others he could come back

111

later and track, because one of those horses had the loose shoe. He followed his prey all that day. Just before dusk, it led him to a white settlement of two cabins, a trading post, a blacksmith shop, and a saloon.

Daniel camped on a rise above the settlement and watched. There weren't many men in the village. It was just a small place where people from the surrounding countryside came to trade and buy supplies from the trading post. He saw two Indians walking into the saloon to buy whiskey, so his presence there would not cause alarm. They were accustomed to seeing Indians around. But he decided to wait until morning to enter the village. He made a cold camp and slept that night, waking at first light. As he entered the settlement, he reined Arrow toward the blacksmith shop. A broad shouldered man was pounding away at a horseshoe on an anvil. Daniel pulled up to within earshot.

"Howdy," he said in perfect English. "Can you board my animals?"

"Can if you've got a dollar a day for both - includes feed."

Daniel flipped the man a coin, and got down from his horse. He un-

cinched his saddle, threw the saddle over a nearby fence rail. He had traded for the saddle two winters ago, but only used it on long trips. Riding bareback for long periods of time made a man's legs tired.

"Can I stow my gear here, also?"

"Jus' throw it there by the fence. No one'll bother it."

Daniel could tell the man had no use for Indians.

"Any place a man can eat here?" queried Daniel, taking his gear from the pack horse.

112

"Saloon's the only place," the blacksmith replied, not looking up. "They'll fix you a good venison steak an' taters an' such for a dollar."

"Who lives in the cabins?" asked Daniel.

"One's mine. The other belongs to the saloon-man. Rents beds for a dollar a night."

"Everything around here cost a dollar?" Asked Daniel.

"Nope. Horse-shooin' cost a dollar four bits." And then he said "Ain't never run across a injun that talks Amerikin as good as you before."

"Raised by a white missionary and his wife," Daniel lied over his Shoulder, walking toward the trading post.

He watched as the two Indians rode their mules out of the settlement and up a trail. The trading post was empty except for its tall skinny owner. It had the usual trading post supplies - rifles, knives, tomahawks, hides, ammunition, patent medicines, which promised to cure everything from coughs to bee stings, barrels of flour, sugar, and salt, animal traps, jugs of molasses and sundry other items.

"Help you?" the man asked, dryly.

"Take some rifle powder, and a can of those peaches," replied Daniel.

"You with that young feller that came in a couple days ago?"

"What feller is that?"

"The one with the scar on his face!"

"Don't know anyone with a scar on his face," answered Daniel.

"Just as well," stated the skinny man," he stays drunk aller time at tha saloon. Shiftless, iffin' you ask me!"

Daniel paid the man, walked out on the porch, opened the can of peaches with his knife, and ate them with the same knife while sitting on an outside bench. He knew he had found his man. After finishing the peaches, he walked across to the cabin that had a sign over the door that read: Beds for Rent. He looked inside and found it empty. He crossed back to the saloon and entered. Only two people there - the owner-bartender and a man about thirty sitting at a far table. He had a long scar down his left cheek.

"What can I getche?" asked the bartender.

"Bottle and a glass," answered Daniel.

He paid the bartender, took the bottle and sat at a table where he could watch the man with the scar. Daniel didn't drink alcohol, but he poured the glass until it was half full. He had formulated a plan to find out where the other three trappers had gone. He could go back and locate the tracks where they had veered off the trail, but if he could find out from the man with the scar where they were going, a lot of time could be saved. From what he had seen, there were only four people in the village: the blacksmith, the trading post owner, the bartender, and the man with the scar on his face. Daniel picked up his bottle and glass and walked over to the man's table.

"Have a drink with me," he said to the half-drunken man. "Never did like drinking by myself."

"Why, sure," blurted the man, with red streaked eyes. "Pour us 'nother of that snake pizin." Daniel filled his large glass and sat down. "Down here sellin' hides?" he asked.

"Yep. Sold a few to the trading post man," Daniel lied. "My partners are supposed to meet me here. You trap alone?"

"Naw," the man belched. "My pardners are over to Moss Point."

"Moss Point? Where's that?"

"'Bout thurty or thurty-five mile east a here. They gotta cabin there. Gotta couple of squaws, too."

Daniel saw the bartender walk outside for fresh air. When he was all the way outside, Daniel stood up as if to pour another drink, instead he walked behind the drunk, pulled the man's head back by the hair of his head and cut his throat from ear to ear. He wiped his knife clean on the man's shirt, then walked outside.

"Say, mister," he said to the bartender, "that man's sick back there. He's coughing up blood."

"What tha! Guess I'd better see what's tha matter."

Daniel followed the bartender across to where the drunk was doubled up on the table. When the bartender saw all the blood, he stiffened like a board.

"What's happened here?" he blurted.

"Just this," said Daniel, as he stuck his knife deep in the bartender's side, then stepped behind him and cut his throat.

Blood spurted forward onto the table as he folded to the floor. Daniel cleaned his knife on the man's shirt, then walked next door to the trading post. Once inside, he asked the owner for another can of peaches. When the man reached up to take a can from a shelf, Daniel grabbed his hair, pulled him back and cut his throat. The owner gurgled as he died, bleeding to death behind the counter. He walked over to a gun cabinet and took two long barreled pistols, some shot, and several more powder horns. He loaded the pistols and stuck them behind his wide belt.

115

Daniel had never stolen anything in his life, but in his state of mind, he figured anything he took from white men could never make up for his loss of Sahani.

Daniel then walked down to the blacksmith shop with the whisky bottle in his hand and shoved it toward the smithy. "Have a drink," Daniel offered the blacksmith.

"Well, don't mind if I do," he bellowed thankfully.

CHAPTER THREE

Daniel Denali

Daniel had found a cave big enough for him, Arrow, and the pack horse up in the hills. By his read of the sky, he knew winter was going to be a bad one, so while he could, he gathered and chopped wood for the cave. The back of his cave stood tall with wood and pine boughs. He hunted deer and antelope, built a smoker, and smoked-cured meat enough to last. He enclosed the mouth of the small cave and covered the front with brush for concealment. There was a stream not far from the cave, but he planned to melt snow for water when winter came.

And winter came with a fury. Cold, icy wind blew in from the north and covered the ground with two feet of white snow on the first day. Winds whipped trough the pines and cedars sounding their lonesome whines and whistles. A man could hibernate and sleep like a bear in weather like this. Before long it turned into a blizzard. Snow flakes came down so hard, aided by the cutting wind, it stung his face. Folks think snow cannot sting, but it can in a blizzard, and it was so thick he could not see beyond two feet in front of him.

117

So he built a good fire close to the cave's entrance where smoke would ventilate and he hibernated. And he hated. He hated the white man with every fiber of his being, even the name Daniel. In his now darkened mind, he changed his name back to Denali swearing never to use Daniel again. Daniel was dead. Daniel died when Sahani drew her last breath. In return, Denali would take the life breath away from as many white men as he could before breathing his own last breath.

White people in the settlements had become enraged over the beheadings. There wasn't much law in the mountains, but there were a few constables here and there. People wrote letters and sent special emissaries to larger settlements and seats of local government for something to be done about the outrage. Before long bounty hunters were engaged to find whoever was doing the killings, but no one had seen the killer and did not know who it was that cut off so many heads. Some placed the blame on crazed trappers. None ever thought it was a Cherokee. The Cherokee were a peaceful people, and had been for many years.

Eight bounty hunters rode from settlement to settlement asking questions and trying to gather any evidence they could find. But there was no evidence, just bodies with no heads. These hunters were hard men who could track almost as good as an Indian, and could shoot an apple from a tree at over two hundred yards. They were a determined lot with only two goals - find the killer and collect the bounty. With the blizzard blowing full blast, they could do nothing until it stopped, so they holed up at the village where the first murders had occurred. The saloon had been cleaned up and had a new owner, as did the trading post and blacksmith shop. The bounty hunters spent their time in the saloon huddled around a pot bellied stove drinking whiskey and telling lies. They would wait for a weather break or news of more murders.

After several weeks, Denali got cave fever and had to get out for awhile. He decided to visit the same settlement where he had killed those first four people. No one had seen him there except the dead, so no one would recognize him as the killer. If the trading post was re-opened, he would buy some coffee, bacon, sugar, and salt. If it was closed, he would break in and take what he needed. He saddled up Arrow, left the pack horse in the cave out of the weather, and struck out for the settlement. It was still snowing hard, but he could see farther ahead than he could when the blizzard had struck. He used his own innate sense of directions to find the village. Looking backward, he could see his tracks already being covered by snow. After two hours of traveling, Denali saw lights coming from the settlement. He rode in, hitched his horse to a hitching post, and walked into the trading post. A short bald man was the new owner behind the counter.

"Howdy." Denali said in a friendly manner. "Sure is nasty out there!"

"Didn't expect to see anybody out in this weather," the short man remarked.

"Aw, I got myself caught headed back home," lied Denali. "Saw the lights - thought I'd stop in, warm myself, and get a few things."

He walked to a nearby pot-bellied stove, took off his mittens, and warmed his hands.

119

"Need a couple pounds of coffee, a slab of bacon, some sugar and salt,"he told the man. "You the only one awake here about?"

"Naw, there's sum bounty hunters next door to tha saloon. They're waitin' for the weather to clear. Been looking for that head chopper," the man said putting together Denali's order.

"Heard about that," grinned Denali.

"Folks seem ta think it's sum crazed trapper," offered the short owner.

"There's a few crazy ones running in these mountains," said Denali.

"Well, here's your order, young man." Denali left the stove and walked to the counter.

"Tell you what, add a couple of those canned peaches, up there on that shelf."

The man had turned to reach for the peaches when Denali hopped the counter, put a knife to the man's throat and cut it from ear to ear. He fell to the floor spurting blood and making gurgling sounds. Denali found a meat saw near the counter and sawed the man's head off. He washed his hands in sink pan, picked up his sacked order, then picked up the man's head by the hair, and walked out the door. After hanging his order over his saddle horn, GE took the head next door and placed it in front of the saloon door where the bounty hunters would be sure to see it. He swung up into the saddle and rode off into the night. The heavy snow was already covering up Arrow's tracks.

When Denali got back to his cave there were still a few dying coals in the fire he had left. He added more wood, then put on a pot of coffee, fried some bacon, and heated up some fry bread he had brought with him. He walked to the cave's opening and saw his tracks were already covered by snow. Sitting by the fire, he drank his coffee with a sinister, dark, grin on his face.

At the settlement, one of the bounty hunters decided it was time for him to sleep. He bade his comrades in arms goodnight and walked toward the door. Outside, a lantern brightened up the saloon's porch. When he opened the door, he saw the head staring up at him and let out a howl that would have waken the dead. The other bounty hunters rush to the door not knowing what to expect.

"Look at that!" he cried. "That belongs to the tradin' post man!"

"Son of-a bitch,!" bellowed one of them. They all rushed next door and found the decapitated body lying in a pool of blood behind the counter.

"That bastard has been here, and with all eight of us rite next door. He's laughing at us!" said the leader.

"Tell you what boys," said one of the hunters, "you can have my part of the reward. Any fool with this much brass - I want no part of. I'm headed home!"

With that, he walked out the door and across to the Beds for Rent cabin, got his bedroll, saddled his horse, and rode away up the snow covered trail. At the saloon, one of the bounty hunters retrieved the head, placed it next to the body, and they all went back to the saloon for several stiff drinks. When the weather cleared a bit, they saddled their horses and rode off on the frozen trail. Not far from the settlement they found the frozen body of the man who had left earlier. His head was setting on his chest. They were unaware of the sinister, dark, grin on Denali's face.

121

After two weeks, the snow storm died down. The cold wind still whistled through the trees, it was still snowing, but not as hard as before. A man could see ahead a hundred yards. The bounty hunters returned to the settlement where Denali had killed the short, bald trading post owner. There were only four die-hard bounty hunters left - the rest had gave up and went home where it was safe and warm. The hunters wanted to scout the area for out-lying shacks, cabins, or other hiding places the killer might use. They figured the head chopper was somewhere in the vicinity. What they did not know was that Denali's cave was two hours from where they were searching, but right now he was watching them from behind a snow bank a hundred yards away. When the storm had lessened, he figured the hunters would return to the place where the killings had started and would search outward from there. They knew about the three trappers killed at Moss Point, but they had already combed that area and found nothing other than the headless bodies.

Denali watched as the men rode single file on a trail that led away from the settlement and around a hill. He eased Arrow down onto the trail, and moved up, following twenty yards behind. The wind covered any sounds he might make, and from his vantage point he could barely see the last bounty hunter through a snowy haze. He knew the trail curved abruptly ahead, and as the trail began to curve, he soundlessly moved Arrow up closer. The last hunter wore a wool cap with ear flaps tied down around his neck. When Denali could no longer make out the three front men making the sharp curve ahead, he quickly moved up behind the last man.

He hit the man at the base of his neck with a tremendous blow with his hatchet. It severed the man's head from his neck-bone and spine. There was only a slight moan - the howling wind muted the sound. The man's head fell forward onto his chest, held together only by skin and gristle. The bounty hunter leaned forward and fell lazily from his horse in two feet of soft snow. The horse stopped, looking around at the fallen rider. Denali dismounted and calmed the horse. With a swift hatchet blow he severed the rest of the man's head from his body. He turned the man onto his back, and placed his head on top of his chest.

Denali pulled the hood of his heavy rawhide jacket over his head and moved on toward his next target, his hatchet in his right hand. The wind picked up its howl, and snow kept falling. As Denali came up on the bounty hunter's right side, the man turned to see who was siding him. At that point,Denali swung and caught the man just below the Adams apple with a powerful blow. The sharp blade went clean to the bone. Only a gurgle was heard as the man fell from his saddle. The horse bolted and raced toward the other bounty hunters. Denali dismounted, and quickly chopped the rest of the man's head off and placed it on the man's chest. He mounted Arrow then disappeared into the night. As the frightened, rider-less horse shot passed the last two bounty hunters, they reined up in shocked bewilderment.

"What tha..?" blurted the leader.

Then it dawned on the two men that something had happened to their comrades.

"We'd better go see what happened to 'em," he said loudly, so the other man could hear his words over the wind. They found the first headless man lying in red snow, but did not dismount. Wide eyed, they backtracked and found the other bounty hunter with his head on his chest, also.

"That son-of-a-bitch is tracking to kill us all!" yelled the leader.

"He ain't human!" hollered the other one, "it's like he wuz a ghost. We'd best be shaggin' our tails outta here!"

They turned their mounts and went racing and sliding down the trail as fast as they could safely go. Denali sat on Arrow some yards away, his two long pistols in hand, grinning his sinister grin. He had planned to let the last two go so they would spread the word. And spread it they did. The stories and tales about the head chopper spread throughout the white mountain settlements like wildfire. Men carried weapons everywhere they went, and they kept their womenfolk and children at home, even though no harm had thus far come to women or children. Only the bravest of trappers went out to ply their trade. Too many stories abounded about lone trappers in the wilds suddenly looking up to see a crazed man with a long pistol in one hand, and a sharp hatchet in the other. There was talk about bringing in the army.

The stories had even reached Tall Woman at Strong Heart Village. A runner she had sent to the army post to learn of their possible building of a reservation nearby, brought the news. By then, the head count had reached thirty dead, the runner told her. Her heart sank. She knew in her heart of hearts that her Daniel was doing these terrible things. He had gone off the deep end - he had gone insane. And she knew what had twisted his mind. The death of Sahani at the hands of the white trappers had set the fuse to burning and he had exploded with hatred and a killing lust for all white men. A hatred so intense that would end only in his death. She bowed her head in her hands and grieved because there was nothing she could do to stop Daniel's hurt or the senseless killings.

Tall Woman wondered if she should tell Hawk and Star. Star was heavy with child - any day she expected a grand baby to be born. This drastic news may cause some abnormal reaction. Daniel was her hero, and had been since her childhood. And Hawk would most assuredly be effected; he would immediately want to find his brother and bring him home. And even if Hawk could find Daniel, what would happen if he attempted to bring Daniel home. Was Daniel so far gone that a death fight might ensue? She did not know. This was one time this great leader, this woman warrior, did not know what to do - so she grieved - she cried bitter tears. But, for the present, no one knew of her turmoil and would not know until she had had time to think it through.

All three of Tall Woman's villages were doing well and in good hands. Brave Bull, in the absence of Star, had proved to be a capable leader at Tall Woman Village. And although, at first, she wasn't sure of how Laughs-a-Lot would be as chief of Lost Valley, he had surpassed her expectations. Many more cabins had been built there, and many families had moved into those dwellings. Through Laughs-a-Lot's capable hands, the horse herds had grown and had become a profitable business. He was an expert at trading and selling horses, bringing in large funds for the

Cherokee settlement. Yona, of course, had been devastated by the loss of his wife and his daughter, but had buried himself in his position of daytime security boss, and had become a great asset to Tall Woman. Nightbird relished his job as night-time security leader and had saved two cabins from burning to the ground. Hawk's leadership at Strong Heart had always been above her expectations, but she knew he badly missed his brother and wished for him to be home. Big Tree had taken over many of the day to day problems of Strong Heart, relieving Tall Women to tackle the larger problems of building an Eastern Cherokee Nation. Now, if only Daniel was home and healthy, she would be a happy woman again.

Brave Bull watched as the army patrol passed through the gate at Tall Woman's Village. A young, clean shaven, pleasant talking lieutenant was in charge of the eight man patrol. Asking who was in charge of the village, he was directed to Brave Bull. The blond haired officer told Brave Bull his name was Lieutenant Travis Judd, and asked permission to rest and water their horses; he said his patrol had been searching the area for a mad trapper who had killed numerous white men throughout the mountains, and the deep snow had caused his horses to tire. Brave Bull asked the lieutenant to unsaddle the horses, put them into the corral so they could be fed and watered. He then invited the men inside the village lodge to eat and rest. The lieutenant agreed, thanking Brave Bull profusely.

After the lieutenant and his men had eaten a hot meal of venison, corn, and Cherokee fry bread, he told Brave Bull that the killer they were after had killed thirty men and chopped off their heads. He said all the white settlers were up in arms about it, and that a group had come to the fort demanding the commandant to do something - thus the patrol. So far the patrol had found nothing. Brave Bull remembered the four trappers that had killed Sahani and her mother and he told the lieutenant about their deaths. The lieutenant's interest perked up. He wrote down the details, adding how hospitable the Cherokee had been to his troops.

"Well, Chief," he said to Brave Bull, "looks like we might be looking for four men instead of just one. I had my doubts that one man could kill so many without leaving a trail of evidence."

The officer asked to talk to Dove's husband and was told he lived at Strong Heart. Brave Bull gave him directions and explained that Tall Woman was the Chief of all Cherokees, and to ask for her when the patrol reached her village. Brave Bull invited the men to stay the night in the warm lodge, which they gladly accepted. The next morning the patrol left, thanking Brave Bull for the hospitality and cooperation. They set out for Strong Heart.

Miles away, Denali sat hunched against the cave's wall, his knees up under his chin. The once clear thinking warrior was having delusions and trouble separating fact from fiction. He had just awoke from a dream where he saw Sahani standing at the cave's entrance beaconing him to follow her, but when he stood and tried to follow, the image faded into thin air. He became despondent at her disappearance and loss, and then the warm, soul satisfying hatred for the white man crept through him filling his

127

tormented being. He saddled Arrow and struck out into the cold dawn of morning.

He rode until mid-morning before he saw a tendril of smoke coming from a cabin. It was a white man's cabin because he saw a snow covered plow leaning against a work shed, and he saw two stout work horses in a partially enclosed shelter. He tied Arrow to a cedar tree and crept quietly to the one room cabin. He peered through a window partially covered by a burlap bag that did not completely cover the opening. Three grown men sat by a fireplace drinking whiskey from a jug -playing poker on a make shift table. They were arguing. One man, disgusted with the situation, raised up, walked to the door to answer nature's call. He walked outside cursing, leaving the door open.

Denali hit him at the side of his neck with his tomahawk severing the man's jugular vein, then quickly cut his throat with his sharp knife. The other two men, hearing and seeing the commotion, stood up knocking the make-shift table over, and one reached for a long rifle leaning against the wall near the fireplace. He didn't make it. Denali's tomahawk caught him on the side of his face. The man screamed and fell to the dirty floor. Denali leaped through the door and rammed his knife deep into the last man's side. He cut their throats while screams reverberated the small cabin. Afterwards, Denali washed his hands in the snow, swung up into his saddle, and rode out leaving three severed heads stuck on fence posts for all to see. Daniel left with a wicked grin across his face.

When the army patrol arrived at Strong Heart, they were met by Hawk who knew of their coming long before the patrol arrived. He greeted and welcomed them.

"You are welcome here, Lieutenant," said Hawk. "Please dismount and rest yourselves. There are benches by our headquarters where your men can sit."

"I wish to speak with Chief Tall Woman," the lieutenant told Hawk.

"Come with me. I will take you to Tall Woman." He led the officer into the headquarters building where they found Tall Woman sitting at her desk.

"Mother, this officer wishes to speak with you." Hawk went outside.

"Chief Tall Woman, I am Lieutenant Travis Judd. I have come to speak with the husband of Dove concerning the death of his wife and daughter,"he said pleasantly. "We are searching for a mad killer. We believe the killer to be one or more trappers, and hope Dove's husband may have some details that might aid us."

Tall Woman called for Hawk and told him to locate Yona.

"Yona, Dove's husband, is in charge of our police force," she told him."He will be here shortly. In the meantime, would you care for coffee and some food?"

"Coffee would be great," he said. "I am amazed that you, and the young man who welcomed us, speak such good English."

"All of our leaders and most of our people here at Strong Heart speak English," she informed him. "I am aware of Dove and her daughter's death at the hands of four trappers. While we wait for Yona, I can give you the details."

Tall Woman explained what she knew of the murders, giving also the descriptions of the men. The lieutenant told

129

her that Brave Bull had given him a deposition and that he would like one from her and Yona. Tall Woman told him that her daughter, her son-in-law, and Brave Bull had found the two dead women."

"Could I get depositions from them as well?" he asked.

Tall Woman sent for Star and Eagle Feather. When Yona, Star, and Eagle Feather had explained what they knew, and had given depositions, the officer expressed his deep regrets, and stood to leave.

"I want to thank you for your cooperation and hospitality," he said with conviction. "I will take my leave now and return to the fort with the information I now have," Touching the brim of his hat, He said "Again, thank you for you cooperation."

As the patrol left, Tall Woman fell into deep depression. She knew the four trappers had, indeed, killed Dove and Sahani, but she doubted they were the killers of all the white men that had been beheaded. She still felt that Daniel was responsible. She told Big Tree to take over at headquarters. She said she had a headache and was going to lie down for awhile. When she was alone, she cried bitter tears for her precious son.

When Lieutenant Judd reported to the Post Commandant, Col. Richard Harrison, he found the Colonel in a nasty mood. Judd brought his commander up on his progress and handed the Colonel the depositions he had obtained. He read them and seemed somewhat pleased. At least, he had something in writing. The Colonel, speaking through a grey handlebar mustache, told Judd that he now had the politicians on his back concerning the beheadings. He said settlers had gone to the State House and complained that the army was doing nothing to apprehend the sadistic killer. He waved several letters in the air as proof.

"So far, you are the only person that has gathered any information on this killer or killers," he told Judd. " I am putting a full company in the field to root out whoever is killing these civilians. Presently, I don't have a captain to command a company, so I am promoting you to Field Captain. Take one night's rest. At daybreak, I want you to search every shack, every cabin, every nook and cranny in these mountains for this outlaw. I want him in this stockade! Do you understand Captain?"

Captain Judd understood. He saluted, then left the Commandant's office determined to apprehend the killer or killers. At daybreak, he was in the field with a full company of combat hardened cavalrymen - a full company looking for one mad Cherokee.

For two months, Captain Judd and his men searched every lean-to, every shack, every cabin, every barn, in the mountains within twenty-five miles of where the murders had occurred. There seemed to be a pattern that suggested the killer worked within twenty-five mile circle, yet nothing or nobody was found to suggest even the slightest suspicion. He was at his wits end until his redheaded top sergeant suggested the head chopper might possibly live in a cave. The company started out again, searching this time every cave within that circle.

There were many caves in the mountains, most of them empty except three or four occupied by elderly Indians who would not have had the energy to accomplish the killer's feats. But it did give the Captain food for thought. What if the killer was not a white trapper as most people believed, but instead, a Indian living in a cave. This thought gave the officer and his men incentive to search even harder. A month into the cave search, two Indian scouts rode hard into the company's tented camp, reining up short in front of the Captain's tent. They told the Captain they had located a cave where a muscular young Indian lived. They said they had laid undercover and watched the Indian bring two horses from the cave to water them at a nearby stream. The scouts told him the man was heavily armed. The cave dweller had not seen the scouts because they were concealed about seventy yards away, and had used binoculars to watch the man's doings. The Captain was on his feet immediately. This was a real sighting - the first solid piece of evidence that had come along. He quickly assembled his men.

"Our scouts have found a probable suspect," he told the men. "There's a cave five miles from here where a stout, young Indian about thirty or thirty-five years of age is living. He has two horses, and he is heavily armed. We will approach the cave from all directions during the dawn hours of the morning.

"We will walk, leaving the horses in camp, under guard. Anything that rattles, get rid of it. Stash your swords, take only your rifles, side arms, and knives. When we reach the cave, I will call for the man to come out. If he is innocent, I will apologize for the intrusion. If he is mot, we will take him into custody. I want this man alive. No soldier will fire until I give the order. Make sure you have ammunition and powder. Now turn in. No bugler will sound wake-up call. You will be shaken awake by our sentries. That is all!"

The cavalrymen were up at two in the morning and ready to leave out by two thirty. The Captain divided the men into three groups. Upon reaching the cave, they would approach from three directions, spread out in a semi-circle with little opening in the line for escape. The men were in place when dawn broke through the trees, casting a foggy luminous glow upon the snow covered ground.

Denali had not seen the scouts when they discovered his hiding place, they had been too far away, but he heard the soldiers when they first appeared and fanned out in a semi-circle. He knew he was captured, there were too many of them to attempt an escape. He would fight, regardless of their number. He would do battle, and if necessary, he would die a warriors death. The Cherokee would sing songs about him recalling his brave stand against so many white-eyes. He loaded his two rifles, and his two long pistols. He laid his bow and arrows near the cave's entrance and stuck his big knife and tomahawk behind his belt. While it was still a little foggy, he took the butt of his rifle and pushed some brush clear of the opening so he would have a field of fire. Lying prone on the cave's floor, sticking his rifle through an opening, he waited for the fog to lift.

"In the cave!" yelled Captain Judd. "We would talk with you! You are surrounded by many soldiers! If you are innocent, you will go free! Come out so we can talk with you!"

The Captain's words were also spoken in Creek and in Cherokee by the Indian scouts. In English, Denali answered:

"I do not wish to come out! I care not of the many soldiers you have! Leave this place or many of you will die. I care

133

not whether I live or die!"

He already had a soldier in his sights. His rifle barked. The soldier died with a red hole in his forehead. Denali rolled over behind the cover of jutted portion of the cave's mouth as rifle fire hammered inside the cave from a hundred rifles. He saw his pack horse and Arrow go down with many holes in their bodies, and bleeding profusely. He reloaded his rifle, took a bead on a second soldier kneeling by a pine tree. He fired. The soldier fell dead at the base of the tree. More rifle balls bounced off of the cave's walls - whistling as they zinged from wall to wall. The soldiers were laying, for the most part, behind clumps of snow - easy targets. Three more died from his deadly fire. He reloaded both rifles and shot two more. Several of the bouncing balls hit him in the right leg and his right shoulder. His deerskins were dirty, and now bloody.

He shot two more soldiers laying in the snow, then a bouncing ball tore into his right arm. He could no longer lift his rifle with that arm. The rifle fire was so intense hitting the cave walls - he took a ball that shattered his left shoulder blade. He was immobilized. Denali could not lift a weapon. He gritted his teeth in severe pain. He almost passed out, but fought it off. Soon they would rush the cave; he did not want them to see him unconscious. He struggled to lean against the wall.

When the soldiers rushed in, they saw that he was incapacitated, no longer a threat. He was barely conscious when they carried him to the fort on a travois. He passed in and out of consciousness along the way although the soldier-medic had stopped most of the bleeding. Because of the snow, the bouncing of the travois was not as hard as it would have been on bare ground.

Denali Greyeagle was in the post hospital under heavy guard for two months before he was able to stand trial. There were casts on his left shoulder and his right upper arm - the bone had been broken by a rifle ball. His other wounds were painful, but healing. The army doctor had told Lieutenant Judd that a normal man would have died from so many wounds. When Denali could stand, he was confined, not in the regular stockade where enlisted soldiers and drunken Indians were locked-up, but on the second floor above the stockade where officers were confined. That floor had two cells and was very seldom used - officers being officers and gentlemen, as they say.

The Cherokee was placed in a cell close to a large window in the hall that looked out over the parade grounds. The window was there for the benefit of any officer or gentleman who may have found their way into a locked cell awaiting court martial. They could look out into the hallway and through the window at the post flag waving in the wind. Regular soldiers confined on the floor below had no such privileges. Denali's wrists were manacled with a foot-long chain, and his ankles were manacled with enough chain length for him to shuffle when he walked. His long hair was dull and matted, his face lined from the pain of his wounds. He ached each time he tried to lie down on the cell's single bunk. He was guarded by three surly soldiers, one on either side of his cell, and one by the stairs that led down to the first floor cells.

Denali was being tried by the army because he was an Indian and because he had killed eight soldiers in the firefight. The thirty plus civilians he had killed were also mentioned in the trial records mainly to appease the politicians. And had not the politicians been involved, the army would have already shot Denali and been done with it. But Col. Richard Harrison wanted a star on his shoulders. He planned to give the politicians a shindig of a trial with no less than five representatives of the American press, and two foreign reporters. The beheadings had been news on two continents.

On the day of the trial, the post dinning hall was used as a courtroom. It was filled with politicians, news reporters, and local landed gentry. Eight army officers sat behind a long oak table - a two-star general was president of the court. He was a hard looking man of sixty years and was grey of head and beard. Beside him sat Col. Richard Harrison. Other officers were to the general's left and right. When guards brought the prisoner in, they placed him in a chair surrounded by a fence-like barrier. The prisoner sat stone-faced and manacled. The general, president of the court, brought the court to order.

"Denali Greyeagle, you have already under oath admitted to the murder of eight army soldiers and over thirty civilians. Do you still admit to these crimes?"

"I killed them," Denali admitted straight away. "If you had not caught me, I would have killed many more white-eyes."

"Do you see any reason this court should not pass sentence, immediately?"

"Do as you wish!" Denali said with a sinister smile.

"Due to your own admission of guilt, and the evidence before me, this court condemns you to death by firing squad, at daybreak tomorrow," the general stated gravely.

"I do not fear your rifles," Denali said loudly. "Your rifles will not kill Denali Greyeagle. I am already dead!" He stood and spat at the eight officers sitting behind the oak table.

"Take that crazy Indian back to his cell!" yelled the general, standing with clinched fists.

Near day break, one of the guards brought Denali his last meal of coffee, fried bacon, biscuits, and white gravy. He shoved the tray back at the guard.

"You eat it!" growled Denali. The guard did.

At daybreak, one of the guards opened Denali's cell and motioned for him to shuffle out. As he stepped out, one guard fell in behind him and another guard was directly in front. The third guard stood near the stairwell. With the speed of a cat, Denali threw his arms over the guard in front, pulling his chain tightly against the guard's neck, then shoving hard against the guard at his back - ramming him out through the paned glass window. Denali dragged the other guard with him out through the window. All three crashed to their deaths on the rock hard parade ground below. They hit on their heads - breaking their necks.

Even in death, there was a dark, gruesome, grin on Denali's face. Fifty paces away, the firing squad stared in shock and disbelief.

CHAPTER FOUR

Growing Pains

To keep the peace between the army and the Cherokee Nation, Colonel Harrison sent Captain Judd, leading a patrol of eight men to bring the sad news of Denali's death to Chief Tall Woman. The Captain did not like this mission, but it fell to him as a soldier under orders to accomplish it.

Tall Woman took the news quietly, without expression, bade the cavalry officer goodbye, then almost sank to the floor in despair. She would have fallen if Big Tree had not caught her. He took her to bed where she stayed for two days without eating. She would not see anyone during that time. Her thoughts went back to an earlier time when Daniel was eighteen years old and carrying the weight of an adult warrior, a time when he was clear of mind and had purpose. She recalled the cave where Daniel, Hawk, and Star had actually grown up, had become men and Star had grown into a beautiful woman. She remembered Daniel's bravery in bringing vengeance to the trapper who had scalped the Cherokee family, and his actions at the Creek village where Star and little Raven had been held hostage. Daniel had been a man of vision when he founded and developed Strong Heart Village and Lost Valley, a tireless worker for the Cherokee people. Without his efforts, the Eastern Band of the Cherokee Nation would not have become a reality. Daniel was her first born. Now he was gone. She would never see his beautiful, smiling, face again. According to Cherokee custom, she was not supposed to mention his name for a year, but she did not know how she could do this.

Tall Woman mourned to the point where her face was drawn, crows-feet appeared at the edge of her mouth, and lines shown on her, still, beautiful face. Her eyes were sunk in and looked old. She aged several years in a few months. She was unable to perform her duties at the headquarters building, things were piling up. Big Tree took it upon himself to bring Star, who was due to give birth any day now, in to take her mother's place. He knew that Tall Woman would never return to her work, which had been her passion.

Four months later, Tall Woman died in her sleep. The strong woman warrior who had led the Cherokee to again become a great Nation, gave up her spirit and slipped into the great unknown.

Over a thousand people attended Tall Woman's funeral at Strong Heart. Cherokees from each of her three villages crowded into the valley, and some came from far away. Chief John Ross was too old and in firm to make the trip from Tahlequah to western North Carolina, but he sent five emissaries to honor the great woman warrior. In the history of the Cherokee people, only one other woman warrior achieved the greatness of Tall Woman. Her name was Nancy Ward, another Beloved Woman. Several high ranking government officials came to pay their respects, and in the crowd was one Army Cavalry Captain - Travis Judd. He had told his superior at the fort, speaking of Tall Woman, that he had twice stood in the presence of greatness.

A few days after the funeral, Star, who now needed her brother more than ever, made Hawk co-leader of the Cherokee Nation. She promoted Big Tree to Chief of Strong Heart, replacing Hawk in that position, and made Eagle Feather one of Big Tree's sub-chiefs. A week later, Star gave birth to twin boys. She named one, Jason, and the other, Jesse. She said one would be wise like the fox, the other would soar above most people. Since Daniel was no more, according to Cherokee custom, Hawk would be their teacher. The uncle was the important male in the life of a sisters children.

Six years passed since the death of Tall Woman. In that passage of time, the Cherokee Nation had grown to well over two thousand families, and out of that there were eighteen hundred warriors. Looking at Star, it would be difficult to tell the difference between her and her mother. The similarities were striking. She was tall like her mother, had the same long, raven black hair, and had the same calm, determined, confident, demeanor about herself. In a word, she was a beautiful and capable Beloved Woman - a leader who had the respect of her people. And now, sitting before her in the headquarters building, were a U.S. Senator, his assistant, and a slender man in a dark suit wearing thin, wire-rimmed glasses. His name was

Adolphus Fry.

"Madam Chief," said the senator, "I don't believe you fully understand the import of my visit. The president and the congress of these United States are determined that a federal reservation be made of this valley. There is a reservation at Tahlequah and they want a reservation here."

"What need have I of a reservation," Star asked calmly. "My people are peaceful. We don't need the government to fence us in, and we don't need soldiers to guard us. After the horrors of the Trail of Tears, my people would not stand for it!"

"Oh, but you do misunderstand," stated the senator. "There would be no fence, and there would be no soldiers - just one Indian agent. The reservation would merely be lines blocking off a large area on a map at the Indian Agency in Washington, D.C."

"And what would be the duties of this Indian agent?" asked Star.

The senator pointed at Adolphus Fry. "Mr. Fry would be permanently stationed here at Strong Heart. He will be the conduit between you, your people, and the Indian Agency in Washington. His primary responsibility will be to advise you and issue certain federally funded food supplies such as beef, flour, cornmeal, and other staples on a monthly basis. It would be a symbiotic relationship."

"In other words, a government spy in our midst," spoke Star. "I see no need for this agent, or the agency in Washington. But, in the spirit of cooperation with the Federal Government, I will build a cabin for Mr. Fry . But let this be clear. He will have no authority over me, my sub-chiefs, or my people. I don't need his advise on how best to lead my people, and we don't need government hand-outs. You have no doubt noticed the great fields of corn, squash, and other foods that grow from the ground, and the herds of horses that we have. We hunt for our meat and take only what we need from nature. My people eat regularly. They are healthy and happy. Do we understand each other, senator?"

"I understand," the senator replied. "I am sure you and Mr. Fry will get along splendidly. Now, I must bid you farewell. I have a long trip ahead of me. Mr. Fry, you will not interfere with Chief Star's operations. You are here in an advisory capacity only."

The senator and his group departed, leaving the agent alone with Star. He seemed ill at ease - his knees together, derby hat in his lap.

"Mr. Fry, I will find temporary quarters for you until suitable quarters can be built. Feel free to look over our land, but you will probable find my people unresponsive to your presence. They are unaccustomed to having strangers around. Whatever you do, do not interfere with their routines." And then to her brother, she said "Hawk, would you find Mr. Fry living quarters?" With that, Star indicated that she had other, more important, matters to attend.

At the age of six, Hawk began teaching his nephews the ways of the warrior. He had given Jason and Jesse each a pinto pony, and was talking to them about horses in general when Adolphus Fry walked up to the corral, leaned on the corral fence, and said:

"I hope you don't mind, Chief Hawk, but I would like to watch the young gentlemen as they learn. I wish I would have had someone with your knowledge to teach me when I was their age. As it is, there is much I do not know about such things."

"It's not too late to learn, Mr. Fry," Hawk told him. "If you are serious about learning the ways of the warrior, you can be my third pupil."

"Could I, really?" Fry asked.

"We meet here three mornings each week. You are most welcome to join us."

And join them, he did. Fry was at the corral regularly, eager to learn. Whatever Hawk taught the young boys, he taught Fry. He taught them how to ride, and over the coming months, how to use the bow and arrow, the tomahawk, the lance, and the knife. Hawk took them into the forest and taught them woodcraft, how to track deer and people, how to walk quietly, how to walk the walk of a warrior - which is to respect all living creatures, and never take a life unless absolutely necessary. He taught them about bravery, courage, self discipline and self reliance and never to lie, but always to speak truthfully.

In time, Fry became close friends with Hawk and the twins, and soon he began to speak enough Cherokee to communicate. He was a slender man of medium height, but he had grit. Hawk found him to be intelligent and quick to learn. Before long, Fry was wearing buckskins and moccasins. He carried a knife and a tomahawk, and had become proficient with the long rifle. Whenever the twins were invited to a pow-wow or a festival, Fry sat with the boys and hawk. Along with Jason and Jesse, he learned the traditions and customs of the Cherokee people. It wasn't long until the Cherokee accepted him as one of their own.

The boys called him Edusti Ta'li (Uncle Two), so the name stuck. Adolphus Fry was not like most of the Indian agents who stole from the plains Indians and gave them tainted food. Whatever Fry did in his official capacity, he did for the benefit of the Cherokee people as a whole. One day he was summoned to Chief Star's office.

"Mr. Fry," said Star, "when you first came to us, I was not sure things would work out between us. You have far exceeded my expectations - you have become one with us. I thank you for that. My sons call you Uncle Two, they have much affection for you, as does my brother, Hawk. I called you here this day to welcome you into the Cherokee family. From this day forward, you are Edusti Ta'li. You will walk as a Cherokee and will be treated with respect."

Star pushed a dark, brown, wooden box toward him. It was a long percussion pistol. It was new - identical to one carried by Hawk. When Fry opened the box, tears almost came to his eyes, but he forced them back knowing that a Cherokee man never let his tears be seen by another person, except in special circumstances. When he spoke, his voice was hoarse.

"Thank you, my Chief," he said earnestly. "I pray that I will always live up to the trust you have placed in me."

He left Star's office, went to his own, sat down at his desk and let the tears of appreciation roll down his cheeks, quietly. Uncle Two had finally found his place in life, a home. In the world he had left, he never felt that he belonged, never had a close friend, always the loner. Here, he not only belonged, but was also liked and was accepted. His reports to the Bureau of Indian Affairs in Washington were always positive, so there were never any problems between the Cherokee and the Agency. He requisitioned cattle. Soon there were a hundred head of Herefords grazing peacefully in Strong Heart Valley. They were a red haired breed of English origin and had a white face. Under the capable hands of Laughs-a-Lot and his men, the herd increased exponentially.

Two years passed when Uncle Two came to Chief Star and informed her he wished to marry a Cherokee woman his own age, whose name was White Flower. She was thirty five. White Flower's previous husband had been killed in a hunting accident. Star asked if he would show White Flower love and respect and provide for her. He said that he would. Star talked with White Flower and found that she, indeed, loved Uncle Two and wished to be his wife. They were married in a Cherokee ceremony a short time later. When the white blanket was wrapped around the couple, cheers went up from the people and a celebration was held that lasted all night long. Uncle Two now had a family and considered himself a very lucky man, indeed.

But Captain Travis Judd at Fort Stone was not feeling lucky. He was ordered by Colonel Harrison to Strong Heart to conscript scouts for the army, the last scouts having been killed in a skirmish with Creeks. This was unpleasant duty for Judd. He did not like ordering a Cherokee Chief to produce a scout whether the chief liked it or not. And he hopped Daniel's death at the fort would not cause animosity. He had been on good terms with Chief Tall Woman, but had never met Chief Star. He was unsure of how his appearance and request at Strong Heart would be taken. He knew the Cherokee were a peaceful people, but he also knew they resented being ordered to do anything by white men. So when he arrived, he was pleasantly greeted by Chief Hawk, whom he had met on a previous visit. Hawk took the Captain before Chief Star, and introduced him. Captain Judd, gazing at Star, stood bewildered for a moment.

"Is there something wrong, Captain?" Star asked questioningly.

"No, Madam Chief," he answered, removing his hat. "for a moment there, I thought I was seeing double. You look so much like Chief Tall Woman."

"I am the daughter of Tall Woman," Star replied. "I have been told there is a strong resemblance. Your words compliment me - mother was a beautiful woman. What can I do for the army?" she asked, showing no signs of animosity.

"My mission is delicate, to say the least," the captain offered apologetically. "The army needs a few Cherokee scouts who speaks English and Creek. We are at odds with the Creeks. We had several Creek scouts, but they led one of our patrols into an ambush and the patrol was completely wiped out. The army is mounting a campaign against the group responsible. The army is not at war with the Creek nation, just a band of renegades led by a warrior called Crowfoot. He leads about fifty warriors. I was hoping you would provide scouts to help us find this band of outlaws. They have massacred two settler families, and they will, no doubt, harm other settlers."

"The Creeks have been enemies of the Cherokee for many years," Star told the captain, "when I was very young, they kidnapped me and a friend. They killed my friend, but my

146

people rescued me and destroyed their village. I can't order my people to become scouts for the army, but I will ask them. If there are any men who want to do this thing, I will not stop them."

"No need in asking," Hawk spoke up." I will scout for the Captain until this band is found and eliminated. I will bring three of my best men." Hawk still remembered what the hated Creeks had done to Star and little Raven. He would not pass up an opportunity to punish the Creeks, if Star had no objections.

"Hawk has spoken, Captain. You have your scouts, but let it be understood. Hawk is my brother and co-leader of the Cherokees. When these Creeks have been rounded up, I want my brother and his men back here at Strong Heart. As long as that is understood, I have no problem in furnishing you scouts."

"Yes, Madam Chief. It is understood. And the army thanks you for your cooperation."

The twins, Jason and Jesse, were eight years old when Hawk left with Captain Judd and his patrol. Their schooling in the ways of a warrior would have to wait until their uncle returned. Hawk took with him three old friends - Laughs-a-Lot, Nightbird, and Yona, the husband of the now deceased Dove. The twins stood beside Uncle Two as they watched Hawk and his men ride out at the head of the patrol. Star was also watching from a window in the headquarters building. She would miss her brother and hoped she had not made a mistake by allowing him to go. But then, she busied herself with naming temporary replacements for the men who left with Hawk.

As she sat at her desk, Star thought of how great it would

be to return to the happy days when she, Daniel, and Hawk were together with their mother in the cave at Tall Woman Village. Most of the time those were good days, days when Daniel was the prominent male in their lives. She terribly missed Daniel in her life now. She missed his strong leadership, she missed his smile and she missed her mother. She rose from her desk, walked outside to the pinto Daniel had given her several years earlier, and rode to where her mother was buried. She let the horse graze while she stood beside Tall Woman's grave. Star still wore deerskin dresses with short fringes at the hem and sleeves. Today, she wore a belt made of rawhide and white bone carved in circles that accentuated her figure, and high top moccasin boots that reached almost to her knees under her dress. Her raven hair fell to her waist.

"Mother, I miss you," she whispered," and I miss Daniel. This burden of being the leader of a nation is heavy. Sometime I wonder if it is too much for me. And now, my brother, Hawk, is gone from me for awhile. I feel as though all my family has been taken from me. Although I have a good husband and two beautiful boys, today, right now, I feel alone. When I was young, I could not wait to be grown-up. Now, I would love to return to those carefree days when decisions were made by others. Today, like you when you were here, I have the responsibility of thousands. The days are filled with problems and decisions. I try not to take them home to Eagle Feather and the boys, but it is difficult to separate being the leader of these people from being wife and mother. I love you, mother, and I miss you."

Star swung upon her pinto and rode to the waterfall. She dismounted and sat beneath the big cedar where her mother, Daniel, and Big Tree had slept on her mother's first visit to Strong Heart. She seemed to sense her mother and brother's spirits there, as a soft breeze waffled through the trees. She let sounds from the waterfall take her away to a time long before she was born, another time when the Cherokee ruled so much land one could not think to the end of it, long before the first white man stepped foot on this soil. She sat there for an hour or so before riding back to her office. She sent for Big Tree and Eagle Feather.

"I need Brave Bull here at Strong Heart," she told them. "Big Tree, go there, choose a strong and wise man from Brave Bull's men to take his place at Tall Woman Village. Bring him and his family back here. You three are going to share in the responsibility of leading our people. I don't know when Hawk will return. In his absence, I need strong, wise men around me."

Uncle Two was a college graduate with a teaching certificate, and had taught school for two years in Chicago before accepting a position with the government. He wanted to travel into what he called the wilderness - that was his reason for applying for, and being granted, a post as an Indian Agent. He had trained his wife, White Flower, to be his assistant in his duties as Indian Agent, and had taught her English. White Flower was a dainty little lady of five foot three inches, and she thought her husband was the wisest man she had ever known. She worshipped the ground he walked on, and the feeling was mutual.

On many days, the twins could be found in Uncle Two's office learning more English and arithmetic. Star had made sure the boys got a good start in English, as well as

Cherokee, from their birth. Uncle Two had found the twins bright and eager to learn. So when he approached Star with the idea of starting a school to teach Cherokee children, she was quick to see the benefit of such a proposal. She had a large, one room school house built, and invited all the children to attend, if they were so inclined. The school was a success from its beginning. Uncle Two sent for a large chalkboard, chalk, pencils, tablets, and books in English, arithmetic, and world history. Chalk has been around since the stone age. The chalk board was invented by a Scotsman, James Pillans, in the 1700's. Simple desks were made for the children, and outside, swings and seesaws were constructed. The children were taught three days each week and on Saturdays. From Star's office window she could see when the children were let out for recess, and enjoyed the laughter she heard from the kids at play. Kids are quick to learn, and it wasn't long before she heard children speaking some English words as they played. She was glad Uncle Two had come to Strong Heart.

As Star watched the faces of the children at play, her thoughts wandered far ahead of where she stood gazing out the window. What was to become of the Cherokee people? Their role in the world had already been changed tremendously. Once a hunter, gatherer, agrarian society, they were now semi-ruled by the white man in a far away state - a government who knew little of the Cherokee heart. The only course for the Cherokee people to survive as a people, as she saw it, would be in assimilation - learning to live with the white man, learning their ways and language. The goal would be how to assimilate without losing Cherokee culture and language. The plains Indians was an object lesson. They had, and still were, resisting assimilation, and many once great nations like the Sioux were all but gone, now on reservations guarded by soldiers. True. On a map in Washington this was a reservation, but so far, there were no army guards or fences, her people could come and go as they wished. But how long would this peaceful co-existence last? She wondered. She must give more thought to this word assimilation. Uncle Two's school, she thought, was a step in the right direction.

Brave Bull lived up to his name. He was six feet tall, broad at the shoulders, and his upper arms rippled with muscles. When he and his family walked into Star's office, she ran around her desk and embraced her old friend, his wife, Fawn, and their two children - a boy of ten and a girl around twelve. Brave Bull had served Tall Woman with distinction and bravery. He had been loyal to a fault, and had led Tall Woman Village with wise decisions. They sat and talked at length with much laughter and camaraderie, then Star, personally, took them to Hawk's cabin where they would live until a cabin of their own could be built. With Brave Bull, Big Tree, and Eagle Feather together again, she felt like part of her family had been restored. Later she would reorganize her top leadership among the three. Much of the burden of running the Cherokee Nation would be taken from her shoulders by men she trusted implicitly.

One of the first items she put before her top men was to widen the trail that led from Strong Heart to the land beyond the ridge. Star also brought in Uncle Two to use his knowledge of mathematics in this respect. The road could not be too steep, and she wanted the road wide enough for wagons to enter and leave Strong Heart with loads of corn and other staples grown in abundance in the valley. This produce could be sold at the marketplace near Fort Stone. She planned a visit to the Commandant for a contract to provide horses to the army. The army always needed horses and the Cherokees were known to breed the best in all western North Carolina. Before long one hundred Cherokees were at work building the road. Within two months a wide, stone filled access road was constructed.

Star and Uncle Two paid a visit to Colonel Harrison at the fort and profitable contracts were made to furnish the army with horses and beef. At the white settlement grain elevator, she made a deal to furnish the owner with wagon loads of corn, which he, in turn, sold throughout the mountain area. Four large wagons were bought and a wagon yard was built at Strong Heart. Although two of her people already had a working knowledge of blacksmithing, Star hired a white blacksmith to teach several Cherokees that trade, and soon a working blacksmith shop was operating, as well as a saddle shop. A covered marketplace, with tables, was built where the Cherokee could sell handmade items, produce, artwork, deer antler knives and tomahawks to white settlers. Market day was held on the first weekend of each month, and an area was set aside for settlers to camp out on that weekend. Like Uncle Two's school, the Cherokee Market Place was a success from the beginning.

The Cherokee Market Place did more than making it possible for individual Cherokees to earn money. It created an air of friendship between the white settlers and Star's people, something the Creeks did not enjoy. The Cherokee were soon welcomed in any of the white settlements. They could go to these settlements and buy goods unavailable at Strong Heart, like guns, gun powder and lead shot ammunition, flour, and even white man clothes. Whether or not Star planned it this way, a certain amount of assimilation was achieved. Friendship and peace existed between the settlers and the Cherokee. And this made Colonel Harrison and the army happy.

As Captain Judd's patrol entered the fort gate, Colonel Harrison was standing on the porch that led to his office. He was hatless, but carried his army issue pistol in a cross draw position on his left side. The gray haired, hard-eyed, cavalry colonel watched as Hawk and his men rode beside four Creek prisoners. Captain Judd left the patrol and ambled his horse toward the colonel. The men were dusty from days on the trail. Judd saluted, but did not dismount.

"Four Creek raiders," he told the colonel. "Hawk and his scouts captured them without firing a shot. They were on their way to rejoin the raider band when we came upon them."

"Any sign of the others?" asked the colonel.

"No, Sir." replied Judd. "There were no renegade tracks where we found the prisoners. We needed to re-supply. We returned to do that, and to deposit the prisoners."

"Very well, Captain. Secure the prisoners, and release your patrol. You and scout Hawk come to my office before you chow down."

With that the colonel turned and entered his office. Once the Creeks were placed in the stockade and the men released after tending to their horses, they headed for the mess hall. Captain Judd and Hawk entered the colonel's office. Judd saluted.

"You men relax," the Colonel said in a friendly tone. " Hawk, I met your sister, Chief Star, three weeks ago. She is quite the business woman, and a seasoned haggler. We contracted with the Cherokee to supply the army with horses. If all her horses are as good as the first group delivered, I foresee a very long and profitable relationship between the army and the Cherokee."

"We breed great horses," Hawk commented.

He was a striking figure standing beside Captain Judd who was several inches shorter than Hawk. Wearing buckskins with the trousers stuck inside tall moccasin boots, a pistol behind his wide belt, and a long knife and Tomahawk. He exuded nothing but confidence.

"Tell me about the patrol, Captain," the colonel looked at Judd.

"We covered all of this area," the captain went to a wall map and with his finger pointed to a large area that included several mountain ranges. "No signs of the large band as of yet, sir. Hawk believes they are somewhere, here, beyond the White Mountains. With your permission, that is where we will focus our search on next."

"What makes you think they are there, Hawk?" the colonel asked.

"Food, Colonel. The Creeks we brought in were hunting, but finding no game. It was obvious they were a long way from the main force. The area Captain Judd pointed out is known for many deer and antelope. Without food and water, fifty men cannot long keep up their strength. Water is plentiful throughout the mountains, but deer and antelope tend to live in areas where there is much good grass. Beyond White Mountain is such an area."

"That makes sense," said the colonel. "Captain Judd, take two days rest, then re-supply your patrol. Concentrate your search beyond the White Mountains. If Hawk is right, you will need more men than a single patrol. I suggest you take half a company. That is all, gentlemen."

With those words, Captain Judd saluted, then he and Hawk went to the officers' mess to eat. After a meal of beefsteak, potatoes, corn, green beans and coffee, Hawk rejoined his men in the cabin reserved for scouts. After assuring himself that Laughs-a-Lot, Nightbird, and Yona had eaten, he lay back on a bunk, folded his arms behind his head, and smiled at Star's business acumen.

Mountain mornings are misty and foggy. Hawk and his scouts lay in damp grass atop a small ridge overlooking a low valley where tendrils of smoke rose through the lifting fog. As the fog slowly dissipated into the quiet morning, Hawk and his men saw the many campfires scattered throughout the Creek encampment below. A remuda of stolen horses was hobbled at the edge of the camp. Four wagons, with stout farm horses already harnessed to the wagons, stood in the camp's center. In the wagons were white women and several children. Their hands were tied with rawhide ropes. The women and children look bedraggled, their heads leaning forward in tired sleep.

A few Creek warriors sat feeding the campfires - these were sentries - most of the warriors, wrapped in deerskin robes, were still asleep when Captain Judd and his sixty man force swept into the camp from all sides, shooting, clubbing, and knifing the startled, half awake Creeks.

Hawk and the scouts' job was to rush through the melee, reach the wagons, and drive the captives to safety. As Hawk, Laughs-a-Lot, Nightbird, and Yona tomahawked their way through the awakening Creeks, the women and children, except for one blond woman, began screaming and crying not understanding what was going on. All they knew and saw was people fighting and dying. Some women were hysterical. When the scouts finally reached the wagons, climbed into the seats and picked up the reins to move the wagons out, the women started fighting them with high-pitched screams and hair pulling.

"Stop it, you crazy women!" yelled Nightbird in English. "We 're friendly Indians!"

With a jolt the wagons lurched forward sending the women and children sprawling backward into the wagon beds. The screaming and hair pulling had stopped. Four scouts driving four wagons with crying women and children, made a mad dash out of the camp while Captain Judd's men fought Creek warriors with sword, rifle butts and vengeance. As Hawk's lead wagon bumped across rough ground, the blond woman, about twenty-two, climbed over into the seat beside him - yelling at the horses to go faster. They must have heard her over the din because they picked up speed. She held out her hands for Hawk to cut the ropes, which he did. Two Creek warriors on either side tried to board the wagon to take the reins, but the blond woman reared back against Hawk; with a swift kick she sent one warrior rolling on the ground. With the reins in one hand and a tomahawk in the other, Hawk sent the other warrior bleeding beneath the wagon. The blond woman grabbed her seat as the rear wheels finished off the

Creek.

"We make a pretty good team!" the woman yelled at hawk. The wagon rumbled on toward safety. Hawk thought he had never met a white woman such as this one. He learned back and let out a war cry that made the woman peal with laughter.

After the battle, Captain Judd had lost only one soldier - five were wounded, but would recover. He had fifteen prisoners, and Crowfoot was captured alive. The colonel would be pleased, he thought. After the scouts had reclaimed their horses, they and Captain Judd rode up beside the wagons.

"We're taking you ladies to the fort," he told them. "The Commandant will make arrangements to return you to your families."

Hawk's horse was beside the first wagon. Without a word, the blond woman stepped from the wagon seat and hopped behind Hawk.

"Ma'am, wouldn't you prefer to ride in the wagons with the other ladies?" asked Judd.

"No, sir." she replied. "This man saved my life. I go where he goes!" There was a finality in her voice. Hawk just smiled and spurred his mount forward. Laughs-a-Lot, Nightbird, and Yona looked at each other and grinned.

The Colonel was pleased - pleased with Captain Judd, the soldiers, and pleased with the Cherokee scouts. The women, about fifteen in number and five children, had been gathered in the officers' mess-hall. Clerks were determining to what families and settlements the women and children were to be returned. Hawk and his men, along with Captain Judd, stood watching. Colonel Harrison sat behind the table with several of his clerks. Greta Edmunsen, the blond woman, was explaining to the colonel that she had no family, that her mother and father had died with the fever six years back, and the family she had been living with were killed by the Creeks, and she was taken captive. Miss Edmunsen looked around apprehensively trying to locate Hawk as she was talking to the colonel.

"There must be somewhere you can live?" offered the colonel.

"I have no one," Greta replied.

"Is not there anyone who would take you in, Miss Edmunsen?"

Hawk stepped up to the table beside Greta, and said "She will go with me."

"This is highly unusual, Hawk," replied the colonel. "I don't know what to say about this."

"She will become my wife," Hawk said pointedly.

"That settles it, then," said Greta. "I told the Captain that where this man goes, I go."

"Am I to take it that you approve of what Hawk has said? " asked Colonel Harrison.

"I do," smiled Greta. "I knew he would become my husband when he jumped into the wagon seat to rescue me. Wherever he goes, I will go. His people will be my people. That's in the Bible!"

"Well," said the flustered colonel, "you both are adults. I will say this, you could not choose a better man, Miss Edmunsen. And Hawk, it looks like you have a spirited woman on your hands."

"That spirit is what attracted me to her," said Hawk. "A spirited woman brings forth strong children. We will be married at Strong Heart."

The colonel said "While you and your men are here, I
want to thank each of you for your brave service to the
army. I have written commendations in each of your
records, and here is a folder for Chief Star. It speaks of your
bravery. I do wish you and Miss Edmunsen a happy life."

With that, Hawk, his soon-to-be wife, and the Cherokee
scouts mounted their horses and rode out the fort gate
toward Strong Heart. Miss Edmunsen's sorrel was a
wedding gift from Colonel Harrison. And that was the
unusual courtship of Hawk and Miss Greta Edmunsen - a
blond, blue eyed, beauty with dancing eyes and a spirit
worthy of a Cherokee Chief. They were married a month
later when the holy man wrapped them together in a white
blanket to the delight of the Cherokee people. In Hawk's
absence, a cabin had been built for Brave Bull and his
family, so Hawk and his new bride moved into Hawk's
cabin, happy as two peas in a pod.

Star liked Greta immediately. She appreciated the way
Greta spoke directly and truthfully, and without fear. She
wore her hair in a braided bun at the back of her head, and
among the all black headed Cherokees, she stood out like a
bright light in a sea of black. Greta liked the soft feel of
treated doeskin dresses and high topped deerskin moccasin
boots. She copied the way Star dressed - deerskin dresses
accentuated her figure, and brought approval from Hawk's
eyes.

The only Indians Greta had known were the Creeks when
she was their
captive. She thought them a backward, warlike people
who treated their women badly, were lazy, never bathed

159

and smelled like bear grease. But, here, living among the Cherokee, although different, it was much like living in any large white settlement. The Cherokee were organized, industrious, and family oriented. The men treated their women with respect and provided for their families. They lived in log cabins, not hovels, and the people went to water frequently. Her new people appeared healthy and well fed. There were herds of horses and cattle. There were large cultivated fields of corn and other produce, and there was the Market Place where, once each month, Greta could interact with white and Cherokee alike. Greta's world smiled, and she had never been happier.

The Cherokee treated her differently than she had ever been treated. In their short time together at the fort, Hawk had not told her that he was a co-Chief of the Great Cherokee Nation, had vast responsibilities and hundreds of men that answered to him, and that by becoming his wife, she had become a princess. Greta felt like she had awaken in a fairy tale world where a prince had brought a glass slipper that fit her feet exactly. She fell in love with her new world, her people, and her handsome Cherokee husband.

Greta was born in America, but her parents came from the old world, Scandinavia, Sweden, where most of the people were light skinned and fair haired. Her mother and father had spoken English with a distinctive brogue, but she had learned to speak the language without the brogue. Now she was learning a new language, new traditions, and new customs. Everyday there was something new, different, and exciting to learn, and since many of the Cherokee spoke English as well as Cherokee, there were few communication barriers.

And there were now two large school rooms where Uncle
Two, the Indian Agent, taught at one and his wife, White
Flower, taught at the other. White Flower taught the lower
grades while her husband taught Cherokee children high
school subjects. Greta would often speak to the children
about the land of her parent's birth when Uncle Two taught
world history. The children would set wide-eyed with
thoughts of such a vast world beyond the oceans. They
were learning that their world consisted of more than just
the mountains that surrounded Strong Heart. But evil also
lurked beyond the mountains.

Fall - 1861

News travels fast in the mountains, and bad news seems
to ride the winds. There had been rumblings about several
Southern States seceding from the Union, and knock-down
drag-out fights had occurred throughout North Carolina
between die hard Union advocates and those who spoke
out in favor of secession. It appeared that war between the
states was inevitable.

Ten years passed since Hawk and Greta married. They
now had three boys, ages three, four, and six. Greta named
them from the Bible she read every night. Isaac was the
oldest, Jacob, in between, and Jeremiah was the youngest.
Star's twins, Jason and Jesse, were now eighteen years old.
When they heard that North Carolina was, indeed,
preparing for war, they were chomping at the bits to join
the Confederate Army as scouts. Star knew something was
up as the boys stood before her in her office.

"I cannot condone you two going to war," she told them.
"This is not our war."

"But it is our war, Mother! "said Jason. "It is every Cherokee's war. This Yankee government has broken every treaty ever made with the Cherokee. They have lied to us time after time. This is our chance to right some of their wrongs."

"Very many Cherokee have already enlisted," Jesse told his mother. "Our young men see an opportunity to force the Union Army out of North Carolina and fight for a new government. If the Cherokee fight, and if the Confederates win, we will have more control over our future."

"Our people are in good shape right now with the present government," their mother told them.

"That is true," agreed Jason, "but it is only a matter of time until this government makes a soldier guarded reservation out of our valley just like they have at Tahlequah. We must never forget the Trail of Tears."

"Have you talked this over with your uncle Hawk?"

"We have, but uncle Hawk says it is not his decision to make. He said only you can give us permission to enlist."

"If I say no," Star told her sons, "you boys will resent my decision, and may even resent me. I see no other course but to say, yes. But understand, I do not enjoy giving my approval. No mother wants to see her sons go off to war."

"We understand, Mother," replied Jason. "If this turns out bad, it is on our heads."

"Very well," Star said sadly. "but do not go off unprepared. Make sure you take what you need without depending upon the Confederates. Their government is new, and their army is new. You are probably better trained than any of the white southern soldiers."

The twins walked around their mother's desk and

hugged her tightly.

"Don't break my ribs!" she laughed. "You boys don't know your own strength."

The twins were strong, and tall like their father and uncles. Star was amazed that they favored Daniel and Hawk so much. It seemed only yesterday that the boys were tiny in her arms, and now they were going off to fight a white man's war. It all seemed so distant, but she knew Strong Heart and all of North Carolina would be affected. Star's dealings with the Union Army at Fort Stone had been good, but Colonel Harrison and his troops had pulled out and rode away north leaving the fort empty. It was a wonder they had not burned the place to the ground, but it was left intact. Perhaps they expected the war would end quickly and they would return to Fort Stone.

Back at the Indian Agency at Strong Heart Village, Uncle Two folded the official letter he had just read and passed it to his wife, White Flower. It was a letter from Washington telling him to close down the agency and for him to return to Washington, immediately. His mind was in a quandary. He owed no allegiance to the Confederate States and cared not for this war between brothers. He composed a resignation letter informing the Indian Agency in Washington that his loyalties were with the Cherokee people - that he had a Cherokee wife and children and had no intention of leaving them. He would not be returning to Washington. He walked outside, removed the sign over the door that read Indian Agent and threw it onto a woodpile. He told his wife that this was now the official office of the Cherokee School System. He said he would have a sign made to that effect. He would inform Chief Star of his resignation as Indian Agent later.

The 69th North Carolina Regiment, CSA, commanded by a former white Cherokee Chief, Colonel William Holland Thomas, and his men occupied the former Union fort and renamed it Fort Cherokee. The unit was commonly known as Thomas' Legion and the command initially totaled 1,125 men, which included an infantry regiment, a cavalry battalion, an artillery battery, and a four hundred man Cherokee Battalion. Many of the Cherokees acted as scouts for the Thomas Legion.

As Chief Star, Eagle Feather, Hawk and Greta rode into the Fort they were met by a bewhiskered sergeant who promptly took them to Colonel Thomas' adjutant.

"I am Chief Star of the Eastern Cherokee," Star said politely. "We wish to see Colonel Thomas."

"May I tell the Colonel the purpose of your visit?" The tall, thin officer asked.

"Yes. I have brought my sons who wish to enlist. But before they do, I would talk with the Colonel." The adjutant ushered the group into the colonel's office.

"You are welcome here, Chief Star," said the heavy set, gray headed commander. "I have heard of you, and once, I met your mother, Chief Tall Woman. She was a great Chief and a fierce warrior. What can I do for you?"

"These are my two sons, Jason and Jesse Greyeagle. As you can see they are twins. They wish to enlist and fight for the Thomas Legion. I do not wish that they be separated. If they can stay together, I will place my sons in your hands."

"Normally, I would not approved such a request," the colonel told Star, "but I need every Cherokee scout I can get my hands on. No one knows these mountains better than a

Cherokee, and if we are to win this god-awful war we must have intelligence, we must know where the enemy is, and what he is doing. You have my word. They will not be separated."

"Captain Wordsworth," the colonel told his adjutant, "these men will serve together as my personal scouts. They will be attached to the Mountain Scout Unit and will be under my personal command. Make that happen, Captain!"

"Yes sir," replied the Captain. "You men come with me."

After the twins said their goodbyes, Star thanked Colonel Thomas and her group took their leave. She knew the day would come when she would have to release her sons to become independent men, but her leaving them here at Fort Cherokee was not an easy thing to do. As Star, Eagle Feather, Hawk, and Greta rode out through the fort gate, she took a farewell glance as the twins walked across the compound with the adjutant. They will serve proudly and with honor, she thought to herself.

On the way back to Strong Heart, Greta said: " If women ruled the world there would be no wars!"

"I don't know about that," Hawk stated. "Fighting and war seems to be as much a part of nature as living and dying. I once watched two wildcats fight until one bleed to death and the other one wobbled off half dead. Horses sometime fight each other to the death, and I have seen even some of our English bulls ram each other until one either gives up or lays down. War rages in the animal world, and it has been a prime occupation of man since the beginning. Uncle Two tells me that the Queen of England is constantly at war with one country or the other."

Eagle Feather was quiet as usual, but you could tell

leaving his sons at Fort Cherokee troubled him. "I hope they get enough to eat," he finally said.

"Hawk," said Star, "when we get home, I would like for you, Eagle Feather, Brave Bull, and your men to create a program for vast storage of non-perishable foods, such as corn and other dry foods. This war is going to effect every family in these mountains. Times will get hard, I feel. Many of our men have gone off to join the Confederacy, but those left will still need to eat. Babies will still be born, mothers will still need to nourish them. Our horses and cattle will still need food.

"Beginning today, we will stop taking wagon loads of corn to the grain elevator. We will store that corn for our people's use if food gets scarce. We will sell no more cattle, and only a few of our horses. I am not sure this new government can back their paper money."

"We will build storage bins for dried corn," offered Hawk. "We can also gather pecans and walnuts from Lost Valley and store them in great quantities. Each family will be asked to store up food and smoked venison for use if times get hard. Apples and pears can be sliced and dried so they will last. Pemmican is also a great emergency food."

"What's pemmican," asked Greta.

"Pemmican is lean meat dried, pounded fine, mixed with ground-up nuts and berries, usually blackberries, and melted fat" Star told her. "Cherokee warriors have used it for years on long hunts."

"We will begin a food storage program starting tomorrow," said Hawk. They were now entering Strong Heart, and the sun was going down, reluctantly.

Another problem bothered Star. Tall Woman Village was

a long way from the Cherokee Settlement. If that village were attacked by Union forces, she did not know how long they could hold out. Already reports were coming in about Kansas Jay hawkers attacking small white settlements in the Smoky Mountains near the Tennessee line. Moving the entire population from Tall Woman Village to Strong Heart and Lost Valley would be a large undertaking. They would either have to tear down the cabins at Tall Woman Village and haul the logs by wagon to the Strong Heart, or build new Cabins. Either way would be an arduous job. She would have to think on this, and talk to her top men.

CHAPTER FIVE

War

Jason and Jesse had crawled up a rocky hill to a stand of cedar trees overlooking what is today Bryson City, North Carolina. In the 1860's Bryson City was a small settlement. Encamped at the edge of the settlement was a company of Union soldiers preparing for muster - morning roll call. The mountain morning fog had just dissipated, but the grass was still damp and the air had a slight chill to it. The Twins could feel the chill through their buckskins, and their long rifles were slung across their backs to keep them away from the damp grass. They had been sent on a reconnaissance mission to locate Captain Goldman Bryson's Federal Mounted Company - the so-called Mountain Robbers.

The Mountain Robbers was an estimated force of a hundred and fifty troops that raided numerous Western North Carolina settlements, and was hated by the settlers for many reasons. Goldman Bryson was a home-grown Yankee and he raided and killed his own neighbors without conscience. For twenty days the Twins had searched the mountains for Captain Bryson and his men when they, finally, ran across their horse tracks. They followed the

168

tracks to where they now lay not fifty yards from Bryson's camp.

"That struttin' peacock down there is, no doubt, Captain Bryson," Jason whispered to his brother.

"We've got 'em, Jason!" Jesse whispered back. "Best we hightail it back to the Fort and make a report to Colonel Thomas."

A hundred yards away, the Twins had tethered their horses. They swung up into their saddles and struck out for Fort Cherokee. They rode at a trot so their mounts would not wear down during the thirty mile ride, and even then, they stopped now and again to loosen cinches so the horses could breath better while they rested. Upon reaching the Fort they rode up to the colonel's hitching rail at a gallop, dismounting before their horses stopped. Running into the Adjutant's office, they spoke between breaths.

"We found the Mountain Robbers," blurted Jason, "thirty miles from here at Bryson City, but appears they might be moving soon"

"They have over a hundred men and they are well armed," said Jesse.

Captain Wordsworth rushed into Colonel Thomas' office with the scouts' report. The Colonel came out immediately and questioned the Twins. When he had satisfied himself with the details, he put together a Cherokee force under the command of Lt. Campbell H. Taylor, a Cherokee. Thomas' Cherokees caught up to the Mountain Robbers at Murphy, another settlement not far from Bryson City. They were dismounted and at ease. The Cherokees surrounded them, leaving no avenue of escape. After an initial barrage of rifle fire that took down many of the Union soldiers, the

Cherokees waded in with knives and tomahawks. The Twins were in the thick of it - swinging tomahawks and slicing with their knives - trying to make a path to get to Captain Goldman Bryson.

The white Federal soldiers were not accustomed to close quarters combat and they fell like flies at the hands of the whooping and hollering Cherokees. Captain Bryson tried to run, and was ordered to halt, but kept running. He was shot dead by Lt. Taylor. Captain Goldman Bryson's Federal Mounted Company, the dreaded Mountain Robbers, were eliminated, all except seventeen prisoners. The Thomas Legion of Cherokee warriors was commended by General Braxton Bragg and the North Carolina governor, Zebulon Vance. Jason and Jesse Greyeagle were awarded Sergeant of Scouts stripes. They had performed their duties as scouts with tenacity, and had fought bravely in the battle. Colonel Thomas sent a letter of commendation to the Twin's mother:

To: Chief Star Greyeagle
        Strong Heart Village
From: Colonel William Holland Thomas, Commandant
        Fort Cherokee, CSA
Subject: Letter of Commendation

Dear Madam Chief,

Your sons, Jason and Jesse Greyeagle, have been awarded Sergeant of Scouts Stripes, an award I do not give out lightly, they must be earned, usually with years of service. In the short time your sons have been at Fort Cherokee, they have conducted themselves with utmost courtesy to their officers, and they are respected by their fellow scouts. You, no doubt, have heard of the Union's Federal Mounted Company, called by settlers The Mountain Robbers, a company of butchers that have sacked and pillaged many civilian settlements with no regard for life or property.

Scout Sergeants Jason and Jesse Greyeagle were sent on a mission to locate these Mountain Robbers. After twenty days in the field they did exactly that. A company of the Thomas Legion was led by your sons to the settlement of Murphy where we engaged the enemy and promptly eliminated them. In that battle, your sons fought bravely and with honor.

They have been commended by General Braxton Bragg and Governor Zebulon Vance.

As a parent, I felt it my duty to send you this letter of commendation.

Respectfully yours,
Colonel William Holland Thomas
Commanding

When Star received the commendation letter from Colonel Thomas her heart swelled with pride, but she already had known that her sons would perform their duties with gallantry. Her thoughts went back to Daniel and Hawk as young warriors, how fearless they had been, how brave they had been in battle. Hawk was still with her and took much of the load of running a nation from her shoulders, and for that she was thankful. But she missed Daniel terribly; she missed his great smile and his reassuring hand on her shoulder when she had become concerned over this or that in her youth. He had always been there for her, and for Hawk. Now, she walked in Tall Woman's moccasins - she wished Daniel was still here to reassure her, to smile and say: It is a good thing you are doing, little sister. She wished, too that her sons were with her.

Hawk's sons, Isaac, Jacob , and Jeremiah, had no uncle to teach them in the ways of the warrior when they became of age. Isaac was already of age according to Cherokee tradition, and his training had already begun by Hawk and Eagle Feather. Had Daniel been alive, that responsibility would have been his. Daniel had been Hawk's hero. It was Daniel who had taught him about the long rifle, the knife and the Tomahawk. It had been Daniel who taught him everything he knew. Several times, after Daniel's death, he dreamed that his brother and teacher had come to him saying: Let us go hunt the deer, little brother. He wished those days were here again. He wished Daniel was here to teach Isaac, Jacob, and Jeremiah. The price of the loss of a loved one is a heavy cross to bear, he told himself.

Hawk and Isaac were inside the corral. He was teaching his son how to guide his pony using only his legs and knees. Little Jacob and Jeremiah were hanging onto the corral fence shouting encouragement to their older brother. The boys had raven, black hair like Hawk's, but their eyes were light blue like their mother's. Whoever heard of a blue-eyed warrior? he smiled to himself. Yet, as he looked at each boy, he could see Daniel in their faces, he could see himself, Tall Woman, and Greta there also. His nephews, Jason and Jesse, were already men and fighting a war. He

172

thanked the Great Holy Spirit that his own sons were too
young for this strange war, but there would be other wars,
there would always be wars. Someday his sons might have
to fight, so the training he and Eagle Feather gave them in
this time might save them in another time.

"How's he doing, husband?" Greta had walked up to
where Jacob and Jeremiah were hanging onto the bottom
fence rail.

"He's a natural horseman," answered Hawk.

"I want to ride too!" yelled Jacob.

"Your time will come, little one, as will Jeremiah's," their
mother said. "Who's hungry?"

"I am!" they all yelled.

"Enough for today, Isaac," his father told him. With that,
Isaac threw his right leg over the pony and slid to the
ground, gracefully.

"Look at that!" Hawk told Greta. "I haven't taught him
that, yet! Like I said, he is a natural."

"Nobody here likes Blueberry Cobbler, do they?" their
mother teased.

"I do, I do, I do!" the boys said excitedly.

"Go wash your hands, then"

"Augh, mother!" Boys are boys no matter their eye color.

When the messenger from Tall Woman Village rode into
Strong Heart,

his horse collapsed and died in front of Star's office. The
rider had ridden his horse to death trying to deliver his
message that Tall Woman Village was under attack and
needed help. Hawk was the first to run to where the dead
horse had fallen, at once angry at the rider, but then

realizing that something was desperately wrong here.

Through gasps of breath, the rider told of the attack. And now Star was standing beside Hawk. She quickly took charge of the situation and raised the alarm throughout Strong Heart and Lost Valley. Before long people were gathered all around the headquarters building, twenty or so deep.

The messenger told Star that more than two hundred Union soldiers and maybe a hundred red-legged Kansas Jayhawkers were attacking his village. He said the villagers were defending the place as best as they could, but the attackers had better weapons. He did not know how long the villagers could hold out, and urged Star to send many warriors immediately. When Eagle Feather arrived, Star told him to take two horses and ride to Fort Cherokee and guide Colonel Thomas and his Legion to Tall Woman Village. She told him when one horse became too tired to run to release that horse, jump on the second mount and keep riding. She gave orders for Hawk, Brave Bull, Laughs-a-Lot and Nightbird to gather as many warriors as possible, fully armed, and to meet her back at the headquarters building. She told Yona to arm at least a hundred or more warriors and protect the road that led into Strong Heart in case there was an attack here. A hundred men could hold off three times that number if they controlled the entrance road to Strong Heart. Soon Hawk, Brave Bull, Laughs-a-Lot and Nightbird had a company of a hundred warriors each. All armed and ready to ride. Yona mustered two hundred men to protect Strong Heart from an attack.

As she rode out of Strong Heart, Star led four hundred warriors in four companies of one hundred each. It would take at least two hours to reach Tall Woman Village. She prayed to the Great Holy Spirit that she could get there in time, and that not one of her people would be killed. She and Hawk led the first company. Behind them rode Brave Bull and his men, and behind them came Laughs-a-Lot with his, followed by Nightbird and his company. They were stretched out for a mile. She set the pace at a trot. At that speed the horses would last. Only Star and Hawk had saddles; the other warriors chose to ride bareback, preferring not to burden their horses any more than necessary. Each warrior carried a long rifle, knife, tomahawk, lance, and bow with arrows.

At Tall Woman Village the battle had been going on for almost two hours. It was a furious battle, but the Cherokees were holding their own, thus far; the Yankees had not breeched the stockade fence made of strong upright logs with portholes for rifles. Three hundred warriors were fighting a life and death struggle for their families. One hundred riflemen were at the portholes. When they fired, they stepped aside to reload while another hundred men stepped into their places and fired. Behind them were a hundred bowmen rapidly shooting arrows up and over the stockade fence, raining fast and deadly arrows down on the invaders.

The Union soldiers had never fought Cherokee warriors - they thought theirs would be a quick and easy victory, but the Union soldiers kept falling - had their officers misjudged these people? Where was the quick victory? Why hadn't they brought canon with them? The whys kept piling up as lead balls and arrows kept killing. Now, of a sudden, there was cheering coming from behind the stockade fence! What possibly could the Cherokee have to cheer about? Then, they looked up through the din of powder smoke and saw the reasons for the cheers. The Union troops were surrounded by four hundred mounted Cherokee. My God, where did they come from?

They were just sitting there on their horses with upraised spears, and they were being led by a woman of all things. What kind of men were these to allow themselves to be commanded by a mere woman? Now what was this crazy woman doing by raising her hand? At that command the warriors reversed their spears and stuck them into the ground on the right side of their horses. They un-slung rifles from their shoulders and aimed them. When the woman dropped her hand, four hundred rifles belched fire and brimstone, smoke and havoc. And many Union men died screaming. Then the woman yelled another command and the men took up bow and arrow. They pulled back bow strings, and when the woman yelled another command. four hundred arrows arched in the sky and fell like sharp, pointed hail.

Each time the woman shouted a command, four hundred more arrows were loosed until there were only a few Yankee soldiers left standing. The woman gave another command. The men shouldered their bows, picked up their spears and rode slowly through the battlefield spearing anything that moved or breathed. The stockade gate was opened and the woman rode through the gate without even looking back! These were the thoughts of the last Yankee officer left standing as Hawk hit him with his tomahawk. The young officer's thoughts and spirit left his body never to return. None of Star's men were killed or wounded, and only one warrior behind the stockade fence died, seven were wounded, but would recover.

Shortly, Lt. Campbell H. Taylor with a company of Thomas' Legion arrived. Eagle Feather and the Twins rode at Lt. Taylor's side as guides because they knew the way from Fort Cherokee to Tall Woman Village. As they rode through the battlefield. Lt Taylor exclaimed"

"My, God! What has happened here?"

"Looks like mother has already been here," said Jason, looking over the bodies lying on the ground and scattered around the Village.

"Yep, Guess you could say that," replied his brother.

The Lieutenant found Chief Star kneeling beside the dead Cherokee. She held his hands and bowed her head, then crossed his arms. He would get a warriors funeral and his wife and child would be taken care of by the wife's family. Star would make sure the warrior's family did not go without. Star hugged the wife and tried to wipe away her tears. Then she walked over to Lt. Taylor.

"Chief Star, I extend to you my condolences for the man you lost; it is difficult to lose one of your men, I, too, share that grief several times over. I had hoped to get here sooner."

"You were not long behind us, Lieutenant. If my men had met with failure, you would have been here in time to save us. I thank you for coming," Star said earnestly.

"Your husband and sons are here with me," he said. "Your sons are very brave scouts. I am proud they are in my unit."

"Thank you, Lieutenant. You honor me by saying that."

Star spent some time with her family, and then gave the

responsibility of burying the enemy soldiers to the people of the Village. She was not immune to the death of so many soldiers - men with mothers and fathers, wives and children who loved them and would grieve at their absence from this life. But she had been cast into a vicious play and given a script with no room to ad lib. She had done what she had to do, her people's lives were at stake, and if necessary, she would have given her own life to save them. She gathered her men outside the stockade fence and told them how much she appreciated their bravery. They knew she was proud of every man there. Her top men organized the warriors again into four companies, then Star and Hawk and Eagle Feather led them as they moved out, a mile long line of quiet warriors.

Star had hoped her sons could have visited with her at Strong Heart a few days. But she understood that duty comes before all else; it was the way of love and war. Star felt calm, confident, and qualified. Tall Woman had taught her well. But she also felt a foreboding, a feeling she could not explain - it was like a hazy cloud, a far gathering storm out there someplace, a Mephistophelean spirit lurking, waiting for the exact moment to envelop the Cherokee people and choke the life out of them.

Over the next several months, there was relative peace in the Cherokee Villages. The war raged throughout North Carolina and surrounding states, causing food shortages for many and limiting travel. Life for the Cherokee took on a seemingly normal daily course. As long as the Confederate Thomas Legion Cherokee was stationed at the nearby fort, Star felt her people would be relatively safe, baring a possible small raid by the Kansas Jayhawkers. However, losing three hundred men to the Cherokee in one battle did not set well with Northern generals or the U.S. Government. They may not attack Star's villages today or tomorrow, but at some point in time they would get their revenge, likely at war's end if the North won. This possibility was a concern to Star.

Star had no problems with either army when one or the other occupied Fort Cherokee. She had developed a good relationship with Colonel Harrison when his Northern Troops were there, and she now enjoyed good relations with Confederate Colonel Thomas and his Cherokee Legion. The Cherokee Nation did side with the South, but Star, personally, held no allegiance to either North or South, her allegiance was to her people. She wanted peace and cooperation with whomever was in charge, but she would take no bullying from either. If the South won she felt her people, in general, would be treated fairly because the Cherokee fought for the Confederacy. But if the North won, she felt her people would have a rough row to hoe. A Northern Government would, most assuredly, turn Strong Heart into a guarded reservation. That, her people did not want.

The Civil war was anything but civil. Union battle deaths reached 110,070, with 250,152 dying of diseases - total dead 360,222. The Confederate States of America lost 94,000 in combat and 164,000 dead of diseases - total dead 258,000. The dying did not stop when the war ended. Sicknesses followed the soldiers and prisoners of war home - diarrhea, typhoid, yellow fever and other diseases decimated the Indians. Twenty-five percent died of white man illnesses.

The North Carolina economy was totally destroyed - homes, stores, barns, buildings, burned to the ground. The Indian population was reduced to poverty, to being homeless refugees. And although Star's three villages had corn, stored for just such an occasion, the Cherokee's immune system could not fight the dreaded diseases brought among them by returning soldiers.

The ravages of war played havoc on the Cherokee people. There was a death mask over the Cherokee. This, Star suspected, was the specter that would choke the life out of the Cherokee people. When a family died of either yellow fever or typhoid, their cabin was burned. When Star looked out over Strong Heart Valley, she saw too many black, ash spots, too many cabins burned. Since Lost Valley was separated from Strong Heart by a waterfall and thus secluded, the fevers had not yet reached there. She was losing her people daily now, and the weight of such a monumental burden was sapping the strength out of her. And her twins, Jason and Jesse, were missing in action.

The prison camps, both North and South, were breeding grounds of death and dying, of savagery and near starvation. Diseases were rampant, putting dozens on the death list daily. And it is to this prison camp that Jason followed after his brother was capture by an enemy patrol. This camp was a temporary holding place until transfer to several Union prisoner of war institutions. This particular camp held twenty-five people. The twins had been separated by about one hundred yards when Jesse was taken. With too many guns pointing at him, Jesse had raised his arms in surrender, knowing that Jason was even now watching and would follow at a safe distance.

Following the patrol was easy for Jason, tracking was something that came natural to him. The trick to it was knowing nature's order, then looking for what is out of order - a disturbed twig or bent grass; nature has a thousand ways to tell of what happened here, what passed this way.

And as Jason watched the camp from his hide, a group of dead blackberry bushes surrounded by ankle deep grass, his eyes trailed a single guard walking his post outside the barbed fence. A tower guard was at the far corner. It was early morning and prisoners were fed outside in the prison yard. Each time the guard disappeared, and the tower guard was looking the other way, Jason would whistle a bird call that his brother would recognize and respond to. On the second day, Jesse heard the call and walked toward the sound. He lingered four feet from the fence. With a hand signal like scissors cutting a wire, and holding out six fingers, meant cut here at six o'clock.

At six is when prisoners were fed the evening meal - if you could call it that, a glob in a bowl that supposed to be stew left over from the day before, and anything else the cooks could find to throw into the pot. Prisoners were milling around, some dabbing biscuits into a small metal bowl they carried. Jesse had positioned himself near the wire; he sat down, pulled his knees up and used them as a table to set his bowl on. He pretended to eat, waiting for Jason to make his move. Jason appeared quickly from out of the brush - he cut the two bottom strands of barbed-wire then disappeared back into the brush, with Jesse low on his heels. It happened so fast that neither the walking guard or the tower guard saw or heard anything. The more simple

181

the plan, the better the odds are of it working.

Jason had brought four horses - two to ride and two to trail. They rode all during the night, and when one horse gave out, the Twins changed mounts on the run. By daylight, they were miles away from the prison camp. They found a gully that would hide the horses and themselves from spying eyes, and went to sleep. When the Twins awoke it was late evening. They ate pemmican, washed down with water from their canteens. When it was dark enough, they saddled up and were on their way.

"They're on to us by now," Jesse told his brother. "We are now wanted fugitives - one enemy escapee, and one who aided in the escape. Patrols will scour the countryside for us."

"Been thinking about that," answered Jason, "might be a good time to leave the mountains and head for Texas. I've heard it's wide open down there, and a man can make a new start with very few questions."

"Never been to Texas, but it sounds good to me," offered Jesse. "I'd like to see mother before we go, no telling when we can come back home."

The Twins encountered two different patrols, but they managed to evade them. And as they rode on toward Strong Heart, the devastation to the countryside became more apparent. Even at night the burnt out homes and buildings were a stark reality that war had destroyed North Carolina. They wondered if Strong Heart had been destroyed - were their mother and relatives still alive? Once well into the mountains, they found a stream where Jesse bathed and changed into buckskins that Jason had brought along.

The shock of seeing Strong Heart as they rode into the Valley hit them like a blast of hot air. Immediately, they felt the gloom that hovered over the once happy village, and their eyes were pained at the sight of so many burned cabins. The harm to the Cherokee village was more than they expected. They just sat there on their horses and soaked in the dismal, moonlit picture unable to speak. This was where they were born, where they grew-up, where they swam as children in the blue waters of the waterfall, where they were taught the ways of a warrior by their uncle Hawk. All the times they were scouting for the Confederacy, fighting for the South, when they thought of Strong Heart, the thoughts were always happy ones, thoughts that would keep a man going, gave him reason to fight for his home and people. But now, as they tied their horses to a hitching rail in front of the headquarters building, they felt only sorrow.

Although obviously tired and drained over the loss of so many of her people, Star was nevertheless ecstatic at seeing her sons walking up the stone path. She ran from the doorway and embraced them with bear hugs - then she stepped back to take a look at her wayfaring twins. They were six feet tall, about one hundred eighty-five pounds and muscled. "Beautiful," she smiled, and hugged them again. Once in her office, star brought them up on everything that had happened, and when she spoke of the people who had died, tears wet her cheeks.

"Thank the Great Spirit our family has not yet been sick. When it first broke out here at Strong Heart, I moved them to Lost Valley. So far, it hasn't made it through the waterfall and no one is permitted to enter or leave without my approval."

"Then why aren't you there?" Jesse asked with concern.

"I am the leader of these people, my son. I cannot walk away from them. I led them during good times, and I must lead them through these bad times. I must stay, but you must go - now. Go to Daniel's old cabin in Lost Valley. The family is there."

The Twins brought Star up on their situation and plans for Texas. She told them that she hated to see them go that far away from home, but that it was probably best because the Army would most assuredly come calling. The Twins hugged their mother and went through the waterfall.

The Twin's reunion with Eagle Feather, their father, their uncle Hawk and his three sons, and Greta, lasted to the wee hours. They listened to the stories of everyone there with much interest because it told of desperate times for the Cherokee people. The future looked bleak. In addition to the fevers, the South had lost the war and now the blue coats were back in power again. They had changed the name of the fort back to Fort Stone. A newly commissioned Lieutenant Colonel, Travis Judd, was back in Cherokee country and in charge. He had already paid a visit to Strong Heart and placed an entry/exit ban on the village because of the sicknesses. He placed no guards, however, because of possible infection. If a soldier caught the bug, it would spread through and wipeout everyone at the fort. He placed Star under the honor system.

But the Twins did not honor the white man's system. Two weeks after they arrived at Strong Heart, they said their goodbyes to family, swung up onto their horses, and rode out into the night with thoughts of Texas on their minds, and the Union Army far behind. They each trailed a pack horse loaded down with supplies. Now if they could get out of North Carolina without being detected, caught, or captured, they just might have a chance for a new life in a distant land. The Twins had heard tales galore about the independent Texicans, Goliad, the Alamo, and Sam Houston. It was said that Houston had lived once with a band of Cherokees somewhere in east Texas. If the Twins could locate that band of brothers they would have a place to live until they figured out what to do. And from these Indians they could learn much about the ways of the Texicans, and how to fit in with them. They rode on as the night closed in behind them.

At Fort Stone, two old buck skinned trappers sat on the gallery in front of the commandant's office chewing tobacco and spitting brown globs at several horseflies. They were watching a search party return with no luck.

"Could've told 'em they wasn't gonna find them two Cherokee boys," spat Beaver Ben. "Them boys are trained scouts besides being Injun."

"Gossip has it that Colonel Judd ain't too anxious to find 'em," offered Blackjack McLeod. "Seems he had a first-name speaking friendship with Chief Tall Woman, the boys' grandmother, and also with Chief Star their mother and Chief of the Cherokees. Hell, Hawk even rode scout for the Colonel way back when!"

"Well, he ain't got much say when it comes to dealin' with the Injuns," retorted Beaver Ben. "He's gotta follow orders, and the word is to keep a tight noose on the Cherokee. This new government got no truck with them what sided with

the Rebs, and they ain't forgot Chief Star's part in the
massacre of sum three hundred Yankee soldiers."

"Ya know, Ben, I wuz wonderin' why the colonel left no
guards on her village? Said it wuz concern over soldiers
catching the crud, but later I found out he put four
sharpshooters along that road that leads into Strong Heart -
told 'em to keep an eye out for the Twins, to capture 'em if
they can, but if the boys put up a fight to shoot 'em outta
their saddles."

The Twins had discovered the sharpshooters, and circled
around them without being seen.

"Don't sound very friendly to me."

"Nope." Blackjack McLoed spat another glob of tobacco
juice, this time clobbering a horse fly.

Besides everything else on her shoulders, Star was
lonesome - she missed her family. But, so far, they were safe
in Lost Valley, and her beloved Twins had headed off to
Texas, a place known for being wild and open. She knew
there were Comanche and Tonkawa in Texas, but was
unaware of the east Texas Cherokee. Star had heard the
Tonkawa had cannibalistic tendencies. Many used to think
they originated in central Texas. Research indicates that the
Tonkawa occupied northeastern Oklahoma in 1601. By
1700, the more aggressive Apache had pushed the Tonkawa
south to the Red River. They kept moving into Texas, where
they made treaties with the Lipan Apache. And in 1824 the
Tonkawa entered into a treaty with Stephen F. Austin,
pledging aid against the warlike Comanche. In 1840 , the
Tonkawa fought as allies of the Texas Rangers .

The east Texas Cherokee had migrated from Arkansas to
Texas in search of a home. Followed by a small group of

sixty families, Chief Bowles set up his people between the Trinity and Sabine rivers. This is the tribe that had adopted Sam Houston, and the tribe the Twins would seek for shelter and Information, if they could be found. Texas was a large place.

But Star found no solace from feeling alone as she struggled to maintain her grasp on sanity, and when the fever took Big Tree, her step father, and advisor, the loss hit her hard. And then Yona died. After that she lost Uncle Two and his family. The deaths of Uncle Two and his family were especially difficult to bear. He would be dearly missed by his students - those that survived. The silent specter had robbed her of many of her top men. As she sat in her darkened office, with only the glow of the fireplace giving light, she wished Tall Woman and Daniel were here to advise her and give her comfort. She couldn't confide in Hawk because she had ordered him and his family and Eagle Feather to live at Lost Valley, and not to leave there until this dreaded plague was gone. So she lived alone in her cabin at Strong Heart. She made her daily rounds throughout the cabins consoling, encouraging the living, delivering food, and burying the dead. Each evening when she returned to her office to record the names of today's deaths, she could have easily just given up, closed her eyes, and allowed her spirit to leave this burdened place. But she could not give up or give in. Some of her people had to live - to live and reproduce, to repopulate. The Cherokee people had to rise, had to again overcome tragedy and rebirth itself. She fell asleep in her chair with her head and arms on her desk, exhausted.

Hawk wanted to be with his sister, to hold her up, to

share the awful burden she carried daily. But Star could not be persuaded. It was important that her family survive the plague, and the only way she knew was to confine them to Lost Valley, even over Hawks repeated protest. Several times he started to walk through the waterfall and announce "I am staying." But that would be a breach of honor. He and his family and Eagle Feather, were ordered to Lost Valley for their own good. Star had also ordered Laughs-a-Lot, Nightbird, and Brave Bull and his family, the last three of her top leaders, to Lost Valley. They protested, but to no avail. To go against their Chief would be open rebellion, not the way of a warrior. So Hawk continued teaching his sons the ways of the Cherokee warrior, Laughs-a-Lot and Nightbird tamed and trained horses, and Brave Bull hunted game to feed them all. That kept their minds and hands busy, but their thoughts often wandered through the waterfall.

Hawk's sons, Isaac, Jacob, and Jeremiah were growing like spring grass. Isaac, ten now, was tall for his age, and it seemed like Jacob, eight, and Jeremiah, seven, were determined to catch up to Isaac. For his sons' sake, Hawk was pleased that Star decided to close Lost Valley, but he still felt he should be by her side. Greta had been teaching the boys from her large family Bible since they were old enough to understand her words. Even Hawk listened with interest as she read by the glow of the fireplace. The boys especially liked to hear about the men they were named after, and Hawk liked to hear about Joshua, the great warrior who became chief after Moses died. Hawk told stories his father, Running Elk, related about the Cherokee having kinship with the Canaanites and coming to this land

188

thousands of years ago.

"All men are related," informed Greta. "Every tribe on earth began with the sons of Noah and can be traced back to their beginnings. In time, people scattered all over the world and created communities, some even crossed oceans, and some came to this land long before the white man. Actually, the white men are new here compared to the Cherokee and other ancient races who have been in this land for thousands of years."

"Why does the white man want to take everything from us?" asked Isaac.

"That, my son," said Hawk, "is the question of the age. "People move into a land, make it their land, and live on it for generations. After a while other people show up and move the first people out. Then later other people come in and move them out. One old Cherokee wise man said it was the way of the circle, the natural progression of people things."

"In other words," said Greta, "some folks think might is right. People have been taking what doesn't belong to them since the world began because they were strong enough to take it. They had the might, but that doesn't make it right."

"Trouble is," Hawk added, "people want more, more of everything whether it belongs to them or not."

"That's where morals and values comes in," said Greta. "This Book I read from teaches the right way to live with others, but few follow it. If every human being lived by the principles of this Book, there would be universal peace."

"And," said Hawk, "there are some who don't want peace. The way I see it there are times for peace, times for war, and times to just be silent. Similar to the fields where we grow corn. We grow in one field for two years, then leave it silent while we grow in another field. Gives the earth a chance to recover. Right now, the Cherokee people needs a chance to recover. We need some quiet time, a time to rebuild and grow strong. This time of sickness will pass. We have lost many people and will lose more before times get better.

"Now, whether the army and this present government will allow us to remain in this land as free as we have been is the question. My feelings are that Strong Heart will be made into a reservation ruled by white men, and that we will have limited movement throughout the mountains and limited access to assimilate into their society. If that happens, our best course may be to find another land."

"You mean move all three villages to a distant place?" asked Isaac.

"Well," replied Hawk, "Moses and Joshua, according to your mother's Book, moved nearly two million people from Egypt to a new land of milk and honey. If they did it, why could not we do the same"

"Have you talked this over with Star," asked Greta.

"I have not, but I plan to soon as this sickness runs its course."

"Father, if this were to happen, where would we go?" asked Jacob.

"I don't know," his father replied. "Before the Twins left for Texas, I asked them to allow their eyes to be mine, to feel out that land as a possible home for us."

Much thought would be given to such an unthinkably large move. The sheer size and logistics of such a move would be staggering. The concept was difficult for the boys to get a handle on - soon they were curled up in front of the fireplace, oblivious to everything but sleep.

Sleep did not come easy for the Twins during their first summer nights in Texas. If Texas was anything, it was big and it was hot. Not even a breeze was stirring under the pines where they tried to sleep, but could not. Jason and Jesse were not accustomed to hundred degree nights. They had traveled long and far and had seen a lot of country, and they had finally made their way into east Texas, found a clear running creek, picketed their mounts, and decided to give themselves and their horses a needed few days of rest. The day before, they had stopped at a small one-horse town called, Alba. A sign said it had been established in 1843, maybe twenty-five years old, but it had a mercantile store and the people were friendly. Buckskins may be good for winter wear, but not good for Texas summers, so the boys bought Levi Strauss denim trousers, light weight shirts, and because everyone they saw in Alba wore cowboy boots, they bought themselves a pair of tall, round top, black boots.

"Appears you boys have been traveling a spell," stated the jovial, gray headed store owner. "Can't say I've ever met Indians that talk as good as you do. Don't believe I've seen any Indians that look more white than brown either"

"Yes, sir," said Jesse, "we've been on the trail for a couple of months. Came down from the eastern mountains looking for Cherokee relatives."

"Ah, you 're Cherokee!" said the old man. "That explains the light color. Cherokees aren't like other Indians - they 're good people and good neighbors. They don't live in tepees, you know. They live in houses or cabins like the rest of us.

Some own farms and a few have small ranches. Quite a few Cherokee in east Texas. You'll have no problem locating your kin. Before you leave, I'll direct you to a Cherokee family I've known for years. They'll be able to help you," the talkative man said.

While Jesse talked to the store owner, Jason had been looking at the rifles and pistols.

"I see you have an eye for guns," said the man. "This here is the Henry, 44 caliber, lever action repeater. It uses a metal cartridge, and as long as you keep cartridges in this tube under the barrel, it'll fire a bullet each time you work the lever and pull the trigger. Sure a lot faster than those muzzle loaders you boys carry."

"We'll take two," said Jason without hesitation. He quickly saw the advantages of a Henry over his long rifle. "What about these pistols here?" he asked.

"That's the Colt 45 caliber six-gun. Uses metal cartridges and will fire each time you cock the hammer and pull the trigger. Again, compared to your percussion pistols, the Colts will seem like greased lightning in your hands."

"We'll take two," Jason told the man. "What's that heavy looking rifle?"

"That, my boy, is a Sharps. Shoots a 50 caliber cartridge, and a good shot can bring down a buffalo at a thousand yards."

"We'll take one of the Sharps and ammunition for all of these. Would you be interested in taking our long rifles and long pistols in as trade?"

The store owner was interested and made the Twins a fair deal - the muzzle loaders, plus some cash closed the bargain. He also threw in saddle scabbards for the rifles and tried to sell them a pair of holsters for the six-guns, but after thinking on it, they decided to carry the pistols behind their belts. They paid the man and also bought two pounds of coffee. It was probably the best day the store owner could remember. Now, they were camped by the creek, under the pines, and still could not sleep because of the heat.

Rifles and pistols were nothing new to Jason and Jesse. They had been using them since they were youngsters, but the weapons they were accustomed to could not compare to the Henrys, the Sharps, and the Colt six-guns. They were already excellent shots, but with the new weapons they were even better. It did not take much practice to hit what they were shooting at, and the Sharps was like the store owner had said, a great long range rifle. Finally, a slight breeze wafted through the trees. Sleep then came fast. They were bone tired.

When daylight shoved dark into the background, morning was still stingy on cool weather, but there was enough breeze to make the morning hospitable. Jesse filled their canteens from the creek and brought water for coffee while Jason built a small fire. They cooked bacon and biscuits and washed it down with strong coffee. The mercantile store owner had given them directions to a Cherokee farmer's place. When they had rested another day, they would seek out this farmer and try to connect with the Texas Cherokee. So far the Twins had not seen any army patrols in their travels in east Texas and that was a good thing, even though Texas was ruled by a Union dominated Reconstruction government. Besides, the army here would have no cause to stop or question them, the

Cherokee Mountains were a lifetime away.

The store owner had informed them that the Comanche were still hostile, but they raided farther west and a bit north. Farther down in south Texas, Mexican bandits and rustlers were more a threat along the Nueces Strip and gave the Texas Rangers a constant headache, the store owner had told them. But east Texas had its problems, also, in the form of robbers, rustlers, and just plain, mean, gunmen who hired their guns to whomever paid the price, and some, like John Wesley Hardin, killed for little or no apparent reason. Texas could be a dangerous place for the gullible, especially after the civil war ended and scalawags of all stripes sought refuge from the law in this big country once owned by Mexico.

The Twins had heard the stories of white warriors, such as Jim Bowie, Davy Crockett, and other fortune hunters and adventure seekers, who had been massacred in a mission called the Alamo in a town called San Antonio de Bexar. After a long chase, Sam Houston and his Texicans finally mustered enough men to stop and fight and defeat the, so-called, Napoleon of the South. Texas became a Republic, then, finally, a State. But Mexico never forgot, nor did many of the Mexicans living in Texas. A white man could still get his throat cut in any number of cantinas in towns predominately Mexican, and a Mexican could still get himself shot in white man saloons. Violence had been an integral part of Texas history, and as Jason and Jesse ate their breakfast beneath the pine trees, things had not changed much.

CHAPTER SIX

Texas

The Twins heard the two riders approaching through the trees before they saw them.

"Hello, the camp," one rider called. It was customary to give notice before riding into someone's camp.

"If you're friendly, come on in," Jesse called back.

"Friendly, we are," spoke a freckled-faced young man of about twenty-

two, wearing a Texas border hat.

"Smelled your coffee. Sure would be obliged for a cup if you can spare some," said the tall, lanky man wearing a wide brimmed hat and a handle-bar mustache. He looked about twenty-five.

The Twins mistook them for cowboys because of their hats, boots, and spurs, and because their skin was browned from the sun and they looked leathery tough. Jason could tell the pair spent most of their time out-of-doors, and not a lot of time at a dinner table. They rode good horses, one was a gray and the other a dun. Both men had lever-action saddle rifles, and both had six-shooters strapped to their waists. Each man carried a large Bowie knife. The Twins'

195

hands were never far from the butts of their pistols. If necessary, they could get to them quick. When Jason and Jesse noticed the Texas Ranger badges on the men's vests, they figured their own pistols would not be necessary.

"You're welcome to the coffee," spoke Jason. "We were just cooking up some breakfast, if you boys are hungry you can join us."

"Hungry we are," said one. "We ain't ate since noon yesterday."

"We thought you were cowboys when you rode up," said Jesse.

"Naw," said the man with the handle bar mustache, "we're Rangers on the trail of six bank robbers. We lost their tracks 'bout a mile from here - smelled the coffee and thought you might be them."

"Once we saw you, we knew right away you weren't them." said freckle- face. "You boys are Indians."

"We're Cherokee," stated Jason. "Came to Texas looking for work. We've had some experience as trackers"

"Where you boys from?" asked the man with the mustache.

"Near the Smoky Mountains," replied Jesse.

"I come from Tennessee," offered freckle-face. "I know about mountains, but 'I've been a Ranger since I was eighteen. That's how old I was when I came to Texas. Say, you boys think you could pick up the outlaws' tracks. It sure would be neighborly of you."

"Be glad to help if we can," answered Jason.

The four young men ate and talked and enjoyed each others company. The Ranger with the handle-bar mustache, they learned, was Ruff Jackson, a native Texan, and the

freckled face young man's name was Abe Gaston, a
Tennessean. The two Rangers had been trailing the outlaws
for three days. A bank had been robbed in Tyler, about
thirty miles away from where the Twin's camped, and two
men had been shot dead - a bank teller and a deputy sheriff.
The Rangers, always short of men, could spare only Ruff
and Abe to trail the robbers. They were called in when the
outlaws left Smith County. Rangers were not hindered by
county lines and could pursue their prey anywhere in the
State of Texas. The Rangers were a tough bunch, and
because of the violent men they pursued they were
sometimes judge, jury and executioners. If they had a creed,
it was get your man or die trying. Consequently, if the
Rangers were on your tail, best you headed for heaven
because hell was following.

After a breakfast of bacon and biscuits and coffee, The
Twins secured their pack horses, saddled up and followed
the Rangers to where they had lost the outlaws' trail. The
earth was hard-packed because of little rain and a hard,
relenting sun, but it was obvious to Jason and Jesse why the
tracks suddenly ended. Whoever had been delegated to
brush the tracks away knew what he was doing, probably a
trained tracker, only faint impressions of his work were left,
and only a capable tracker would have been able to notice
the difference.

"They've done a good job of covering their tracks," Jason
told the Rangers. "If you boys will tend our animals, my
brother and I will walk circles to where the tracks pick up
again."

About fifty yards away, the Twins found the outlaws'
tracks, and motioned for Ruff and Abe to bring up the

197

horses. They trailed the robbers until the sun was in the two o'clock position, then more brushing, but the Twins got right back on the trail. After two hours, they came to a shallow creek and the tracks ended. Jason asked the Rangers to wait at the bank while he and Jesse rode in the creek in opposite directions looking for the spot the outlaws pulled out and onto the other bank. Before long, Jesse found the spot. He rode back to the Rangers and gave a bird call that brought Jason back, then the four men were again on the trail. The sun was setting, a blazing orange when they noticed a tendril of gray smoke off in the distance.

The men staked their horses on what little green grass the sun had not withered, removed their rifles from their saddles, and began to move toward the smoke. Jason brought along the Sharps .50 caliber rifle. They were far enough away that the horses would not nicker back and forth giving away their approach.

"Looks like an old line shack," whispered Ruff. "they're either boiling coffee or cooking somethin'."

The six horses staked and saddled off to the right of the dilapidated shack fit the descriptions given by witnesses of the robbery. The structure appeared about ready to fall down - a strong wind would probably do the job. There was still enough light left to challenge those in the shack, and the Rangers were not of the opinion to wait until morning.

"Hello, the shack!" yelled Abe. "you're surrounded by twenty Rangers. Give it up or die in the shack! you're choice!"

Two of the killers suddenly burst from the shack's

weathered door, shooting as they ran for the horses, but the Rangers brought them down with a hail of bullets. Then quiet. Smoke still drifted up from a tin stove pipe.

"Jason, think you can knock that stove pipe to kingdom come with your Sharps?" asked Ruff. "That'll put some smoke in there."

"I hit what I aim at," replied Jason, taking a prone position. The others followed his lead.

The Sharps sounded like a canon when it knocked the stove pipe off of the roof, sending it twisting and tumbling over the rear of the shack. Soon black smoke filled the shack and men began coughing. Abe told Jason to put another round into a weak stud that held one corner of the dilapidated structure. When the .50 caliber bullet hit the stud, the roof sagged a little. He shot two more studs and the front roof started to collapse.

With the smoke and the roof collapsing, the remaining four outlaws filed through the door coughing, arms raised, and yelling, "Don't shoot, we're givin' up!"

The Rangers tied the killers hands behind their backs while Jason and Jesse kept them covered, then the Twins walked the outlaws' horses over and helped them into the saddles. Abe tied the two dead men across their saddles while Ruff gave cover. Soon the Twins brought up their own mounts. Everybody was mounted except Abe. Before he saddled-up, he unfurled two ropes and threw them over two of the outlaws, pulling the ropes tight around their waist and handing a rope each to Jesse and Jason.

"Boys, if these two try to run, jus' yank 'em outta the saddle," Abe told them. "If these other two try anything, me an' Ruff'll just shoot 'em. Guess we'll have to press you boys into temporary Ranger service 'till we get these mongrels back to camp."

Most lawmen would have waited until daylight to transport their prisoners, but the Rangers did not play by any known rules. They had a few guidelines, but, mostly, they made their rules as they went along. As long as they had a good moon, they saw no sense in stopping. The Twins liked these Rangers, they got the job done.

They arrived at the Ranger camp just after the morning meal. Ranger Captain Jonas Simpson was standing by the door of his tent watching the men as they rode in. Simpson was a stout looking man in his mid forties with a black mustache and long sideburns. During the war, he had been a major in the Confederate Army. He was a tough Ranger and expected his men to be tough. Ruff and Abe dismounted and walked over to the Captain who was eying the Twins, trying to figure out what they were doing riding with his men.

"Two bank robbers dead, four for the lock-up, Captain," said Ruff.

"Good work, men," growled the Captain." Who's the Indians?"

"That's Jason and Jesse Greyeagle, Sir. They're Cherokee from up around the Smoky Mountains. We came up on their camp when we noticed smoke from their coffee fire. We had lost the outlaws' tracks, but these two found it and led Abe and me to a line shack where the robbers were holed up. They helped us subdue the outlaws on top of that. Never met anybody that can track as good as these two."

"They can shoot, too, Captain," said Abe. "Jason there

shot out the shack's stove pipe with his Sharps, causin' the place to smoke up, and damn near brought down the shack on top of these killers. I asked them to help us bring back the prisoners."

"Good work," the Captain said again, "that's thinking on your feet. Secure your prisoners, go down to the chuck wagon and eat. You look like you can use some meat on your bones. Feed your friends, also, then bring them to my tent."

At the chuck wagon, the men ate a hearty breakfast of beefsteak, potatoes, gravy, and biscuits. They lingered over coffee awhile and talked.

"You boys ever thought about joining the Rangers?" asked Ruff.

"Never heard of the Rangers until we met you two," replied Jesse.

"Well, I think the Captain will offer you a job. He wants to see you soon's we finish eatin'. If he does, I hope you boys join up. We can use good men like you," Ruff told them.

"Besides that," said Abe, "you 'd be the first Cherokee ever to be a Ranger. Now, that's something' to crow about. Wonder what the Captain would do if you was to bring in a scalped prisoner."

The four men had a good laugh at that, then Abe and Ruff took them to the Captain's tent. He was setting behind a small desk signing arrest warrants when they walked in. He put the warrants aside and told the Twins to stand easy.

"The Rangers appreciate your help," the Captain said earnestly. "Not many civilians care to help a Ranger out when he is in need. The reason we have such a strong bond, is because the only people we can count on is ourselves. As I understand it, you helped willingly. It's obvious you two have qualifications we could use. What would you think about a Ranger job?"

"Well, sir, like we told Ruff and Abe, we haven't really thought about it - didn't know about the Rangers until we met them. We are looking for a job, but if you were to accept us, there is one request we'd like to make," Jesse told the Captain.

I like that, the Captain thought - courteous and straight to the point. "And what would be that request?"

"We're twins, sir," replied Jason. "We haven't been separated since we were born. We work well together. If we were Rangers, we'd want to work

together."

"I know about the tie between twins," said the Captain. "I was a twin, believe it or not. My brother and I served together in the army. I lost him at Bull's Run. Never have gotten over the loss. You have my guarantee. You will not be separated. Are you boys wanted for anything serious?"

"Well, sir, I imagine the Union Army would like to get their hands on us. We scouted for the Confederacy in the Cherokee Mountains of North Carolina. don't think they like us very much," Jesse informed the Captain.

Truthful, the Captain thought. "The Rangers are not political. We have ex-Union and ex-Confederates in our ranks and they get along just fine. They put Rangering above all else. If any Union people come around here looking for you, as far as I'm concerned you don't exist."

"Then if you will accept us, sir, we'd like to join up," said Jason.

"Accepted," the Captain smiled. " Put your animals in the corral down by the creek. Until I can assign you a tent, you can sleep down by the oak grove. That's all for now."

When the Twins walked out of the Captain's tent, they were Rangers. Ruff and Abe were waiting for them with slaps on the back. They walked the Twins down to the corrals, then took them around and introduced them to the other Rangers in camp. They were met with smiles and genuine acceptance. Not one Ranger showed any animosity about the Twins being Cherokee. The Twins felt they were in the right company - they felt good about joining the Rangers. They especially liked their new friends, Ruff and Abe. For two weeks, the Twins stayed in camp tending their horses and listening to the older hands telling about life in the Rangers. They were told they sometimes got paid, when headquarters had the money. The Captain had assigned the two a tent, and had told them he appreciated the fact that they could read and write, a fact uncommon with most Rangers. While in the camp, the Twins had developed a healthy respect for the Ranger Captain. They decided it was time to write their mother and uncle Hawk back in the Cherokee Mountains:

Dear Mother,

We are well. The trip was long, but we made it to Texas in good health and as we write this, we are Texas Rangers - the top law enforcement agency in this wild place. For your information, we are shielded from the Union forces from which we ran, so there is no need to worry about that problem. Here we are the law. We both wish to thank you for educating us as Cherokee warriors, but also in the white man's way. Many years ago, you told us that the only way for the Cherokee to continue to exist as a people was to assimilate into the white culture. You were right, and that is what we are doing.

Believe it or not, we hunt down and bring white men to justice. We never thought a Cherokee would be doing this. Here, the Rangers do not care whether you are white or Cherokee as long as we bring in the outlaws. We do our jobs. There are many opportunities here for our people. Cherokee here legally own their own farms or ranches and are not looked down upon. Property here is reasonable and we are looking for a suitable place for you and our family.

This is to our uncle, Hawk: Uncle, you asked us to find a place for our family to live. Texas, we believe, is that place. We are convinced of that. But, we do not think this state would appreciate a whole Cherokee Nation coming here at one time to set up a community. What we suggest is that our family move here, along with Brave Bull and his family, Laughs-a-lot, and Nightbird. You could start a horse ranch. You and Mother have had the weight of responsibility of a nation way too long. It is time for both of you to retire from leadership. Give it to other of our people, and come and live the remainder of your lives with only the responsibility of our family. Uncle, and mother, this is our recommendation, but we will live according to your wishes. You can write us at the Ranger camp. Address is on the envelope. Your loving sons and nephews,

Jason and Jesse

When Star received the letter from her sons she was happy they were alive and well. She was also open to their suggestions. She was tired. She needed a break from her awesome responsibilities. She was tired of death and dying. Tired of being a woman warrior. She wanted to be just a woman, a wife, and a mother. She called Hawk in to ask him his opinion. It was the first time he was allowed to leave Lost Valley.

"My brother, I need your advise, she told him." Star handed him the letter. After giving Hawk time to read the letter, and time to think about its contents, she asked "What do we do?"

"We go to Texas," he said flatly. "I trust my nephews, and I believe what they have written. It is time we think about the Greyeagle family. You can assign qualified people to take our places. The mountain Cherokee will always exist, maybe not like in the past, but they will continue to be a people. In Texas, we can raise horses and live like a family is supposed to live without the weight of so many people on our shoulders. You asked my advise - you have it, sister"

"So be it," said Star. Like her mother, never one to be indecisive. "Inform our family to start preparing for the move when we hear again from my sons. In the meantime, sell all of our horses, brother. We will buy more when we get to Texas. We will need four of those large covered wagons, like the white men use, and we'll need to keep strong horses to pull them. It is a long way to Texas."

After making the decision to relinquish her leadership, although it would be a few months before the Greyeagle family actually left Strong Heart, Star felt relieved for the first time in ages - like a heavy weight had been removed from her shoulders.

Back at the Ranger camp, Captain Simpson had asked for volunteers for a supply trip to Austin, about twenty-five miles away. The Twins volunteered. After hitching a pair of mules to the supply wagon, they set off, their horses tied behind the wagon. In Austin, they dropped off the Captain's supply list at a mercantile store to be filled and stored in the wagon. The Twins were impressed at the size of the seat of Texas state government. The city was settled in the 1830's on the banks of the Colorado River. Originally, it was called Waterloo, but renamed after Stephen F. Austin, known as the father of Texas. It was not a one-horse town like Alba. It had several streets and many shops. The boys looked around and found a gun shop on Sixth Street.

They explained their wants to the owner, a man accustomed to serving Rangers. The Twins decided to order special made holsters for their Colts and a waist cartridge belt to carry their holstered guns. Pistol holsters of the day were made to protect a gun, almost enclosing it, but wasn't worth a damn for a fast draw. They sketched out a crude picture for the owner, showing a holster that allowed the gun hammer and trigger guard to be exposed to enable a fast draw. They wanted it wet, form-fitted, so the Colt would not jiggle in the holster, and a rawhide loop that could be pulled over the hammer spur - a safety feature that would keep the gun secure while riding at gallop.

They told the man they wanted backup weapons, one, a smaller Colt sheriff's model to be worn in a holster in front and to the left on the cartridge belt, angled in such a way as to permit a right hand fast draw while seated. They each bought a .45 caliber derringer, with over and under barrels, to wear in their boots. They wanted the shop man to sew a small holster on the inside of their boots to hold the derringer. The owner could have the holsters ready in a week, but could sew the boots that day, he said. The Twins paid the man, then walked back to the mercantile store. While waiting for the Captain's order, they bought an extra pair of Levi Strauss denims, an extra shirt, a leather vest like what Ruff and Abe wore, and black, flat brimmed western style hats. The Rangers had warned them about not wearing a hat in the hot Texas sun. Without a hat, the sun sapped a man's strength, they had said.

The mercantile store clerk told them to come back later that evening, it would take a while to fill the Captain's order, so they found a silversmith the Rangers had told them about, and bought Ranger badges made from a silver Mexican coin with a star at its center. Austin being Ranger headquarters, the silversmith kept several on hand. Once outside they stuffed their trousers inside their boots, made sure the derringers were secure, pinned their stars on their vests, and put on their new hats. The Twins were beginning to feel like Rangers. Within a week the boys would be wearing their special holsters.

With nothing to do until evening, they walked around town, just looking at different shops and noticed the townspeople gave way to them as they walked. Several kids starred at the new Rangers, and a deputy sheriff touched the brim of his hat as he passed. They found an eatery called Scholz Garten. On a sign it read: established 1866. The Cherokee Rangers went in and ordered a breakfast of venison steak, eggs, potatoes, biscuits, and coffee.

"Never seen an Indian Ranger before," said the pretty waitress as she served them. She was blond headed and talked with a German accent. She was also attractive and had a shapely figure.

"We're Cherokee," Jesse told her smiling. "Actually, we 're not Indian. Indians come from a country called India. Never have figured out why folks call Native Americans, Indians."

"We're the first Cherokee Rangers," Jesse told the pretty lady. "He's called Jason and people call me Jesse."

"I am Hanna," she said. Jesse could tell that Hanna had an eye for Jason. "I work every day except Sunday. Hope you boys will stop in whenever you're in town."

"We will," said Jason, "you can count on it." The lady smiled and walked back behind the counter to serve a couple of minor politicians.

"Ah ha," chided Jesse, on their way back to camp. "Old Jason has an admirer."

"She is a pretty thing," Jason smiled at his brother, "has hair the color of Aunt Greta's."

It was dark when the Twins drove into the Ranger compound; Captain Simpson was waiting for them. A year ago, two men, Cobb Aikins and Clem Taylor, shot a young Ranger to death in the streets of Sulfur Springs - the reason: they didn't like Rangers. A massive manhunt had been organized by the Rangers, but Aikins and Taylor were never found. Now, the Sheriff of Dallas had seen the two men wander in and out of the Hob Knob Saloon for the past week. The Dallas Sheriff was an old man with only a few months left until retirement, and said he wasn't capable of taking the two hard-case killers, and requested Ranger help since the man they had killed was a Ranger. All of the Captain's men were out on various arrest warrants. The only men in camp were the cook, his helper, and an injured

Ranger recuperating from a gunshot would to his leg.

"Boys, I don't normally send new men out on such a dangerous job," the Captain told the Twins as they still sat on the buckboard," but you're all I have available right now. If I don't get Rangers over to Dallas right away, they might run off like they did last time. They've already killed one Ranger. No telling when they'll decide to kill another one."

"Here's what I want you to do, it'll take a awhile to get to Dallas, so trail an extra mount. By switching back and forth, you can cut that time down a few hours. Sheriff says that saloon stays open all night and the killers usually wobble out about mid-morning. He'll go with you into the saloon and identify the pair. From there it's up to you. If it were me, I'd go in guns in hand. Tell 'em once they're under arrest, and if they even look like they might put up a fight, I' d shoot 'em dead."

"Watch out for the bartender. He's a distant relative and we don't know how He'll react. If he does react, shoot him, too. Aikins and Taylor are stone killers. We 're not about to give them a break of any kind. You boys understand?"

"Yes, sir," they responded. "Any chance there's a sawed off shotgun around?"

"I see you boys have got your heads screwed on right. Go get your mounts. I'll have a shotgun waiting for you as you ride by."

Noon had not come to Dallas the following day when the two Rangers rode in. The town was quiet except for a mongrel dog who barked at the Rangers. The settlement's streets were dirt and dusty. They found the Sheriff's office, a small brick building, not far down the street from the Hob Knob Saloon. There was a lamp shining through an opaque window that badly needed cleaning. The old Sheriff was brewing coffee on a pot bellied stove. The Twins tied their horses at the hitching rail, and knocked on the door. The first thing the Sheriff saw when he opened the door was two Ranger badges on what looked like two Indians. He blinked, backed up and let the men in.

"Damn!" he exclaimed, "when did Indians start wearing Ranger badges?"

"We 're Cherokee," said Jason dryly. "You ready to go?"

"How about some coffee first?"

"We'll drink coffee later," Jesse said smiling. "First we've got two pale faces to scalp."

"You mean that?" stammered the Sheriff.

"Sure," smiled Jason. "Why do you think they sent Indians? We 're gonna hang their scalps over the Captain's tent door."

"Now I know you're joshing." The old Sheriff gave a belly laugh.

"When we get to the saloon," explained Jesse, "you go in alone, locate where they're sitting, come back out as if nothing's happening and tell us. Then go on back to your office. don't want you getting hurt this close to retirement."

"Don't have to tell me twice," the red-faced Sheriff said.

When the Sheriff came out of the saloon and told the boys where the killers were sitting and drinking, they were the saloon's only customers at that time of the morning, he then ambled on back to his waiting coffee. Jason broke the stage gun down to make sure two double-ought buck shells were in the breach. When the Twins walked in, the bartender was wiping down the small wooden bar. Jesse was in front of him before the man pulled back his bar towel. Taking no chances with the man, Jesse hit the bartender upside his head with his gun barrel knocking the man flat on the floor and unconscious. By this time Jason was standing five feet from the killers' table.

"You're under arrest!" barked Jason.

Aikins went fumbling for his pistol, but before he could fire, Jason unloaded one barrel of double-ought buckshot in his face, knocking the man backward with only half a face left. Taylor stood up to draw his .44 caliber pistol, but Jesse was already at the table. He shot the killer between the eyes. Taylor died with his pistol falling from his hand. The Sheriff heard the shooting, ran to the saloon door and peeked through the bat-wings. When he saw the two killers dead on the floor and the bartender unconscious behind the bar, he let out a whiz.

"Damn! You boys don't need to scalp a man, you just shoot their hair off!"

The Ranger Twins dragged the dead men out of the saloon by their feet, leaving a trail of blood on the saloon floor. The Sheriff pointed out the outlaws' horses - the only two tied outside the saloon. The Twins hefted the killers across their saddles and tied them down for the trip back to Ranger camp, then swung up into their saddles.

"Almost forgot, Sheriff. Here's their arrest warrants," said Jesse.

"Damn! It don't pay to mess with you Cherokee Rangers!"

The Sheriff just shook his head as the Twins rode out of town. Noon was just now shining over Dallas, Texas, and the dog was still yapping. When the boys got back to camp, they rode up to Captain Simpson.

"Two dead Ranger killers, Captain," said Jason.

"Good work, men. Get yourselves some breakfast." Those boys are going to make fine Rangers, the Captain thought.

The incident in Dallas traveled fast throughout the outlaw community and towns around the area, giving the Twins a reputation as Rangers you don't want on your tail. When Abe and Ruff heard the news, they whooped and hollered because they were the ones who brought the Cherokee Rangers into the fold.

Two months passed since the Dallas shootout, and the Cherokee Rangers had successfully served eighteen warrants bringing all the culprits in alive. The Twins were well like by other Rangers, and the Captain was pleased with his two new men.

Three months after the Twins had written their mother, they received a letter from Star with a bank draft on her account in Asheville, North Carolina. The letter said the money was to purchase an already existing ranch, if possible, with a large ranch house, barns, corrals, and acres of good grazing land with accessible water. Star told her boys that as soon as she received word of the purchase, the Greyeagle family would leave for east Texas. The Twins were in high spirits when they deposited the draft in a bank in Austin, recommended by Captain Simpson. The Twins told the banker to search for real estate according to the letter's instruction and to let them know immediately when several properties were found. The property did not necessarily have to be in the area, but they wanted several options from which to choose. The banker was amazed that two Texas Rangers had access to that much money, and Indians at that. What the banker did not know was that the Greyeagle family had, over the years, become financially comfortable and were very astute when it came to business matters.

In time, the banker did find several ranches for sell, but the property Jason and Jesse chose, was located in Travis County on the Colorado River, about forty miles from Austin - close enough for the Twins to travel for visits. It was a large rancho owned by a wealthy Mexican cattleman who had fought with Texas against Mexico. The expansive two story ranch house was made of adobe and had an adobe wall around the house, all painted white. The ranch house had a red tiled roof, a walkway of stone, a garden area, shade trees, and several cactus plants. There were three large barns made of logs, four corrals, a bunkhouse, two windmills with water tanks, and enough acreage to accommodate many horses. There was grass aplenty.

There were many rooms inside the ranch house with a tiled stairway leading up to the second floor. There was a large kitchen with indoor water provided by a hand-levered pump, and the large family room had a giant, tiled fireplace. The place was furnished with heavy mahogany Mexican-style furniture. The bedrooms had beds with hand carved relief projecting detailed ornaments and figures. The Twins told the Mexican rancher that they would buy the property if the furniture went with the sell along with all the hay stored in the barns. After a price haggle, the Mexican agreed.

The final sale agreement was handled by the boys' banker and an attorney, also recommended by Captain Simpson. Funds were transferred and the rancho became Greyeagle property. While in Austin the boys had a woodcarver to carve a large, heavy wooden sign to hang over the rancho entrance that read: Rancho Greyeagle. That same day, the Twins wrote Star of the purchase with directions on the shortest route to east Texas and the Rancho Greyeagle.

As the Greyeagle family began their long trip to east Texas, the Cherokee Rangers were given a mission that required four men. A band of Comanchero - outlawed Comanche, Mexicans, and a few violent whites - had attacked the small village of Quitman and massacred several of its in habitants. Jason and Jesse had been promoted to corporal of Rangers, and Captain Simpson gave them the choice of picking the men to accompany them. The Twins chose Ruff and Abe. Their mission was to find the twenty man band of raiders and eliminate them - no arrest warrants, no prisoners.

The Rangers, from the beginning, had always been under-manned. Once, in a county where a general riot had ensued, the Rangers sent only one man. When the Ranger arrived, the city fathers asked "Where were the other Rangers?" The man replied "Only one riot, only one Ranger." That Ranger asked who was the leader of the riot? When told who the man was, the Ranger walked up and shot the man dead. No more riot. Violent times requires violent men with authority. You cannot send a school teacher to face violent people who are out of line. It takes men who are willing to lower themselves to the depths of depravity to end the problem, once and for all. The souls of those warriors is between God and themselves, not to be judged by the general populace.

The Greyeagle family, Star, Hawk and his family of four, Greta, Isaac, Jacob, and Jeremiah, Star's husband, Eagle Feather, Brave Bull and his family, Laughs-a lot and

Nightbird, had bought four schooner type covered wagons, each wagon pulled by six stout horses. Laughs-a-Lot had been adamant - extra mounts would be trailed behind the wagons. In addition, the men rode alongside of the wagons as added security. Following the Twins advise, star had provisioned her group with white man clothes. They were glad to be leaving North Carolina with all of its sickness and problems.

The four Rangers rode into Quitman for information about the Comanchero raid, and, hopefully, to add a few men to their group. The Sheriff of Quitman told the Rangers the Comanchero had headed north toward the Red River after the raid. He mustered fifteen locals who would join the manhunt - several had lost family members to the Comanchero. The Twins were familiar with parts of north Texas, having crossed the Red River from Oklahoma when they came to Texas. The Comanchero' trail was not hard to find or follow - twenty men riding horses and herding other, stolen horses, plus driving three wagons loaded with loot, left a wide trail.

"They won't cross the Red River;" Ruff told Jason. "They normally operate in northwest Texas. Up a-ways, they'll veer west toward the Llano Estacado where they can hideout for awhile and trade with the Comanche."

The Llano Estacado, commonly known as the Staked Plains, is the southern extension of the high plains of North America. It lies south of the Canadian River in northwest Texas and northeast New Mexico. It is a high mesa sloping toward the southeast, and is one of the largest tablelands on the continent. The Llano Estacado covers all or part of thirty-three Texas and four New Mexico counties with approximately 32,000 square miles. It is a semi-arid region with average annual rainfall of eighteen to twenty inches. The soils are dark to reddish brown sands.

There is water there if a man knows where to look for it, and is a perfect place to conceal horses and people. Outlaws and Indians alike have used the place to escape the eyes of Texas authorities and the army for years. Sure enough, the Comanchero turned west, and the wagon tracks became easier to follow. The tracks were so clearly visible, the Rangers could follow at a trot. The Comanchero were either stupid or they did not care who followed, thought the Twins. Either that, or they were leading their pursuers into a trap. They were in the dry prairie now, mile upon mile of open grassland that led eventually to the escarpment of the Llano Estacado.

They were also in Comanche country. Few white men traveled this far into Comanche territory, which was probably why the Comanchero felt safe and bothered not about their tracks. The Comanchero conducted business with the Comanche, trading them stolen goods for buffalo hides which they resold. The sun bore down unmercifully - making the brown grass hills in the distance shimmer and wavelike - like a mirage. Water was scarce unless a man knew where to look.

Jesse and Jason were thankful for the flat-brim hats they had bought and the extra canteen they had thought to bring along. They passed the word along to conserve water, and for the men to place a small pebble in their mouths. This would help to create saliva. It did not take the place of water, but it helped. Most of the men had buttoned the tops of their shirts to keep the sun from baking their breastbones. Suddenly, Jesse held up his hand for the men to stop. He looked at Jason, who nodded affirmatively. They smelled wood smoke.

Dismounting, the Twins handed their reins to Ruff and Abe and told them to keep the men here, while they scouted ahead. They walked to a brown grass covered rise, then crawled to the top. The wood smoke became stronger. There in a depression, hidden by the small mound, were the Comanchero. They were cooking and drinking whisky from jugs as they sat in what little shade the wagons offered. The horses were tethered beside a stream of clear water that came from somewhere beneath the earth. A man riding fifty yards away could have easily missed the stream altogether. There were twenty men. They were so unconcerned about being followed into Comanche country, they did not even post guards. The Twins backed away from the rise and made their way back to where the men had dismounted, trying to keep the horses from nickering, because they smelled water.

"They're over that rise," Jason told them. "Twenty men getting liquored up. By dusk, they'll be drunk. That's when we'll hit 'em. We'll ride in from two directions, blasting away until everyone of them are dead. No quarters, no mercy. That's the way the Captain wants it. They had no mercy on the citizens of Quitman, so we will show them what retribution feels like at the hands of Texas Rangers."

Jesse told them: "Move the horses back away and rest until just before dusk. Drink as much water from your canteens as you need. There's plenty of clean water just over that rise. You men will be divided up and led by us Rangers. Ruff and Abe's groups will attack from the west,

217

while mine and Jason's will come in from the east."

"Check your weapons," Jason told them. "Make sure they're loaded. Ride in fast and close and blast away. The Comanchero have one more man than we have, so it'll be pretty much an even fight, but we'll have the element of surprise. You boys rode a long way for this fight. When the time comes, let them feel the justice of your fury."

Just before dusk, the Rangers and the men from Quitman rode into the Comanchero camp from two directions. They rode in with rapid gunfire and vengeance and surprise. Some of the outlaws were drunk, a few were asleep, and the few that managed to draw their weapons were shot dead in their tracks before they could fire a shot. The fight lasted about forty-five seconds - every Comanchero lay dead on the ground. They were not buried. They were left as a sign to others about Ranger vengeance and audacity.

A hunter's moon shone brightly over the Prairie. Wanting to get out of Comanche country as quickly as possible, the men herded up the stolen horses, while several men climbed aboard the wagons and headed them out toward the town of Quitman. It was somewhat cooler riding at night, but not much. At Quitman, the four Rangers cut out the Comanchero horses and herded them toward the Ranger camp. It was mid-evening on the second day when the boys herded twenty horses into the Ranger camp. Every Ranger in camp watched as they were driven to the camp corral, and Captain Simpson came out of his tent because of the commotion.

"Twenty dead Comanchero," Jason told the Captain. "No prisoners. All stolen horses and three wagons loaded with stolen property taken back to the people of Quitman. The horses we brought in were Comanchero horses. Thought you might want them for extra Ranger mounts."

The Captain just shook his head and grinned from ear to ear. "Good job," he told the four men. "You boys deserve a couple of days off. Enjoy them, but don't wreck any saloons." The Captain was a man of few words.

Jason, Jesse, Ruff, and Abe rode into Austin for two days of rest and

recuperation - the Twins to pick up their custom-made gun holsters, and possibly a visit to Scholz Garten to eat and visit with Hanna, the waitress. Ruff and Abe invited the Twins to their favorite watering hole, a run down Mexican bar called Red's Scoot Inn. The Mexican patrons knew Abe and Ruff, but one man eyed the Twins with suspicion even though they wore Ranger badges. Ruff and Abe ordered Tequila and the Twins asked for coffee.

In many bars there is always some mean drunk who takes exception to anyone they view as different. One such mean drunk was a stout Mexican who did not like Rinches- a name Mexicans called the Rangers. The Mexican's name was Apache Gomez. He did not like the fact that two Indians were in the bar, even though he was of mixed blood, and started loud talking the Twins in the Mexican language. The Twins could not understand what the half-breed was saying, but Ruff and Abe could.

"Senior, If I wuz you, I wouldn't mess with these two Cherokees," said Ruff in Spanish. "They are muy malo hombres. We want no trouble, but you keep mouthing off , you'll get more than your share."

"Gomez," don' like Gringos either," the half-breed spat, standing and pulling a large Bowie knife. "I slice you first, and then I'll bleed them!"

Grinning, Ruff stood up, pulled his Bowie, and started toward the half-

breed. But before he could engage the Mexican, the bar owner came from behind the bar with a sawed-off shot gun.

"Gomez," the owner said, "this is the last time you will ever cause trouble in here. Now, git out, and don't ever come back!"

"I go," the half-breed barked, "but I see the Rinches later. He left through the back door.

Ruff explained to the Twins what the Mexican had said, and told them to be careful because the half-breed could be dangerous when drinking, and was known as a gunman. The Twins just grunted - it did not bother them. After awhile, Jesse and Jason left to get their new holsters and eat at Scholz Garten. Ruff and Abe stayed to drink Tequila. At the gun shop, they strapped on the holsters and liked the feel. They could now draw their six-guns fast and with ease. They thanked the owner for doing a good job, and walked down the boardwalk to eat with Hanna. Jason noticed the half-breed following them on the opposite side of the street, staying in the shadows. He looked at Jesse and Jesse nodded that he had seen the man, too.

Hanna smiled when the boys walked through the eatery's door, and brought them coffee. They had liked the venison steak they had eaten on their last visit and ordered the same, with hominy and green beans. While they were finishing the meal, a young Mexican teen came in and found the Twin's table.

"Seniors," the kid said, "this is not from me, but from the man across the street. He challenges you to a gun fight, said if you do not come out, he will come in here. The man paid me to give you the message."

Hanna heard what the boy had said, and pleaded with the Twins not to accept the challenge. She said the half-breed had already killed two men in gun duels in Austin.

"We are the law," answered Jason. "It is against the law to threaten to kill a Ranger. I have no choice but to go outside and arrest the man. If I let him go, others will think the Rangers weak."

"I'll go," said Jesse.

"No, brother. I will accept this gunman's challenge," replied Jason. "I'll try to arrest him, but if that doesn't work, I'll shoot him dead."

Jesse told Hanna that she was a witness to the man's deadly threat, that if it came to a court case, Jason would need her to testify. Hanna said she would. The sun was in the twelve o'clock position, and a breeze stirred the dusty street. There were several citizens milling around when Jason stepped out onto the boardwalk. Across the street stood Apache Gomez, his left hand almost touching the butt of his pistol. Jason's black eyes took in everything about the man. Gomez had his left hand close to his six-gun, but his right hand was behind his back. A second gun, thought Jason. Jesse stood just inside the eatery - he, Hanna, and several other customers watched through the café's window.

"You're under arrest," spoke Jason, loud enough for those on the street to hear, and have time to clear the street, "for a death threat against a peace officer."

Instead of drawing his holstered gun, Gomez swung his hideout pistol from behind his back, and leveled it at Jason.

221

Jason's gun came out so fast, the people watching could hardly see his draw. Both men fired. The half-breed's bullet struck the eatery's door face, not twelve inches from Jason's head. But Jason's bullet found its mark between the Mexican's eyes. He was knocked backward three feet by a .45 caliber bullet that tore his head apart. If a man is hit by a .45 bullet, that man is going down. Jason calmly reloaded his gun, then walked across the street and retrieved the half-breed's guns. Jesse and Hanna were on the boardwalk by now. When Jason walked back to where they were standing, Hanna threw her arms around him. She was shaking.

"You could have been killed!" she cried. Jason felt her body against his, and he felt odd.

"Goes with the job," he smiled down at her. They all went back into the café, and Hanna brought more coffee. She set it on the table, her hands trembling.

When the Sheriff finally arrived, he questioned the Twins, Hanna, other customers, and a few people on the street. He told Jason that Gomez had been a threat to decent people, and got what had been coming to him for several years. The witnesses told the Sheriff that the Ranger had tried to arrest Gomez, but that he had pulled a gun. The Ranger was just faster on the draw and more accurate. The Sheriff told Jason it was justifiable homicide, no action by his office was required. The Sheriff took the dead man's guns from Jason. He sent for a wagon to pick up the body, then went back to his office and filed a justifiable homicide report. That was the end of it.

By now Abe and Ruff had heard about the shooting and came running.

"I told that fool he shouldn't mess with you," grinned Ruff.

The Twins bought their Ranger friends dinner. Jason was not ready to go - he wanted more time with Hanna.

CHAPTER SEVEN

Rancho Greyeagle

Over the months that followed, whenever the Twins got a day off, or whenever Ranger business took them to Austin, they stopped by the Scholz Garten to eat, but the purpose was for Jason to visit with Hanna Franks. Hanna's German-Jewish family owned a small, well-kept farm not far from the Austin city limits. Herman and Ruth Franks had a herd of dairy cows, a thriving milk and cheese business supplying most of Austin with good milk and superb round blocks of yellow cheese. Whenever people in the area bought cheese, they asked for Franks Cheese.

Hanna had three older brothers who did most of the dairy work and delivered their products, while Mr. Franks made beautiful old world clocks in his home workshop. Hanna's sister, Ester, helped her mother keep house and feed the family. Hanna was nineteen and only one year older than her sister, Ester. One day when Jason and Jesse were eating at the café, Hanna introduced Jesse to Ester who was visiting her sister at the cafe. The two were immediately taken with each other. From that day forward, the Twins and the Franks sisters were together whenever time allowed. Romance for the Cherokee Rangers was in bloom.

This Sunday evening, they were having a picnic under a giant oak tree on the banks of the Colorado River. The Cherokee twins were struck by the sisters' beauty and femininity. By the same token, the Twins' shoulder length black hair and black eyes intrigued the girls.

"Aren't you concerned about your dangerous jobs?" Ester asked Jesse. "Hanna told me about the gun fight Jason had, and about some of the killers you two have either captured or killed in gun fights."

"Not too concerned," Jesse told her. "It's just a job, but I feel we are as qualified as any Ranger to do the job. Someone has to do it."

"Will you always be a Ranger," she asked.

"I haven't thought that far ahead. My family owns a large ranch not far from here. They are, now, on their way to Texas from North Carolina to settle it and raise horses. Who knows, maybe one day my brother and I will raise horses."

"Your family has never seen the ranch?" Ester asked.

"No. Jason and I selected the property. My mother sent the money to buy it. It's a long story. When our folks get here, my brother and I would like for you and Hanna to visit and meet our people."

"I'd like that," Ester told Jesse. " Maybe you'd like to meet my family?"

"I would. Do they know you and Hanna are seeing Cherokees?"

"Yes, we told them, and they are anxious to meet such famous Rangers. They think you are guardians of Texas," Ester said.

"Guardians? Some folks call us gunslingers," laughed Jesse.

"My father says it takes strong men to bring law to a wild place like Texas, men with grit. Hanna and I feel the same way."

"Someday Texas will be a safe place to raise families," Jesse told her. "But right now, the Rangers are a necessary evil. I guess that's why Jason and I believe in what we do. Without the Rangers, families out in the frontier areas would be open game for outlaws and Comanche. Even towns the size of Austin have problems now and then. That gunfight Hanna told you about is a case in point."

While Ester and Jesse talked on the blanket under the Oak, Hanna and Jason had walked down near the water. Ester's back was to them, but Jesse watched over her shoulder as the two kissed, and he wanted to kiss Ester, but he felt it was not time. Soon, he thought. One day I will marry this beautiful girl. He kissed her on the cheek; she softly touched his hand. As the girls drove their buggy home, the Twins rode along beside until the Franks farm could be seen, then they headed back to Ranger camp. Both were absorbed in thought as they rode along. When the boys got back to camp there was a message for them.

"Your uncle Hawk came by to tell you your family has arrived safely at the ranch," Captain Simpson told them. "I know you men have been waiting for this, so I'm giving you a few days off to visit. Your uncle is an interesting man. We had a good, long talk about your scouting service to the Confederacy, and about the sickness that took so many of your people. I am sorry for your loss."

"Thank you, Captain," said Jason. "uncle Hawk helped

226

train us as trackers. He, himself, is a great tracker. He and our mother were chiefs of the mountain Cherokee. Now, it is their time to retire and build a new life."

"If there are any more like you two, I could sure use them," stated the Captain.

"Uncle Hawk has three sons that will one day be of age. When they are, I could bring them to you, if you would like, sir?"

"Do that," said Captain Simpson. "Now, you men ride along and visit your family. Come back as soon as you can. I have a stack of arrest warrants that need serving and few men to serve them"

Star's family, and the men she had brought with her from the Cherokee Mountains, had settled in at Rancho Greyeagle. Star and her husband, Eagle Feather, had taken the master bedroom on the ground floor, which also included a separate sitting room and an office joining the sitting room, with a door that led into the spacious living room. Upstairs, on the left, Hawk and his family, Greta, Isaac, Jacob and Jeremiah, had a suite of rooms. Brave Bull and his family, Fawn, his wife, his two children, Little Fawn, twelve, and Stonecalf, ten, had the suite of rooms on the right of the staircase. They all shared the common living room and the dinning room downstairs. Willow, the cook, had a room off the kitchen with two smaller rooms for her helpers. Laughs-a-Lot and Nightbird lived in the bunkhouse, but took their meals either with the family at the big house, or at the bunkhouse kitchen.

They were all pleased with the ranch the Twins had selected. Star had bought Levi Straus denims, western boots, shirts, and western hats for the males of Rancho

Greyeagle, and several dresses for the ladies. Hawk had bought lever-action rifles and Colt .45's for the men, and two buggies for the ranch. They already had the sixteen stout, wagon-broke, horses that had pulled the schooner wagons from the Cherokee Mountains, and, also, the riding horses they had brought with them - a total of eight. Star had visited the bank the Twins had bought the ranch through, and transferred all her funds from North Carolina - a sizable amount, the banker had told her.

While in Austin, she advertised with newspapers throughout Texas for Arabian breeding horses - only the very best will do - the article had read. She told the banker to locate a small herd of Hereford beef cattle, not for resale, but for her family's use. She visited two local hardware stores and bought every kind of ranch and farm equipment she would use, and quickly became a favored customer of Austin businesses. She bought chickens - laying hens and roosters, saddles, bridles, ropes for lassoing ranch animals. She had a blacksmith to make several branding irons with the Greyeagle brand, the bar -G. With Laughs-a-Lot, she bought the medicines and salves needed on a working horse ranch. She opened up accounts at the stores she had visited so her top men could sign for whatever the ranch needed.

Star passed the word along that Rancho Greyeagle was hiring cowboys and vaqueros - only honest, loyal, hardworking, top hands need apply. These cowhands would have to pass Laughs-a-Lot's muster, because he would be

their boss. She told Brave Bull and Nightbird to hire five men each for day and night security, with Brave Bull taking the day shift and Nightbird the night shift. She bought cords of firewood for ranch use, and had a fence built completely around the large ranch. She bought dishes, pots and pans, silverware and linen, sheets, towels, and quilts. When Austin shop owners saw any of Rancho Greyeagle personnel enter their stores, they jumped over themselves to wait on them. The Greyeagle name became a name much admired and respected.

At the ranch, Star gave the ladies responsibilities. Star would keep the ranch books while Hawk supervised the working ranch. Eagle Feather became Hawk's assistant. Greta would teach English, history and arithmetic to the children three days each week; Willow, with the help of two Mexican women, would cook and feed her household, while two Mexican male cooks would feed the ranch hands at the bunkhouse; Fawn, Brave Bull's wife, would help out in Star's office when needed. The ranch soon became organized and functioning - Rancho Greyeagle became known throughout the area. Neighboring ranchers came by with their wives to pay their respects to the new neighbors. They were treated royally, and when they left, they nodded their heads approvingly, the wives stating what a great hostess Star Greyeagle was. She was the chatelaine of the vast Greyeagle enterprise. They envied, but respected her.

The youngsters were playing in the yard and were the first to notice Jesse and Jason riding down the long entrance onto the ranch. They ran into the house, all talking at the same time about how grand their uncles looked in their tall boots, Stetson hats, six-guns and stars. The expansive house became a flurry of action. Star rush outside and waited eagerly to embrace her sons. Willow, the cook, who had fed

229

the boys many times at Strong Heart, stood smiling beside the large, mahogany double doors with her hands clasp together in front of her apron. Eagle Feather, the boys father, stood beside Star beaming with pride. The whole family watched as the Twins tied their horses to a hitching rail and walked up to hugs and pats on the back. The Twins felt like celebrities, smiling from ear to ear.

"We will have a great feast for all our family and friends in honor of my wandering sons!" Star exclaimed

And a feast is was. Willow and her helpers out did themselves with beef, venison, fried chicken, mashed potatoes, green beans, green peas, sweet potatoes, hominy, brown gravy, and biscuits as big as cat heads. The great mahogany table was stretched with food, including pecan and pumpkin pie.

Star sat at one end of the long table, and Eagle Feather at the other end, with all others sitting wherever they wished to sit. The Twins sat on either side of their mother. Greta said grace and thanked the Creator that the family was once again together, happy, and in good spirits.

Hawk and Laughs-a-Lot brought the Twins up on the family's trip from the mountains, and the plans they had for breeding and raising the finest horses in the State of Texas. The family, Hawk told them, had only one breakdown, and that was a wheel that Brave Bull and Nightbird had expertly repaired. They ran into no hostiles, no hassles with the Union Army other than searching the wagons for contraband, and crossing the Red River. It took a while, Hawk said, to find a shallow crossing, and they had to cut logs to attach to the heavy wagons so they would float across the muddy water. They lost no livestock and no one was injured during the trip.

Jason and Jesse talked about their experiences since coming to Texas, and told them all about the Texas Rangers, Texas itself, and the Texas people. Jesse told the family that most Texans were hard working and honorable people, but that there were outlaws and Comanche that were violent and was a real threat to the people at large, causing the Rangers untold hours of tracking them down and bringing them to justice. They told Brave Bull and Nightbird to be watchful of any strange tracks on ranch property, especially where the ranch ended at the Colorado River. They explained that the Comanche were expert horse thieves, and occasionally made raids, even this far south from their homeland in northwest Texas. Jason smiled when he told the family about Hanna and Ester.

"Mother," he said, "they have the most beautiful hair - the same color as aunt Greta's."

"They want to meet the family," explained Jesse. "With your permission, we would like to bring them here to meet everyone. Their family has a dairy farm and makes cheese, and their father makes the most beautiful grandfather clocks."

"I must meet these sisters that have captured my sons' hearts," said Star. "Bring them soon. They and their family will be welcomed here at Rancho Greyeagle."

"What is their lineage?" asked Greta.

"They are German Jews," replied Jason.

"Ah, that is good," she said. "The Messiah was born of the Jewish people. I must meet and talk with these girls." The youngsters giggled among themselves because their uncles had sweethearts.

The Twins stayed three days at the ranch and felt guilty because of the stack of arrest warrants on Captain Simpson's desk. They bid their farewell to family and friends, swung up into their saddles straight and tall, and rode out of Rancho Greyeagle toward the Ranger camp as the mid-day sun blazed orange in the sky. As they rode out through the ranch entrance, they turned in their saddles and waved - the faces of those waving back would remain with them for days on end. They were content with the fact that their family was safe from the turmoil in the Cherokee Mountains, and now settled safely in Texas.

Strong Heart, Lost Valley, and Tall Woman Village were no more. All the Cherokee had been herded into what was previously called Strong Heart and renamed the Cherokee Reservation of the Eastern Band of the Cherokee Nation. A new and strict Indian Agent had been sent from Washington, with new rules that made those who remained alive after the dreaded yellow and typhoid fevers had taken its toll, feel less than human. Union soldiers were ever present. They patrolled the reservation and the areas around it. The proud Cherokee felt like they were living in a glass house, running against an invisible wall they could not understand. They had a chief, but he was hemmed in on all sides and had little authority.

A civilian town grew up adjacent to the reservation called Cherokee, North Carolina. Many of the once proud Cherokee warriors were reduced to making and selling trinkets, wood carvings, peace pipes, tom-toms, to gift shops in the town in order to survive. Few walked with their heads up, all the town people saw were stone faces. After all, they were only Indians. The lands that had been handed down through the centuries to a people that had built one of the greatest nations ever known in North America, had been taken away and given to the white man, a relative new comer.

Dogs were treated with more respect. Once a vibrant and healthy people, they had become withdrawn, downcast, and reclusive, with no hope for tomorrow. This caused problems between husband and wife, between Families, discord was everywhere. Alcohol became a problem. It was not unusual to see a once clear-eyed Cherokee face down drunk in a ditch, self respect gone. Hope gone. Life not worth living. Who cared? No one. No one cared or tried to understand what it is like to lose that spark of life necessary for the spirit to hold a person up. No one cared. Not even the Cherokee, not anymore.

When a child bruises a knee and sheds a tear, a mother can take away the

hurt of that bruise, and the tears, with love and a few simple kisses. But when a mother loses the instinct to care, the child cries and cries and with no one to care, the hurt and pain moves inward and develops into hate. The child becomes anti-social. It seemed that mother earth no longer cared for the Cherokee; she no longer saw the silent tears of her children; she no longer gave them solace, and the sky no longer gave them sunshine, just rain, cold, impersonal, rain.

Eagle Feather was awaken from his sleep. Star was

having a nightmare. She was sobbing - twisting and turning - grabbing her pillow with both hands, burrowing her knees into his side. The ranch operation was in full Swing; the ranch was now stocked with Arabian breeding horses, cowboys and vaqueros branded horses and cattle, and the ranch was alive with productive activity. Yet, she sobbed in her sleep. It was almost dawn. He took her from the bed and carried her into the sitting room and sat down in a large, comfortable chair and held her close to his body with her face nestled against his strong chest. He slowly and tenderly rocked her back and forth in his muscled arms, feeling her tears roll down his breast.

He held her tightly and close. He was not a part of her dream, but wished he could be inside her mind so he could protect her from whatever spirits that had caused her mental pain. There are times when a man just needs to hold his woman, with no words, until she cries out the reasons for her tears. He just needs to wait, to hold her and wait until she is ready to speak. And when she speaks, he still needs to be quiet and listen until she has talked herself out. So he held her and waited, patiently. Finally she spoke in sobs.

"I have let our people down, husband," she told him. He said nothing. "I ran away and came to Texas to save my own family. I should have stayed. I knew what was going to happen. Maybe I could have done something to forestall the inevitable. But I ran away with my family. I am not deserving to have walked in Tall Woman's moccasins. I feel terrible." Eagle Feather remained quiet.

"Our people are suffering, and look at me! Look at this magnificent house, this great ranch. I should be back in the

234

mountains suffering with our people. I was selfish. I was thinking of my immediate family, of our sons, and I ran away afraid that our family would die with the sickness - afraid that my family's liberty would be taken from them. Right now, I feel so unworthy of ever having been the Chief of the mountain Cherokee." She sobbed great sobs of grief. He held her close, but remained silent.

"Like you, I was trained as a warrior, not a person that runs away from sickness and danger, not a person that leaves her people. I have lost Tall Woman. I have lost my dear brother, Daniel. I have lost Tall Tree, Yona, and so many more. I had a dream and I saw their faces. Their faces were gaunt and out of shape. They looked as pale as death. They were staring at me. I saw the Cherokee with no hope - mothers and babies crying - men not knowing what to do. I woke up screaming, gasping for air. I did not want to wake you, but I did with my sobs. Please forgive me, dear husband."

"There is nothing to forgive," Eagle Feather told her. "And you have nothing for which to feel ashamed. Since you were young you devoted every waking hour, and your nights, to our people. When Tall Woman died and you became Chief, you devoted your whole life to our people. You gave everything you had until there was nothing more to give. You did not run away, you escaped an out-of-control situation that no human being could have stopped in order to, somehow, keep the Cherokee spirit alive in a different place.

"Your mother, and later you, understood that the only path for the Cherokee people was to assimilate into the white culture. It was the only way for us to survive. We may assimilate, but we will never forget our heritage, our traditions, or our language. Like your mother, you looked far into the future. When you brought us here to this flat land of many cultures, you were doing what a Chief is born to do - to keep the spirit of her people alive. That is what we are doing. What good would it have served if we had all died in the mountains? What good purpose would we have served if every Cherokee was confined to a reservation with no freedom to grow?

"I should have told you this before now, but in addition to loving you, I have respected you for being the greatest leader I have every known, and that includes Tall Woman, whom I respect to this day. Do not feel discouraged because life has thrown stones in your path. Right now, you are kicking the stones from your path and leading us into a new way of life. Your tears may be justified because of your deep feelings for our people, but it does not change the fact that you, like your brother, Daniel, are a leader with great vision. The Great Spirit has given few people the gift to see into the future, and the courage to act upon that vision. You have the gift and the strength to make it happen.

"You are hurting now because of the stones, but your vision and courage and strength will lead this small band of Cherokee you have brought from the mountains, to grow into a great force within the white culture. Do not look back in anger or sorrow. Look to tomorrow, and beyond that."

"I will try, husband. Right now, I need you to hold me, to love me. I need to feel your body against mine. I need to feel your own inner strength - I need to draw from your quiet strength, your masculinity - carry me to our bedroom."

236

Around noon, Star sent for Willow, the cook. They walked out of the ranch house to where Laughs-a-Lot was training horses in one of the corrals. Star knew that Willow loved to watch Laughs-a-Lot tame the Arabians. Willow was getting up in years, now. She had fed the Greyeagle family since Tall Woman had moved to Strong Heart.

"Mother, Willow," said Star, "I don't want you to work hard in the kitchen any longer. You have two assistants. The Kitchen is your responsibility, but I want you to only supervise. Let the other women do the work. You are their boss. Tell them what to do, but let them do the labor. I want you to take it easy."

"You are not taking my job away?" Willow asked.

"Never! You have been a loyal cook and member of our family. I am rewarding you for your years of service. From now on, you will take your meals at the family table. You will be served by your assistants like the rest of our family. I am giving you a substantial raise, and making one of the buggies available to you anytime you choose to go into Austin. One of the ranch hands will drive you whenever you choose."

Willow reached her arms around Star and hugged her. "I am the most fortunate woman in the world. I have always known that I was loved, but you have made me a part of the Greyeagle family. From now on, I will be known as Willow Greyeagle."

Star called one of the ranch hands over. His name was Rusty. He was twenty-one years old, a very capable cowboy with a great attitude. Eagle Feather had recommended him as a driver for Willow whenever she went into town.

"Rusty, please hitch a horse up to a buggy and drive Willow Greyeagle into Austin. Take her to the Ladies' Dress Shoppe. I want her to have a nice new wardrobe. She will sign for whatever she wants. When she is finished shopping, I want you to escort her to one of Austin's better eating places. Both of you are to eat a leisurely meal. She is precious to me, so make sure she is treated with respect. Here is some money. A man should pay for a lady's meal."

"Yes, Ma'am," Rusty replied, taking the money. "Rest assured, Miss Willow will be treated with respect." Then he said, "Miss Willow, I will have the buggy in front of the ranch house shortly."

Star and Eagle Feather watched as Rusty drove the buggy out through the ranch entrance with Miss Willow Greyeagle sitting in the back seat dressed in her finest dress. She turned and waved back at them, smiling. She felt like royalty.

Charlie McCall, "Rusty", was a natural people person. He got his nickname from his rust colored hair. His smile was contagious. He had no family, and since the age of fifteen, he had raised himself. His family had been killed by Comanche and he was taken captive. When he had turned fifteen, he escaped form the Comanche. He had worked as a cowboy from that age and was an expert horseman. He was also good with a gun. He was honest, loyal, and hard working, and since Laughs-a-Lot had hired him, he had accomplished every assigned job to Laughs-a-Lot's satisfaction. Rusty and Laughs-a-Lot had become friends. He had now finished his training and was ready to teach other ranch hands Laughs-a-Lot's method of taming and training horses.

Most ranches employed bronc busters - taming a horse by riding the mount until the horse either crippled the rider, or gave up and lost its spirit. At one time Rusty had been a bronc buster, but this was not Laughs-a-Lot's way. Laughs-a-Lot had singled out five ranch hands with a good attitude and a temperament he felt would make good horse whisperers. He assigned the five men to Rusty. They were in the small corral when Rusty climbed over the corral fence. Star, Eagle Feather, Hawk, Willow, and Laughs-a-Lot stood leaning on the corral fence to watch Rusty's first group of trainees.

"Boys," he said smiling, "what you are about to learn goes against everything you have been taught about breaking horses. Here at Rancho Greyeagle, we don't break horses - we tame them. Once tamed, we train them. First, I will explain how we do it, then I will show you, then each of you will be assigned an Arabian to tame and train. Take your time on your first horse. As you gain confidence in our method, your progress will increase.

"Get the horse used to having you near it - doing things that feel good to the horse so it relates you with pleasure, like hand feeding, grooming, and rubbing the horse all over. Then begin haltering the Arabian as soon as possible and train it to follow you on a lead rope. If the horse resists leading, loop a large cotton rope over the hind quarters and pull gently on it as you go forward with the lead rope in your other hand. Tie the horse up after it is leading well and train it to stand tied. Use the large post buried deep at the center of the corral for this. Use a rope halter with a strong, lead rope. Tie a quick release knot in case of an emergency and make sure there is nothing close to the horse that it can hurt itself on if it jumps around. Handle the legs and feet after it has become accustomed to standing tied. Pick up each foot and hold it for a few seconds. Rub and praise the horse as you do this.

"Saddle and bridle the horse and let it wear them while you lead it, or just tie the reins up and turn the horse loose for a while in the corral, as you closely watch. Put long reins on the horse and run them back through the stirrups, then get behind the horse and drive it from the ground. Do this in the small corral the first time and take it very slow. This teaches the horse what you want when you pull on the reins. Mount the Arabian for the first time in the small corral. Go up slowly, even letting yourself back down a few times from a half-mount, until the horse is no longer concerned. If you have done the ground work correctly, the horse will already know what you want it to do when you turn it or pull back on the reins. Ride the horse an hour at least four days a week at first. Keep graduating to the larger corrals until you are riding free and the Arabian accepts you as just a part of its day. You can now teach the horse other things as the occasion demands.

"These horses are not mustangs, they are Arabians" Rusty told them. "They are intelligent, and they cost a lot of money. After they are tamed and trained, we sell them for a lot of money. This method is a bit slower than busting a bronc, but the results are much better. Have you noticed how they walk and prance with pride? That's because they still have their spirit. After you have tamed and trained a few horses, you will have earned the title, horse whisperer."

As Laughs-a-Lot's star trainer of horses and men, Rusty
had become a master of the method, and Greyeagle horses
were soon sought by distinguished horse fanciers
throughout Texas. Other capable ranch hands were taught
by Laughs-a-Lot and Rusty, and soon more corrals were
built to accommodate these trainers. Star was so pleased of
the number of trained Arabians, she gave Laughs-a-Lot and
Rusty raises in salary and bought more Arabians. The men
were proud to be called horse whisperers - a name new to
Texas horsemen.

One night in an Austin saloon, Rusty and a few men he
had trained walked through the saloon's batwings, went to
the bar, and ordered whiskey. A couple of cowboys from a
neighboring ranch were sitting at a nearby table. They
knew Rusty, and were friendly toward him.

"There's the Greyeagle horse whisperers," said one of the
cowboys. "They don't break horses like we do, they talk to
them."

"Talk to them!" said the other cowboy.

"Yep. I've watched them work. Damnedest thing I ever
saw. You'll not find a stoved-up bronc buster on Rancho
Greyeagle. They whisper to the horses."

"You gotta be joshin'" the other cowboy said.

"Nope. Hey, Rusty, you boys come on over and have a
drink," he called.

Rusty and his friends joined the cowboys, and answered
their questions about taming Arabians. Before the night was
over, the cowboys had asked for a job. They were tired of
being thrown, bitten, and stomped on. The next day,
Laughs-a-Lot hired the boys and gave them to Rusty to
train. Before long, owners of nearby spreads came to

Rancho Greyeagle to watch the training. After several days of watching, two owners asked Star if they could send a couple of their men over to be trained as horse whisperers. In a spirit of cooperation, Star agreed. Laughs-s-Lot's method caught on. Soon horse whisperers were on many of the larger spreads. Star Greyeagle was touted as being an innovator.

Nightbird was sitting astride his horse looking up at the Texas sky. He loved the night; he loved the sounds; he loved watching the stars, especially the Big Dipper. He was familiar with the night sky and could find his way by the stars - once he located the North Star. He had been named because of his love for the night. When Star Greyeagle had brought him to Texas, he wasn't sure he would like this wide open country. He thanked the Great Spirit that Star realized his love of the night, and had assigned him as security chief of the ranch during the time when most people were asleep. She had given him authority to hire five men to patrol the vast property of Rancho Greyeagle.

Most times it was quiet, except for the night sounds - an occasional coyote calling his lonesome song to a female somewhere in the dark, crickets that filled the night's void, tree frogs sounding their unusual bellyache, a dead limb falling from a tree, the snort of his horse, the crick of his saddle. Nightbird was at home wherever he was when it was night. He had assigned two of his men to ride the fence on the property's extreme right, and at the same time, sending two more along the fence on the far left. He and one man patrolled the center. The ranch was so large, they seldom saw each other until they had made a complete circle of the ranch and met back at the corrals. Tonight, he

and his partner were headed toward the Colorado River
where Rancho Greyeagle property ended and the river
flowed gentle to the south.

The Colorado River is the eighteenth longest river in the
United States and the longest river with both its source and
mouth within Texas; its drainage basin and some of its
usually dry tributaries extend into New Mexico. The 862-
mile long river flows generally southeast from Dawson
County through Marble Falls, Austin, Bastrop, Smithville,
La Grange, Columbus, Wharton, and Bay City before
emptying into the Gulf of Mexico at Matagorda Bay.

Tonight, the river did not seem right to Nightbird. His
native intuition told him something was out of kilter. He
dismounted, telling his partner to stay mounted and alert,
while he walked the river's bank. Soon, he found the tracks
of unshod ponies, Comanche, he figured, five horses,
headed toward the corrals. The tracks were fresh. He
swung up into his saddle and told his partner to follow.
They followed the tracks until they were in sight of the
corrals, then stopped to listen. There ahead, they saw five
Indians opening the gate to one of the corrals full of already
trained Arabians. Nightbird had never seen a Comanche.
He had only been told that they were expert horse thieves,
and were dangerous adversaries. As he watched, he figured
these Indians were just a small band of an equally larger
band raiding other ranches in the area on this same night.

They were not brothers; they were not Cherokee, and
they were attempting to steal horses from Rancho
Greyeagle. This he would not allow no matter who they
were. His mind worked quickly as a Cherokee warrior. He
would kill four of them, but capture one for Star to question

and decide what to do with him. Nightbird told his cowboy partner to dismount, take his rifle, and move to within rifle range of the corral. The cowboy was to shoot the two Comanche trying to rustle up the horses on the right, while he shot two on the left inside the corral. They would capture the Comanche holding the corral gate.

Both men fired about the same time. Four quick shots. Four Comanche horse thieves lay dead inside the corral in a matter of seconds. The Comanche holding the corral gate was so stunned, he hesitated. That was enough time for Nightbird to run the short distance between them and knock the Comanche out with the butt of his rifle. By this time Nightbird's other men were on the scene, guns in hand. The situation was under control. Hawk had heard the shots at the corral and came running. Soon, Star and Eagle Feather and Brave Bull was there - ready for battle.

"Everything under control?" asked Hawk.

"Four Comanche thieves dead, one out, but alive," replied Nightbird. "You want him dead, too?"

"No," said Star. "Anyone here speak Comanche?"

"Only Rusty, said one of the men.

"Wake him," spoke Star.

When Rusty arrived at the corrals, his shirt tail hanging out, six-gun in hand, he surveyed the scene, and asked "What tha' hell's going on?"

"Find out from this Comanche how many is in his raiding party," Star told him.

"Yes, Ma'am," he said. "Excuse my dress."

Rusty questioned the Comanche at length and finally determined that there were twenty in the raiding party. "Miz Star, we need to warn the other ranches as soon as possible," Rusty said.

"Yes," she replied. "Nightbird roust the hands and send them in all directions to warn the other ranches. Meantime, I will question this thief. Rusty, find out where they came from. Hawk, when the men get back, we will back track these Comanche warriors and wipe out their whole camp."

"Done," said Hawk. He had not seen action since the Cherokee Mountains, and was ready to go.

"Rusty," said Star. "Tell this Comanche if he wants to live and if he wants his family to live, he will lead us to his village - that will save time tracking them. He and his family will be given jobs on this ranch, and will be treated with respect. If he don't, he and his family will be destroyed."

"Ma'am?"

"Tell him!" said Star.

"Yes, Ma'am," said Rusty.

The Comanche did not believe what he was being told, but Rusty convinced him that Star, although cold when necessary, was an honorable woman and meant what she said. The Comanche wanted only that his family to be saved.

"Ma'am, he says he he'll do it, if his family is spared."

"Tell him, I mean what I said," replied Star. "But when we bring his family back to Rancho Greyeagle, his loyalty will be only to us."

Rusty told the Comanche what Star had said, and the Comanche nodded his head in agreement. The men had returned from warning the other ranches, and they were in time. Most of the raiding party had been run off, and no threat now existed. Star, again, had become a hero in their sight.

"Gather the men," she told Rusty. When the ranch hands had assembled, she told the men "If any of you do not want to go with us, it is okay. Nothing will be held against you. We are going to wipe out a Comanche camp. If you have no guts for this type thing, I will understand." Not one man backed down.

At day break, Lum Taggart, the fat bellied Sheriff of Travis County and two deputies showed up.

"Ma'am, you have no authority to do this," he said. "This is a job for the Rangers."

"Where were you when I needed you," Star replied.

"We can't supervise the whole county," he said.

"Then get out of my way and off of my property," Star told him. "There's only one way to deal with horse thieves. I have much experience with this."

"I'll arrest the whole bunch of you," the Sheriff belched.

"Do it," Star said belligerently. "You are like all of the non-essential politicians in this area. Not worth a damn! If I wanted or needed help, I'd send for the Rangers myself. Not a lackey like you!"

"You're talking to a Sheriff," he bellowed.

"I am talking to a worthless badge," she said. "Now get the hell out of my way, or I will put you under citizens arrest for not doing your job. Do you want to pursue this any father?"

The Sheriff and his men left with their heads tucked beneath their tails.

"Ma'am, I think you've made an enemy of the Sheriff," spoke Rusty.

"I don't need friends like him," said Star. "He's worthless.

The only real law we have around here are the Rangers. They get the job done, and that's exactly what I am going to do."

Star and her men, plus thirty ranch hands gathered from surrounding spreads, left Rancho Greyeagle with the Comanche leading the way. By noon, they came upon the Comanche camp, a temporary meeting place for the raiders once they had stolen enough horses. Star rode with Rusty, and the Comanche, into the camp to his tent. The Comanche horse thieves did nothing because of the many white men surrounding them.

To Rusty, she said, "Tell the Comanche to gather his family and go back to the men, and stay there."

The Comanche did as he was told. When the Comanche and his family were out of danger, she signaled her men to attack. The attack was brutal. Not one Comanche horse thief was left alive, except two.

"Tell these two warriors," she told Rusty, "that if ever they decide to raid other ranches, best to bypass Rancho Greyeagle, or I will find their village and wipe it out. Tell them to take that message to their chief."

"Damn, Ma'am," said Rusty. "You have killed twenty Comanche."

"I have done worse in my time," she replied. "Gather the men. We go home. Make sure no harm comes to the Comanche or his family."

Two nights later in an Austin saloon, Rusty was drinking alone. Two friends from a neighboring ranch came in and set down at his table.

"Hey Rusty, why the downcast?"

"Nothin' he said. Have a drink."

"Bull shit," one of them said. "why the gloom?"

"No gloom," he said. "Just reality."

"What the hell you talking bout?"

"What do you think of when you think of a woman?"

"Well, sugar an' spice an' every thin' that's nice."

"What about a stone, cold-ass killer woman?"

"You got somethin' on your mind. Spill it."

"I know a woman who's everything you said, but is a stone killer; but in between, she is as sweet as you would ever see."

"Bull shit!"

"Nope, I am telling 'it straight."

"Who you talkin' 'bout?"

"Star Greyeagle."

"Bull shit."

"Telling you straight, Ain't never seen a woman like her. Damned if she don't jack my head around."

"Ah, shit! Rusty has done gone an' fell in love. Ain't that a bitch!" Best you bark at the moon, pal. You'll keep your scalp longer."

"You think?"

"Yep, Hey, bartender! Bring us another round of who shot John."

The cowboy was wrong. Rusty was not in love with Star - she was old enough to be his mother. He just didn't understand how any woman could wipe-out an entire camp, then bring a Comanche and his family back to the ranch like they were long lost cousins. I'll never understand the Cherokee mind, he thought. But Star's method worked. Never again did the Comanche raid Rancho Greyeagle.

Brave Bull had gone into Austin to restock the ranch with

ammunition. Lum Taggart, the Sheriff, happened by and saw all the ammunition that Brave Bull was loading into the ranch's wagon. He stood with his hands on his hips, watching.

"That's a heap of fire power," he belched. "Your boss startin' a war?"

"Never can tell," answered Brave Bull. He did not like the pot-bellied Sheriff. Not many in the county did. The only reason he got his job was because his ex-father-in-law was a judge.

"Think you'd better come down to my office," The Sheriff told Brave Bull. "I need to check and see if there's any warrants out on you."

"No warrants on me," Brave Bull told the man. "I can't leave all this ammunition here. Somebody might take it."

"Are you resisting arrest, boy?"

"Didn't know I was under arrest."

"Git up in that wagon seat and follow me to my office."

"You're making an big mistake," Brave Bull told the Sheriff, "arresting a man without cause. When Star Greyeagle hears about this, you'll be lucky to get a job sweeping out the jail."

"Enough of your sass! Stick out your hands! You're going to jail!"

The store owner saw and heard the Sheriff arrest Brave Bull with no legal basis. He sent one of his clerks to Rancho Greyeagle to inform and fetch Star. When Star, Hawk, and Rusty came to town, she stopped to thank the store owner, then to her lawyer's office, then they all went to the Sheriff's office. She walked into the Sheriff's office spitting fire from her eyes.

"Release my man, immediately!" She demanded. "I talked to the store owner. He is a witness to your unlawful arrest. We both know why you did this - to get even with me because I ran you off of my ranch. My lawyer is filing charges against you for misuse of your authority. When I leave here, I am going to the governor's office. When I get through with you, you might wind up in your own jail!"

"Now, Miz Star," the Sheriff mumbled, "ain't no use in stirring up a fuss. This is all a big mistake. I had already intended to release your man." He told a deputy to release Brave Bull.

"You will be hearing more from my attorney very soon, and I am still going to the governor's office. If it takes every cent I have, and I have a lot, I will see you either in jail or dismissed from office. I have two sons that are Texas Rangers. I will be filing charges with the Rangers, also."

"Miz Star, I am sorry - no use in bringing in the Rangers."

"Sorry is not the proper word for you," Star told the Sheriff. "You are disgusting!"

Star did talk to the governor, the governor called the Sheriff's ex-father-

in-law, the judge, to his office and told him he had received too many complaints against his ex-son-in-law, that he had ticked off most of the big ranch owners, and that they were his vote base. The judge called the Sheriff to his office and relieved him of his duties, putting the chief deputy in charge until voting time. The ex-Sheriff moved out of Travis County nursing a strong hatred for Star Greyeagle.

"Damn!" said Rusty to Brave Bull as he rode along beside the wagon back to the ranch. "Star Greyeagle is no woman to mess with! I have see her destroy a Comanche camp and get a Sheriff fired all in the same week!"

Fall arrived on time in Texas bringing cooler weather and multi-colored leaves scattered on the ground. The ranch hands had flat refused to have the Comanche live in the bunkhouse, so Star had a small cabin built for him and his family. She told the family to bathe frequently and to dress wearing clothes she had bought for them in Austin. The man's name was Wolf. Through Rusty, Wolf told Star that he had been a horse trainer in his village, and would like to work with horses. Star assigned him to Rusty to train. Wolf and his family seemed to like living and working at Rancho Greyeagle. The Comanche was a natural horseman, and soon proved his worth under Rusty's guidance. Star called Rusty to her office and asked him
about Wolf's progress.

"Didn't like him at first," Rusty told her, "but he is a good horse trainer. Fact is, I wouldn't mind having more like him."

"Can you teach him English," she asked.

"Never had much schoolin' myself, Ma'am, but I'll try. He looks a lot different with a haircut and store bought clothes, and those two kids of his has taken a shine to me."

"Children are the same no matter their race," Star told Rusty. "Keep me informed about Wolf's progress, and let me know how his family adjusts here."

"Yes, Ma'am, I will." Rusty left the ranch house and went back to his work.

At the corral, he watched Wolf work with an Arabian, and appreciated the tenderness which he showed the horses. During a break, Wolf told Rusty that he was not

251

treated well by the Comanche because he would not let the braves have their way with his woman. He said he had had many fights because of it, and had decided to leave the Comanche band whenever opportunity presented itself. Wolf said that was the reason his family came with him on the raid.

CHAPTER EIGHT

Legacy

In 1837, the Texas Rangers arrived in what is now Waco, Texas. They were intending to build a fort at Waco Village. Texas Secretary of War William S. Fisher ordered them there to protect the white frontier after a Comanche raid at Ft. Parker near Groesbeck. The Rangers spent three weeks cutting a road through the woods and building a bridge over Cow Bayou. However, it was decided the outpost was too far from any white settlement to offer any protection.

It was now 1870. When Lum Taggart, the ex-Sheriff of Travis County, left Austin after being fired because of a set-to with Star Greyeagle, he moved to Waco and bought a sleazy saloon with funds embezzled while he was Sheriff. He still nursed a bitter hatred for Star, and had become acquainted with two gunmen that frequented his saloon, the Half Dollar. Lum Taggart had been married once, but his wife left him after a month citing that he was lazy, unscrupulous, and generally no account. Over a period of several weeks, he had broached the two gunmen about assassinating Star Greyeagle. He had agreed to pay them four hundred dollars each, half in advance.

"I have heard of the Greyeagle ranch," said one gunman, who wore two six shooters in a cross draw position, butts forward. "Be best to catch her away from the ranch."

"No problem there," belched Lum Taggart, "she usually goes into Austin each Saturday for supplies. She'll probably have two ranch hands with her, but they're not professional gunmen."

"What about the law in Austin?" asked the other gun slinger. He also wore two guns - one on his right hip and another stuck inside his belt in front. Both gunmen dressed in black and wore black Stetson hats.

"Two deputies," answered Taggart, "but they ain't much, couldn't hit the side of a barn with a canon. You Can't miss Star Greyeagle, she parks her buggy at the mercantile store, then walks to other shops in town. Her horses wear the Bar-G Brand. Hang around the mercantile store 'till she pulls up. She's a good lookin' middle-aged woman with cold black hair - she's a Cherokee."

"Don't like Indians," said the gunman with the cross-draw pistols. "No hair off my back when we plant her six feet under." The two gunmen left for Austin that same day.

Star Greyeagle had decided to take Wolf, the Comanche, and his family into Austin so they could become familiar with the interactions of a white man's town. Over the months, she and wolf's family had become accustomed to each other, and Wolf, because of how Star treated him and his family, was dedicated to her. He had become a productive ranch hand and horse trainer, and had learned a few English words from Rusty - barely enough to communicate. Wolf was a tall man with a muscled body, and since his getting a haircut and dressed in denims, he

looked civilized and much like the other Greyeagle ranch
hands. Although most of the ranch cowboys wore guns,
Star had not yet permitted Wolf to wear one. But she
allowed him to carry his knife - a razor sharp knife - with a
seven inch blade, sporting a stag-crown horn handle.

Star instructed Rusty and Wolf to hitch her two favorite
horses, Arabian sorrels, to her buggy and to collect Wolf's
family. She intended to buy additional clothes for them -
more denims and shirts, western boots, and a hat for Wolf,
and dresses for Wolf's wife, Dawn. She planned to buy
Wolf's two boys denims and shirts and boots. The two boys
were eight and ten. They smiled a lot and were friendly,
although they did not talk much. They were well
mannered. Star told Rusty that Wolf would drive the two-
seated buggy while he rode alongside. It was a cool spring
day as they came into Austin. A slight breeze was stirring
the dust on sixth street when Wolf pulled up to the
Mercantile store.

Lum Taggart's two gunmen watched from across the
street as Star's group entered the store. While Star shopped,
the gunmen walked across to the store, looked at the brands
on Star's horses, and took positions to the left and right of
the store's entrance. Earlier, they had been drinking at one
of Austin's many saloons, were red-eyed and smelled of
liquor. There were a few citizens in town, milling around,
but most were at the Stock Show at the edge of town. The
store owner came out first and loaded Star's buggy with
packages, then Rusty, Star, and Wolf's family. Wolf
followed a few steps behind the group. He noticed the two
men in black on each side of the store's entrance, and did
not like their looks - something about their eyes. His

Comanche intuition told him something was wrong here, but this was his first time to a town, maybe all town people gave off this feeling.

As Star's group assembled at the edge of the store front, except for Wolf who trailed behind, the gunman on the right pulled his pistol. He shot Star in her right shoulder. She crumbled to the plank walkway, blood gushing from the wound. The noise of the shot reverberated throughout the store. Wolf, seeing Star go down, and realizing what had happened and who did the shooting, drew his knife and plunged it to the hilt into the shooter's heart.

The man died gurgling, fell forward into a heap, blood oozing from his mouth. Rusty, was quick on his feet. He turned abruptly toward the gunman on the left, drawing his pistol as he turned. The gunman fired and hit Rusty a grazing blow to his left arm, a flesh wound. Rusty shot the man twice in the stomach. The gunman went down howling in pain. Wolf, by this time, had Star in his arms, looked at the store owner, and yelled "Doctor!" The owner told Wolf to follow him. They both ran a block down the street to the doctor's office as fast as they could. Blood soaked Wolf's shirt.

Rusty, seeing that Star was in good hands, leaned over the dying gunman he had shot and said:

"You're dying. Who hired you? Speak quickly, you don't have much time!" The gunman was in terrible pain.

"Taggart," he groaned, "Lum Taggart."

"Where can I find him? Talk quickly!"

"Waco - the Half Dollar Sal..." The man whizzed his last painful breath. His eyes rolled back into their sockets. He died with his eyelids open.

256

Rusty left the dead men and ran down the street to the doctor's office. Wolf's family stood on the porch in shock.

When Rusty busted through the doctor's office, he cried "Will she live!"

"The bullet went clean through," the doctor told him. "No vital organs hit, and no bones broken. She will live. But if this Indian had not got her here as quick as he did, she might have hemorrhaged. Now you two wait in the outer office so I can do my work."

"I stay," said Wolf. "She Boss. I stay!"

"Can't you get him out of here?" the doctor asked Rusty.

"No, sir. If he said he was going to stay, fifty men couldn't drag him away."

"Tell him to stay out of my way then."

"Rusty, leave Wolf." Star said through painful lips. "Take his family back to the ranch. Send my husband, Eagle Feather. Tell Hawk to ride to the Ranger Camp and bring my sons, and take care of your arm."

"Just a graze, Ma'am. I'll tend it at the ranch. I was goin' after the man who hired the shooters."

"No. leave that to my sons - who was it?"

"Lum Taggart. I'll be back shortly," he told Star, and left the room.

"I have given her a sedative," said the doctor to a fleeting Rusty. "She will sleep awhile. You go on and do as she told you." The doctor was glad to get him out of the office.

Before much time had passed, Eagle Feather and Rusty were back and stood beside Star's bed. She had dozed awhile, but was now awake, and still felt a lot of pain.

"Did Hawk go for Jason and Jesse?" she asked Eagle Feather.

"He did. Now you rest. The doctor says you are going to be alright. You will be here a few days." Wolf had not moved. She told him to go back to the ranch with Rusty.

"I stay," he said. "Maybe, more bad men come." No one could talk Wolf into leaving, so they let him be.

When the Twins arrived, Star and Rusty told them the story. After talking to the doctor and satisfied their mother was out of danger, they went to the courthouse and got warrants for Lum Taggart, and headed for Waco. Star had told them not to kill Taggart - she wanted to see him come to trial. When they found the Half Dollar Saloon, they went in and broached Lum Taggart.

"You're under arrest for attempted murder," Jason barked. "Up to me, I'd shoot you dead right now!"

"Bat an eyelash the wrong way, and I'll scatter your brains all over that Back bar!" said Jesse, between his teeth.

"No, sir!" managed Taggart, "no use shootin', I'll come peacefully." As the Rangers took Taggart out through the saloon's batwings, Jesse hollered over his shoulder, "Drinks are on the house, help yourselves!" The bar patrons did.

There was a crowd waiting at the courthouse in Austin when the Rangers brought Taggart in, handcuffed. At the jail, the Rangers told the deputies they understood they had worked for the ex-Sheriff, but if Taggart escaped, the Deputies would be held personally responsible. The Deputies told Jason and Jesse there was no love lost between them and the ex-Sheriff.

Three months passed before Lum Taggart was brought to trial. The courtroom was packed. Star, her shoulder still in a bandage, sat with her husband, the Twins, Hawk, Rusty, and Wolf. The prosecution had presented his case with

conviction, but the defense was equally prepared. Rusty
and Star testified to what had happened, the store owner
had also testified to what he saw, but Wolf, being a
Comanche, was not called by the prosecution. The defense
rested his case with the fact that not one witness had been
presented proving that Lum Taggart had had anything to
do with hiring the gunmen. The judge had no recourse but
to let Lum Taggart go free. He ordered the deputies to
release the ex-Sheriff.

As Taggart walked past Star, he grinned and mumbled
something about "white man justice", then walked out of
the courtroom and to the nearest saloon.

When Wolf asked Rusty "Why bad man go free?" Rusty
just shook his head and looked at his boots. "White man
law no good," said the Comanche, then he, too, walked
from the courtroom to where his horse was tied.

The next morning, Lum Taggart was found dead with his
throat cut from ear to ear in the alley next to a saloon. No
one had seen the killer. But Star and Rusty had their
suspicions. They kept their thoughts to themselves.

During Stars recovery, and the several months that
followed, Eagle Feather and Hawk had come to the
realization that Star, like Tall Woman before her, needed a
bodyguard. They had considered Rusty, but because of
Wolf's devotion to Star, and because of his experience as a
Comanche warrior, they decided to give the job to him.
Hawk brought in the Twins to teach the Comanche how to
handle a six-gun, and Greta, with the help of Rusty, taught
Wolf English. He was quick to learn, and in several months
he could not only speak fair English, but Jesse and Jason
found him to be quick and accurate with a gun. Satisfied

that Wolf could handle the job of bodyguard, he was given that responsibility. From that day forward, wherever Star went, Wolf was always close, his eyes cognizant of every movement around his boss.

Texas, during the 1870's, was a violent place to live. Reconstruction had produced many outlaws in the Lone Star State, and the hated State Police, instituted by the federal government, was not much better than the outlaws.

Although the Comanche never again raided Rancho Greyeagle, they did cause havoc to other ranches and settlements farther north and west. The Rangers were hampered by the state police, but through the efforts of a few die hard Rangers, and a few honest politicians in the Texas State Capitol, they managed to exist, but in a more subdued role. When the state police was, finally, disbanded, the Rangers were re-commissioned, and many of the outlaws were slowly imprisoned or eliminated. Some said the Rangers were a brutal bunch, but, at least, they got results.

Over the years that followed, Star led Rancho Greyeagle to become one of the most respected thoroughbred horse ranches in the state, and eventually, the whole southwest. She and her Arabians were known and respected throughout the country. She was never far from her beloved ranch, and the ranch hands who had helped her build a dynasty. Star Greyeagle lived to the age of eighty-nine. The great Cherokee woman warrior had led her people in the Cherokee Mountains during good and bad times. Her two sons, Jason and Jesse, did marry the Franks sisters, and took over Rancho Greyeagle. They had many children and grand-children and great-grand children. They and their families carried on in the Star Greyeagle tradition of never giving up or giving in. Some of her descendants moved back to the mountains of western North Carolina and live there still.

The Cherokee Mountains - December 2010

In the mountains of his ancestors, Robert Greyeagle, a descendant of Star Greyeagle, built a two bedroom cabin from logs cut on his property. The cabin was near the cave where his far distant relatives, Tall Woman, Daniel, Hawk, and Star, had lived during the Trail of Tears and the Civil War. Now, sitting astride his pinto pony in a foot of snow in front of the cave where his distant relatives once lived, visions came to mind of all that had happened since Tall Woman to the present time.

Today, he had finished his historical fiction novel. It had been an emotional journey tracing his distant ancestors. Although brush had grown up around the cave's entrance, and snow was piled up in front of it, the cave was still there.

He started to shovel the snow away and enter the cave, but thought better of it - he did not want to disturb the spirits that, no doubt, still lived there. And he did not feel qualified to walk where Tall Woman, Daniel, Hawk, and Star had walked so many, many years ago. So, he just sat there on his pony while mind visions crossed behind his eyes. It was like watching a movie. He could clearly see Beautiful Tall Woman and Star, Dynamic Daniel, Steady

Hawk, Loyal Big Tree, Brave Bull and Nightbird, Uncle
Two and Greta and Laughs-a-Lot. So many spirits roamed
nearby the majesty humbleness of Tall Woman Village, the
majesty of Strongheart Valley, the largess of Lost Valley.
And the family love in Rancho GreyEagle.

He rode down to the stream where they had drank. It
was the same stream, only now wider. He dismounted,
broke the ice, and drank from the stream. He could have
been standing in the same spot where Star and Raven had
been kidnapped so many years ago.

Suddenly, hairs stood up on the back of his neck, and
unconsciously, he looked about for any Creek Indians who
might be lurking - how foolish! Odd how these mountains
can play tricks on a man's mind, he thought.

He swung up onto Tomahawk, his pony, not realizing
that he was cold until he felt his pony quiver beneath his
legs. He reined the pony around, rode at a fast pase back to
his cabin, his long hair blowing in the wind. He put the
pony in the barn out of the weather, trudged through the
snow to his cabin, and wrote the last words to his novel.

"Hell of a long ride!" he wrote. It had been a long mind
journey through the history of his ancestors. At times, he
could feel their spirits as he rode through the mountains,
walked where they walked, stood where they stood. They
stood tall and strong. And that was his opus unto these
hills.

End

Made in the USA
Columbia, SC
13 October 2023

24418179R00146